Cry, Wolf

ALSO BY GLENN SLADE CLARK, JR.

The Great Debate

Metrognomes: The Shaman's Apprentice

The Chronicles of Nightfire, Texas, Volume I: The Vampire Murders

Cry, Wolf
Shadow of the Werewolf

Glenn Slade Clark, Jr.

2014

Cry, Wolf: Shadow of the Werewolf
Special Edition

First Edition: December 1999
Second Edition: May 2014

Published by Clark Ink, LLC.

This novel was originally published in 1999 as *Cry, Wolf.*

Cover art by Sean Seybold.

ISBN-10: 1-61815-095-2
ISBN-13: 978-1-61815-095-0

To John Burke and Cathy Johnson,
who taught me freedom through creative writing.

PROLOGUE

Nightfire, Texas
January 3, 1851

Reverend David Paul coldly surveyed the basement of the newly restored church building, barely suppressing a frightened shiver, as he considered the tale of historical horror that he must now pass on to his successor—a tale that, despite its incredible nature, must be believed, and kept secret, by all who would follow in his footsteps at the little church in Nightfire.

Reverend Paul led the way, followed by the young minister who would hopefully be the first in a long line of men who would do just that; for, the preservation of the town relied upon it, and he could not bring himself to leave such secrets in the hands of someone who was unwilling, or unable, to believe in the pure, devastating power of supernatural evil. The bishop had assured him that he would send a man he thought reliable in such matters.

Reverend Paul spoke at last, as they left the stairs of the basement behind, lanterns in hand, and made their way to a little closet. "Did the bishop give you any idea what you were getting into here?"

The other man answered, "He said you'd fill me in; that I am to keep an open mind and believe every word you say with the whole of my heart for the safety of the whole town for generations to come." He laughed shortly. "Heck of a way to introduce me to my new appointment. Very mysterious. So what is it?"

Reverend Paul stood by the closet door. "This is no sacristy, Peter. Before we discuss what lies beyond this door, I'd like to give you some feeling of just how incredible a thing it is. It has to do with the town's crisis this past summer."

"I'd been told the disaster left the town with very little; that you'd had to rebuild almost everything; but I wasn't told any of the specifics. Was it Indians?"

"Oh, Indians played a role, but they certainly weren't the problem. Tell me, Peter, have you heard of such things as werewolves?"

The man laughed, then noticed the look of solemnity painted on Reverend Paul's face. He collected himself. "I can't say that I have given the old stories much thought, but I am open minded. I've seen my fair share of the supernatural." He paled at a memory. "I was involved in an exorcism once, back in my first parish. While I'd rather not share the details, I can say that I'd never dismiss a claim of otherworldly horrors from another pastor offhand."

Reverend Paul smiled. "Good, because what lies beyond this door is a little thing, but it must be protected with all the faith of a believer." He opened the door. "The town was nearly destroyed by the monsters, five months ago." He reached in and pulled out a small object and a book. "What I hold in this glass vial is the only thing that will keep them out. And the book. The book is my testimony; the story that's to be passed down from pastor to pastor, for as long as Nightfire endures."

"What's in the vial?" Peter asked, unable to make it out in the dim glow of their lanterns.

"The blood of the monster who started the plague. The blood of a werewolf. And I can't emphasize enough that the tale I'm about to tell you must *never* be forgotten. The blood in this vial must *never* be lost, lest the demonic shadow of the werewolf should once again leave the people of Nightfire, Texas in darkness. The nightmare must never resume; this evil must not be allowed to finish what it began. If you understand the gravity of this, then I will tell you the story of how the monsters attempted to overrun our town, how we ultimately defeated them, and how this vial of blood will prevent the horror of their kind from ever getting near us again."

Peter nodded his head quietly in a state of controlled alarm. "I understand."

"Then may God always be with you." Reverend Paul opened the book, and he read aloud his testimony to the man who would now be the protector of the most sacrosanct artifacts in all of Nightfire, Texas.

That was how it happened, the first time. From that day forward, generation to generation, the chain remained unbroken, and the story was handed down from one pastor to the next. The people of Nightfire remained safe from the threat that befell their forebears, most of them unaware that those dark events had ever occurred, or that creatures such as werewolves were anything more than myth.

Throughout the generations, in spite of the people's naiveté, the appointed pastor of that little church in Nightfire prayed, under the light of every full moon, that they never need learn how very wrong they were.

I

January 10, 1997

146 years later.

Daniel Mason stood by his car, vigilantly awaiting the one he loved. School had been out for ten minutes now, but it always took Roxanna fifteen to find her way out of the building. Daniel never did mind the wait, because it always gave him time to stop and think.

Today, as he thought, he found his mind focused on the beat up, old station wagon he was leaning against. He had been driving the old thing, without complaint, for about two and a half years now. She was a good, sturdy car and, even though his friends made fun of her fondly, she always got them where they wanted to go.

Soon though, Daniel would be getting a new car. He had been saving up for a long time to buy his dream car: a black '93 Mustang convertible. He was very close to having the money that the three resident used car dealers of Nightfire, Texas had wanted for a down payment. Daniel fell to daydreaming about what it would be like to drive his friends around in the new car, but he was soon interrupted.

"Daniel?"

The voice was a beautiful and melodic hook by which he did not mind being dragged back to reality. "Hey, Roxy." He opened his eyes, which he had only just realized were closed. "I didn't see you standing there." As always, Daniel could not hold back a broad smile at the sight of lovely Roxanna Stillwaters. He looked her over as she stood there holding her books. She was wearing a tight, white T-shirt branded with the school mascot: a vampire bat named Ned. Her shirt and her jeans fit like a glove to her ideal figure. Her dark-golden hair was pulled back in a pony tail that reached down to her waist. Her face had not a scar on it and required no make-up to radiate with beauty; although, Daniel noted, she usually wore a small amount anyway.

What enticed Daniel's love for her most, of all her features, were her eyes. He could never figure out exactly what color they were. Sometimes they looked gray, other times blue, but always somehow on the verge of violet. No matter what color they really were, (and she absolutely refused to resolve the mystery) Daniel found them irresistible. They beckoned him.

At the instant the smile crossed Daniel's face, Roxanna could not help but return it. "Of course you didn't see me standin' here, ya' goob. You had your eyes closed." She waited briefly for a response, but soon found impatience to have gotten the better of her. "Well, are you just going to stand there staring, or—?"

He leaned forward suddenly and kissed her gently on the lips. No one had ever made her feel the way he did. His kisses, even the small ones like this, made her want him as she had never wanted another. The feel of his after-school stubble against her face, the way it felt as if he had reached inside of her and embraced her very soul. She forgot altogether what she had been saying.

Daniel leaned back against the car. "Did you call me a *goob*? Nobody says *goob*!"

"Yeah? Well what're you gonna do about it?" She loved him. With every fiber of her being she loved him. Everybody did. He was known all over town for being an all around good guy. He always went to church, with the full intention of going into the ministry himself someday, even though he did not come from a church-going family. He made straight As in school, had a perfect driving record, got along with everybody, never swore, and, physically, he was very attractive to boot.

"What am I gonna do about it? Well, I'll just have to retaliate. You're a goob-kissin' witch-nose."

"And you're a goob-kissing-witch-nose-kissing toad-face," Roxanna retorted humorously.

"That means nothing, coming from a goob-kissing-witch-nose kissing-toad-face-licking ..."

"All right, cut that out," a new voice interrupted. "The intellectual level of your conversation is giving me cancer!"

Daniel turned to see that his friend had walked up behind them. "Greetings, young Tom! How are ya'?"

"I'm fine," Thomas Raymond Don answered indignantly. "And don't call me *young* Tom! In two years I'll be older than you, and then who'll be calling who *young*?" Tom was not seriously this stupid. He was just joking in his weird way, and both Daniel and Roxanna knew it.

Tom was seventeen years old, a junior, and he was one of Daniel's closest friends. He stood about five and a half feet tall, wore baggy pants and a baggy, untucked, plaid, button-up shirt. He had large, round, blue eyes set on a narrow head, which was topped with a mop of unruly, yet attractive, blonde hair. His absurd sense of humor kept him from having many friends, but Daniel had taken the time to understand Tom and had never regretted it. "So are we leaving, or are you two gonna stand here and insult each other with those idiot grins on your faces some more?"

Roxanna responded, "Oh, where are you guys going?"

"Hilltop," Daniel answered her. "We're just going up there to see if anyone's there. Wanna come?"

"No, I've got too much homework, and I want to get it out of the way before the weekend really starts."

"Mr. Krandall?" Daniel guessed.

"Who else? Algebra is his life. He's under the delusion that it's important or something. Didn't he give your class any homework, or are honor students too good for that sort of thing?"

Daniel smiled mischievously. "Got it done in study hall."

"You would. Oh, why doesn't Mr. Krandall understand that weekends are for recreation?"

Tom added his own opinion of the algebra teacher. "Mr. Krandall is Satan's minion. The invisible nymphs who orbit my head told me so."

"You know, Tom," said Daniel, "you really are psycho."

"*Dang!*" was all Tom said.

Daniel returned his attention to his girlfriend. “So, you need a ride home today?”

“No, my dad’s picking me up today. See?” She pointed to a gray Cadillac with a frustrated-looking middle-aged man at the wheel, which is exactly what Marc Stillwaters was. “But say hi to the guys for me if you see ’em!”

“Oh, I’m sure we’ll see ’em,” Daniel assured her.

“Yeah,” Tom put in, “it’s not like they have anyplace better to go.”

The drive to Hilltop was not a long one, and little was said on the way. After Daniel and Tom drove away from the school, Tom was silent for a full five minutes. Daniel finally asked him what he was thinking about. Tom responded simply, “Paper-clips.” Nothing more was said for the remaining three minutes of the trip.

Daniel and Tom arrived at Hilltop to find everyone that they usually found there. Trevor Stevens was sitting on one of the two short, cement walls that supported the six brick pillars that held up the large, cement roof at the picnic area on the very top of Nightfire’s highest hill. He was smoking one cigarette in the right side of his mouth, as he let an unlit one hang from the left side of his mouth. He was leaning against the brick pillar closest to what, from Daniel’s point of view, was the front, left corner of the structure. His eyes were closed, and it was difficult to tell whether or not he was even awake.

Nic McDoogle was seated at the cement table by the same wall. He was playing a game of solitaire.

Nic's shadow, Bert Jameson, was shooting hoops at the basketball net right beside the covered picnic area. Nobody really liked Bert much except for Nic, who knew him from school, but all of Nic's friends tolerated him.

Daniel knew Nic from church, and he knew Bert through Nic. Unlike the rest of them, Nic and Bert went to the Catholic high school, even though Nic proudly attended the Methodist church. Daniel knew Trevor from both church and school.

Daniel walked over to Trevor and regarded the two-and-a-half inch cigarette butt burning from the right side of his mouth. "Hey," Daniel asked, as he tapped his friend's cancer stick, "you awake?"

Trevor responded dryly, without opening his eyes or moving his lips, "No."

"Oh."

"Don't even try talkin' to 'im Dan," Nic offered, without looking up from his cards. "He's in one of his moods. He's been sittin' up there since before me an' Bert got here, an' he ain't said more than, 'Leave me alone,' to either of us. My guess is Brenda's involved. 'Course, I suppose that's a lot like guessin' that Tom has blonde hair."

"I see. So, Trev, wanna talk about it," Daniel asked carefully.

Trevor opened his narrow, brown eyes, looked at Daniel standing in front of him, spit the cigarette from the right side of his mouth to the ground, lit the one in the left side of his mouth, moved it to the right side, and said, "No. But I'll end up talking about it anyway, like I always do when you show up."

"Oh. I see how it is," Nic spoke up with mock insult. "You can't tell me an' Bert about it, but once Daniel gets here, you sing like a bird!"

Trevor looked over to Nic. "That's right."

"Well, what's wrong with me an' Bert?"

"You, Nic, always try to fix my problems by yapping your opinions at me. As for Bert, Bert just sucks." This last part Trevor spoke purposefully louder than the rest.

For the first time since Daniel and Tom had arrived, Bert stopped bouncing his basketball. "What was that? You wanna come say that to my face, punk!" Bert was never one to laugh things off.

The four other young men spoke in unison, "Shut up, Bert." Fortunately, for all his bluster, Bert was generally a coward when people stood their ground with him. He simply muttered, "That's what I thought," which was perceived by the others as the dumbest possible comeback, and he went back to his hoops.

"So," Daniel returned his attention to Trevor, "Brenda?"

"Yeah. Need you ask?" Trevor responded.

"Here it comes," Tom teased. "Trevor's going to complain about how he has to have sex all the time. Day and night." At this point, Nic abandoned his cards and turned completely around on his seat to face Trevor. Tom went on in his most patronizing tone. "Poor Trevor. Let me find you a gun, so that you can end the misery."

If anyone other than Tom had dared to speak to him that way, Trevor would have been furious. Fortunately for Tom, Trevor counted him among his closest friends and, no matter what his mood, he always found Tom amusing. He smiled ever so slightly and said simply, "Careful. You might talk me into it." He then looked back at Daniel, whom he considered the closest of his closest friends.

Daniel smiled at him. "So what happened this time?"

"I hate that Mexican-Irish-American nymphomaniacal witch. She never lets me alone. I have to do everything she says, when she says. If I don't, she…" He paused and shook his head. He inhaled deeply on his cigarette before going on. "She just doesn't handle it well. She's insane. God, I hate her. Today she made me screw her all day, because she didn't want to go to school. I had to skip—no buts. Then she took my paycheck from me and told me all these things she needed it for, as if it was her money to begin with! And she never lets me do anything without her explicit permission, like I'm her freakin' kid or somethin'! And she freaking makes me *perform* all the freakin' time! Like I'm a machine! How did she get to be such a fucking bitch!? To think I only went out with her the first time because she looked easy. Well, she was, and now here I am, six months later, unable to escape the wrath of her sexual hunger. God, I swear I never want to have sex again."

Nic almost said something, but then remembered Trevor's earlier comment about yapping his opinions and said nothing. Daniel spoke up first, "So what do you want to do?"

"I want to dump her skank-queen butt and become a monk!"

"So, why don't you?"

"I can't! She's evil as Hell! Once I dump her, she'll turn every girl I know against me. Then my life as a man is over."

"I thought you said you wanted to be a monk anyway."

"Yeah, well, a monk who has occasional sex. Okay, I don't *never* want to have sex again. I just don't want to have to if I don't want to. And I for once want a girlfriend who isn't completely insane.

"Trevor," Nic finally said, "brother, any girl's gotta be a little nuts to go out with you in the first place."

Daniel and Tom chuckled.

"Thanks. I'm touched by your high opinion of me." Trevor was starting to feel better. Even if the problem was still there, it helped to rant and get it all off his chest.

Bert, who had been listening while he tossed the basketball around, finally stopped and walked over to the others with the ball held under his left arm. "Dude, dump 'er! You're so weak! I've never stayed with a girl like that. I just love 'em and leave 'em, man. You should follow my example. Dump 'er and just sleep around. You'll be happier in the long run, I guarantee."

In absolute disgust, Tom and Nic rolled their eyes, Daniel cradled his face in the palms of his hands, and Trevor tightened his jaw, rolled his eyes, and made a small, unpleasant sound in his throat. Bert was constantly trying to make himself sound like a stud, and even if he wasn't lying, which he was, his claims would not have made him any more likable. Daniel noticed Trevor's demonic expression and set his mind quickly to finding a nonviolent ending to this gathering.

Trevor spoke, "Shut the hell up, Bert!"

"What? I don't think I heard you, Trev!" Bert spoke challengingly.

"You heard me!" Trevor didn't move from his position on the wall. "I said, shut the flaming, red hell up! You're so full of it!

You've never been with a girl in your life! You sure as hell haven't been to bed with one." Suddenly, Trevor's anger dissolved, and gave way to amusement. He started to laugh.

Daniel saw a crazed look come over Bert and tried to cut off the oncoming tirade before it began. "So, what's everybody got planned for—?" He was cut off.

"Punk, Trevor! I'll show you who's never been with a girl!" Bert reached to his back pocket and pulled out his wallet.

Nic groaned horribly. "Not again."

"See, punk, here's who's never fucked a girl!" Bert opened his wallet and revealed a mosaic of females on photograph, and a yellow condom. "See all these girls? And what would I need this for," he pointed out the condom, "if I never got any?"

Nic could take no more. "Bert, sit down. You've been showin' off the same rubber since seventh grade! You stole half the pictures in your wallet, and all the rest, except for the one of your sister, were given to you by girls who felt sorry for you. You don't need to lie to impress us. We don't care how many, or whether or not you've been with any girls. You're makin' a fool outa yer self!"

Bert was visibly flustered. His entire face, including his eyes, was turning red with rage, but Trevor just couldn't let it go. He was still laughing mockingly when he said, "Bert's a loser." He continued to laugh.

Bert lost it. "Man, Trevor, I'm gonna kick yer—!"

"Hey!" Daniel put his arm on Bert's chest as he saw him poised to physically attack Trevor. Bert glared at Daniel, but Daniel spoke first. He spoke calmly, clearly, and sternly, but without the venom of anger, "It's okay, Bert. No hard feelings.

Trevor was wrong to deliberately anger you, and you were wrong to judge him without standing in his shoes. It's over now."

Bert backed down. Daniel was the one person who could control Bert single-handedly. Bert knew that if it ever went so far, Daniel could beat him stupid. More importantly, having never actually seen Daniel driven so far, he respected the silent understanding that Daniel was the leader of the pack. To cross Daniel was to cross the entire group. Looking down with clinched fists, Bert said, "I guess you're right." He was clearly no less angry. "I've got homework."

Trevor continued to giggle as Bert walked away angrily.

"Good save, Dan," Nic praised. "I'd better go offer that fool a ride home, before he walks the whole way himself. If he does that, he'll be in a bad mood for a week, like last time. Call me if y'all wanna do anything later." Nic waved once with a smile as he scooped up his cards and walked after Bert. Everyone said a one or two word goodbye, and he was gone.

"Gee, Trev," Tom spoke up, "your people skills have certainly improved over the past year."

"Ya' think so?" Trevor smiled, and they all three chuckled.

"So," Trevor asked, "you think I should rebel against the Evil Galactic Brenda this weekend?"

"That's up to you, pal," Daniel insisted.

"I'll help you, Trevor!" Tom offered enthusiastically. He didn't like Brenda anyway.

"Thanks, Tommydon!"

"Don't call me that."

"Why not? It's your name, isn't it? What about you, Dan? We can all go out tomorrow night and keep Brenda in the dark about it, just to see what happens."

"I don't know. I'll have to see what's going on tomorrow night. You two still wanna go car shopping with me in the morning?"

"Of course," Trevor answered for them both. "What else have we got to do?"

"Good. I'll appreciate the company." Daniel looked at his watch. "Whoops! I've gotta get to work. My shift starts in twenty minutes. Need a ride home, Tom?"

"I'll drive you home, Tom," Trevor offered. "That way you can hang out with me for a little while longer."

Tom responded simply, "Okay."

"All right then," Daniel said. "I'll see you guys later."

Daniel got home at 9:47 P.M. He lived with his parents in a small, two-bedroom house, in a quaint little lower middleclass neighborhood. He opened the door and smelled food—chili—though he had no real interest in the smell of the food that he knew was no longer there. His mother had called him at work and asked him to get his own dinner on his way home. She had only prepared enough food for three, and Uncle Jeff had shown up. Daniel had under stood and eaten at Mr. Greasy on the way home. Right now, tired from spending hours on his feet, Daniel's only interest was in getting to his room, calling Roxanna, and going to bed.

After walking through the front door and closing it behind him, Daniel found his father in a state of excitement. "Danny boy! Come'ere an' say hi t'yer Uncle Jeff!" Robert Mason had not even sipped an alcoholic beverage since 1981, yet it always amazed Daniel how drunk his father could appear when in the company of people who really were drunk. Uncle Jeff was always drunk.

Daniel approached his uncle and shook his fat, sweaty hand. Jeff Mason was very fat and, for a man of only forty, extremely aged. Uncle Jeff broke his grip and took a big swig of his beer, "So, Daniel, yer ol' man's been chewin' my ear off 'bout how good yer doin'."' Uncle Jeff paused to release a long, ungodly belch before going on. The smell of beer surrounded and radiated off of him. The stench hit Daniel like a vengeful spirit. He had to push his will near its limits to keep from turning away from Jeff's glassy eyed stare or reaching up to hold his nose. Either of these actions would have hurt Uncle Jeff deeply, but Daniel loved his uncle regardless of his bad habits and unbearable smell, so he fought the urges.

His mother was never so considerate of Uncle Jeff's demons. She never even spoke to him if she didn't absolutely have to. Normally she just gave him razor sharp *go to Hell* stares and fanned the air in front of her nose whenever she was in the same room with him.

The Herculean strength of Uncle Jeff's breath threatened to knock Daniel down, as more words shot out of his toxic mouth, "He's always goin' on 'bout how yer in good with God, got'cherself a good woman, make good grades. Shoot, boy! I wish yu'd do somethin' terrible for a change so's I don't have to hear about it." Uncle Jeff chuckled, causing his entire body to jiggle obscenely, as he nudged Daniel's cheek with his sweaty, fat fist.

Daniel could feel the thick sweat trail still on his cheek after Uncle Jeff's hand had left it, but he managed to hide his disgust. "Oh, I'm not all that, Uncle Jeff." Daniel was even able to manage a warm smile as he spoke.

Daniel's father spoke up eagerly, ever proud of his only son, "See, Jeff! He's modest too! My boy, takes after—"

"Takes after Christ if ya' ask me," Jeff said playfully. "Not healthy. Prob'ly end up sittin' in the desert for forty days talkin' to rocks an' shit."

"Daniel," his mother interrupted sharply, with a familiar *I'm an unappreciated martyr* look in her eyes, "Reverend Jordan called for you while you were at work." She spoke as if he should have known better than to be visiting with his uncle. "You'd better call him back before it gets too late."

"That's right, boy," Uncle Jeff added as, without looking, he felt through all of his pockets. "Put in a good word for yer ol' Uncle Jeff! I ain't getting' ta Heaven otherwise." He smiled. Then he swore, in a way that would have made the devil cringe, and shouted, "Outa' ciggies! Well, I'd better be on my way." Uncle Jeff said little, as he left in a state of controlled panic.

"Well, I'm gonna go get ready for bed. I'm so exhausted," Daniel said after Uncle Jeff was gone. He hugged his father good night, "G'night, Dad."

"Night, Son. No work tomorrow, right?"

"Yes, Sir."

"Going car shopping?"

"Yes, Sir."

"Well, have fun, boy."

"Oh, I will, Dad," Daniel said with a hearty grin.

Daniel went to hug his mother, but she stopped him, wiped an unnoticeable spot of dirt from underneath his chin and said, "Shouldn't show up to see your uncle looking like a heathen."

Daniel's father rolled his eyes in annoyance.

His mother continued, "Now go call the reverend." Then, as if she had just remembered, she hugged Daniel and wished him sweet dreams.

Daniel went into his room and closed the door. With great relief, he kicked off his shoes and pulled off his socks. He fell onto his bed with a sigh. His day at the movie theater had been grueling. He was so tempted to just let sleep take him, but he had to keep his word to Roxanna, and he had to return Jim's call. He decided that he would first get ready for bed, then he would make his phone calls and slip immediately afterwards into merciful slumber. He rose from the irresistible softness of his bed and went to his bathroom.

The house hadn't come with two bedrooms, but when Daniel had been born his father and Uncle Jeff had personally added on an extra bedroom and bathroom for him. Daniel was endlessly grateful that they had built him his own bathroom, which he loved, lopsided though it was.

Daniel brushed his teeth and washed his face. Leaving the bathroom, he removed his shirt, then his pants. With his thumbs in the sides of his briefs, ready to remove them, Daniel made the last difficult decision of his day, and left them on. Daniel then allowed himself to plummet face-first, down to his soft, comfort able bed.

He picked up his phone and dialed Roxanna's number. He had called her during his break at work, but her father had interrupted their conversation with his own need of the phone. Daniel had promised to call her after he got home.

"Hello?" Roxanna answered.

Daniel silently thanked God for not letting Mr. Stillwaters pick up. "Hey, Rox," Daniel said groggily.

"You're tired," she observed.

"Am I?" Daniel asked innocently.

"So, how was work," she asked.

"Oh, it was okay. The pop-corn machine broke, the soda machine exploded, the ticket machine would only print tickets for one movie, and the computers crashed. But I survived. It could have been worse. At least I got paid."

"How do you always find the bright side? If I were there, I would have quit. Anyway, I want you to come over tomorrow night."

"When?"

"About nine?"

"That's fine. But I thought your dad didn't like me coming in the house."

"Oh, don't worry about that."

"Why not? What's up?"

"That's a surprise. I think you'll like it though. Are you lying on your stomach? You sound funny."

"Yeah." Daniel turned over, and his voice became clearer. "How did you become so perceptive?"

"I dunno. Just that way I guess."

"So, what did you do today?"

"Oh, well, I went home. Did my algebra home-work. Bleck! Then I sat around the house eating Cheetos and watching TV Oh, Carey called."

The name Carey always caused Daniel's stomach to knot up. She was an ex-girlfriend who had not parted happily. "Oh? What did she have to say about me this time?"

"How did you guess?"

"Ha."

"Oh, well, she just says that you're gay."

"Gay? That's interesting. Where did she get that idea?"

"Well, we were talking about how..." She stopped suddenly, realizing that she had said more than she should have. She didn't want to spoil the surprise. "Well, you know. You just look gay sometimes," she lied.

"Do I?" Daniel knew she was lying, but chose not to probe. He appreciated the escape from another conversation about his less than pleasant relationship with Carey. "Hm. I'll have to do something about that, won't I?"

There was a long silence. Daniel almost fell asleep, but Roxanna finally spoke up, "So, what will you wear to my house tomorrow?"

"I don't know, a suit and tie, I guess. Your dad doesn't like slobs."

"You're not a slob!"

"Your father thinks so."

"Oh, Daddy thinks Bryant Gumble is a slob. You can't win. Just dress casual. Nice casual, but still casual."

"I don't know, Roxy, I don't want to irk your dad."

"You won't! I mean, it doesn't matter. If you dress up, it'll make me uncomfortable."

"Okay. Hey, I'm gonna have to let you go, Rox. I need to call Jim before it gets too late."

"Okay, sleep tight."

"You too. Love you."

"Love you too. G'night."

"Good night." After Roxanna hung up, Daniel called Reverend Jim Jordan.

The phone rang three times before Daniel heard Jim's voice. "Hello!" The reverend answered as if he were making an announcement, not in the usual interrogative way that people tended to answer the phone.

Daniel answered his greeting, "Hey, Preacherman! What's up?"

"Daniel Mason! Thank you for calling me back. I was just calling to ask you a favor."

"Sure thing, Jim. What do you need?"

"Well, Tuesday is the only day I have free next week to clean the junk out of the storage rooms in the church basement. Would you be available to help me out? It's a big job, and I don't think I can get it done alone in one day. I don't even know if just the two of us can do it."

"Sure we can, Jim. I'll get Roxy and the guys to help out. I don't think I have to work on Tuesday, but if I do, I'll try to get someone to work my shift for me."

"Daniel, I appreciate it, bud. I'll let you go now, you sound exhausted."

"Good call, Jim. See you Sunday?"

"Of course! Good night, Daniel."

"Good night." Daniel waited for Jim to hang up before he hung up himself.

After a few moments of lying unmoved, Daniel stood up, pulled back the sheets, and slid into his bed. It was warm and soft; oh so refreshing after his long day. As Daniel lay waiting for sleep, his mind wandered. He thought of Roxanna. What was this surprise? He feared he knew, but he would deal with that when he had to. He thought about Tom and Trevor. Had they come up with a plan to spite Brenda? How would she handle it? He had always wondered about Brenda's attitude towards others. Who did she think she was? She was worse than Carey had ever even thought about being. Was Carey still mad about how their relationship had ended? Would Roxy react the same way when she found out?

Daniel's mind drifted away from his worries as he thought of a '93 Mustang convertible. Maybe tomorrow. Maybe. Daniel silently thanked God for blessing him with Roxanna, and friends like Tom and Trevor, and Nic and Jim, and even Bert. Daniel loved them all; God first and foremost.

Daniel drifted off to sleep.

II

Daniel walked through the front door of his house the next afternoon, having just revisited all three of Nightfire's used car lots. Trevor and Tom were with him. They had all gone to see if any of the salesmen were willing to negotiate down from the maximum Daniel could afford. None of them had been, so now it didn't really matter which one Daniel bought from. Daniel's mother was in the kitchen making lunch, and Daniel's father was sitting at the kitchen table reading the paper. The three young men entered the kitchen and were greeted warmly. "Hello, boys," Daniel's father said with a big smile and an uncharacteristic gleam in his eyes. "Have any luck today?"

The three boys spoke in unison, "Not really."

Daniel's mother regarded Tom and Trevor with a hateful glare. "Looks like I'll have to make some more sandwiches."

"No, Mom. I'll do it. You sit down and eat," Daniel offered sincerely. Trevor and Tom were visibly uncomfortable. Daniel wondered why his mother always had to let people know how inconvenienced she was by any favor she offered them. He went to make some sandwiches for his friends, and his mother sat down to eat.

"You know," Daniel's father began, "Gordon Kile's son has a '93 just like the one you're after."

"Sure he does, Dad. He's your rich boss' son. He can have whatever car he wants."

Mr. Mason turned his attention back to the newspaper. "I know. It's true. That's probably why he's getting a new car next week." He looked up at Daniel. "Mr. Kile knows you're looking for a '93. He got Steven to agree to give you the first shot at buying his old one, now that he's gonna be selling it."

"Cool. Do you know how much?"

"He's asking for the same price as the other guys were asking for a down payment."

"Oh."

"But nothing after that." Mr. Mason smiled and looked back to his paper.

"What? You mean, that's it? Nothing after that at all?" Daniel was glowing with excitement.

"Yes, that's what I mean. Give him a call, and he'll let you look at it this afternoon." Daniel's father was smiling brightly behind his paper, completely satisfied with himself for brightening his son's day.

Daniel's eyes lit up. "Cool! Thanks, Dad!" He handed his friends their sandwiches, which neither of them had really wanted in the first place, and he ran to the phone. Tom and Trevor followed—unappetizing sandwiches in hand.

After the boys had left the kitchen, Mrs. Mason spoke venomously to her husband, "Honestly, Robert, I don't know where you get off making things this easy for him! He should have to work hard for what he wants, if he's going to know how to handle things in the real world!"

"Daniel does work hard! And he very well does understand that it takes hard work to afford a new car! Do you know how long he's been saving up for that down payment? He's been working himself to death. I didn't own a decent car until I was thirty years old. Daniel's driving that car now, and it's liable to fall apart at any given moment. He could end up stranded someplace awful in that thing. As long as Daniel is trying to help himself, I'm gonna do whatever I can to help him out!"

"Well, you're going to make a weakling out of him. I still think he should have to work harder for such a luxury."

"That's easy for you to say, Barbara! You don't even *have* a job!" As far as Robert Mason was concerned, the matter was closed.

After letting the phone ring for what felt like an eternity, Steven Kile finally answered, "Hello."

Daniel spoke with confidence, though he and Steven had never met, "Hello, this is Daniel Mason. I'm calling—"

"About the car. Right. My father tells me I gotta give you the first shot at it. Well, look, I can't actually let go of 'er 'til a week from today. That's when I get the new car. But you can come look at it now if ya' want. She's in pretty good shape. Not to brag, but I'm a fairly good mechanic for a rich man's son." Daniel noted the slightest hint of bitterness in the last of these words, but opted to keep the conversation light.

"Great!" Daniel responded. "I'll be right over."

"Okay. I'll be parked in front of the house. You know how to get here?"

"Just give me the address, and I'll find it."

"7748 Deerbrook Road. It's the big, white house." Steven laughed to himself.

"Okay, thanks, Steve!"

"No prob." Steven hung up.

Daniel then relayed the message to his friends, "Come on, we're headed to the rich people street." This is what just about everyone who didn't live there called Deerbrook Road.

Trevor cringed.

"Oh boy! Maybe people will give us money!" was Tom's response, as he bolted merrily towards the front door. Trevor and Daniel laughed as they followed him.

"You know," Daniel said to Trevor when they got to the car, "you can stop carrying that sandwich around if you want."

After passing at least twenty *big, white houses,* the trio finally arrived at the Kile residence. There was a black '93 Mustang convertible parked in the front. Steven was lying on the hood. Daniel, Tom, and Trevor left Daniel's station wagon and approached him. Steven sat up and slid down. He stood to meet them. He was about six feet tall and looked to be about three years older than Daniel and Trevor. He had jet-black hair, pulled into a small ponytail, and he was dressed all in black—a tank top and jeans—with the exception of his white sneakers. Judging by his dress and demeanor, he was not at all a stereotypical resident of Deerbrook Road. "Hello," he said.

"Hi," Daniel replied. "I'm Daniel Mason." He reached out to shake Steven's hand. Steven took it and shook it once firmly before Daniel went on. "These are my friends, Trevor Stevens and Tom Don."

Steven looked them over. "Hi."

Tom, feeling insecure, always felt the need to act extra bizarre around new people. "Hey, Trevor, he has the same first name as your last name. May be he's your cousin."

Trevor lit a cigarette and glared at Tom.

Tom looked the other way to see that neither Daniel nor Steven was amused at his choice of stupidity. Seeing that he had failed, Tom went into an even weirder mode. He looked at Trevor's cigarette. "Hey, Trevor, can I have one?" Trevor looked down at Tom. Knowing that Tom had never smoked in his life, Trevor decided that it would be funny to watch him choke on his first. He handed Tom a cigarette. Tom took it. "Thanks!" Trevor offered him a light, but Tom responded with, "Oh, I don't need a light thanks." He then crumpled up the cigarette and ate it.

Trevor stared expressionless at Tom, with his lighter still on. The flame went out at the second Trevor went into a fit of uncontrolled laughter. Daniel and Steven both giggled slightly as they looked at Tom and Trevor, but they were both preoccupied with the matter at hand.

"What?" Tom asked, as if he didn't know what was so funny.

"Yeah, anyway, that's Tom," Daniel explained to Steven, "and he better not throw up in my car."

"Like it would matter if I puked in ol' *Clunk*," Tom teased.

Steven went on to show off his car. He showed them several things that he had fixed with his own hands. The car seemed to be in perfect condition. After about twenty minutes of checking out the car, Daniel finally asked, "So why are you letting this car go? She seems to be in top condition."

"Yeah, well, like I said, I'm getting' a new one next Saturday. My dad's makin' me sell it, 'cause the neighbors have been complainin' for years."

"Complaining? Why?" Daniel asked.

"They say my car's too old. They think it hurts the image of the neighborhood, not being a '97 and all. Bad for the property value, or some bull shit like that. I hate this neighborhood."

"Yeah, me too," Trevor offered all too eagerly.

Steven continued, "Yeah? Then you must not be insane. Money makes people crazy. I don't care if I'm ever more than average, you know?" Steven drifted into silent thought, but soon returned. "So, you buyin'?"

Daniel looked at the car. It was in perfect condition. It shined like new. Steven's neighbors *were* crazy to consider it junk. "I think so, Steve."

"Okay then." Steven extended his hand and gave Daniel another brief handshake. "You don't have to pay 'til you come back next Saturday to take her away."

"Alright. Thank you very much for your time."

"Sure thing. See ya Saturday." Steven walked off to the house. Daniel made a victorious gesture and ran back to his station wagon. Trevor and Tom followed.

As they drove off in the car so lovingly dubbed *Clunk* by Daniel's friends, Daniel asked, "So, what's the plan for tonight?"

Trevor answered him, "We're going to the arcade to spend Tom's allowance on video games and air hockey. Then we're going to The Witch's Tree to see if her ghost shows up. You comin'?"

"Will we be back before nine?"

"No way. That wouldn't irk Brenda nearly enough. We'll be out all night. Why?"

"I have to be at Roxy's house by nine. She won't tell me why, so I can't be late. Sorry."

"Oh, that's okay. You can come next time. Hopefully Brenda will dump me after this. I'll pretend to be upset, then it'll be over. After that, we'll have every night just to do whatever." Trevor stopped and sniffed the air. "Oh, God! What is that smell!?"

"Sorry!" Tom spoke up defensively. "Must be that cancer stick I ate."

"Oh, God!" Trevor repeated with his nose pinched.

Daniel laughed as he gagged and rolled down his window.

III

It was exactly 9:00 P.M. when Daniel arrived at Roxanna's house. He rang the doorbell and waited. Roxanna opened the door with a bright smile on her face. Daniel's own face immediately curled into a smile at the sight of her, despite his nervousness regarding her father. She was wearing a red, silk gown, and her hair was down. She was beautiful. Daniel handed her the rose he had brought for her. "What's this for?" she asked.

"Honestly? To impress your father I'm afraid."

"Oh, Daniel, stop worrying. He's not even here. He went out of town on a business trip. That's the surprise. I planned a special night just for us!" She smiled warmly.

"Oh." Daniel was now more worried than before. His expression strongly suggested that he had just seen a ghost.

"Well?" Roxanna asked. "Aren't you coming in?"

"Uh," Daniel decided to give her the benefit of the doubt. "Sure!"

She took his hand and led him inside.

Roxanna's house was big. Not as big as the houses on Deerbrook Road, but big enough. Her father was very well off. Paintings were hung on every wall. Daniel was afraid to touch anything. Everything looked so expensive all around the house. Daniel's eyes locked on to something in the living room. There was a candle burning on the floor in front of the fire place. It stood in the center of a little, round rug. There were two plates—one on each side of the small rug. Daniel found it charmingly cliché. He relaxed, but only a little. Maybe she really did just want to have a romantic dinner with him. That was no problem.

Roxanna let go of his hand and said, "Wait here." She then went to turn out the living room lights.

Daniel was soon surrounded by darkness in an unfamiliar place. This was never the best of feelings. The only light was the dim glow of the candle on the other side of the room. That would only be enough to see by when he was right next to it. "Rox?" Daniel asked, trying to hide his discomfort.

He jerked, as a hand touched his right shoulder.

"I'm right here, Daniel." She laughed. "You're so tense. I'd almost think you'd never done this before. Come on." She took his hand again and led him towards the candle.

"Never done this?" Daniel asked. "I've had dinner in the dark before. Usually in a more familiar house."

Roxanna was puzzled. Could he really not have known what she was talking about? Maybe he was just teasing her. She sat him down on one side of the rug, in front of one of the two plates. "I'll go get the food," she said. Then she went to the kitchen.

Daniel hoped he was wrong about her intentions, but there was something a little too sexy for comfort about the way she'd said "done this before." It was also obvious, even in the dim light, that Roxanna was wearing no bra. Daniel prayed silently.

God, please help me. Get me out of this. I don't want to lose Roxy. Please don't let it end like this.

"Here we go." Roxy dropped a slice of pepperoni pizza onto Daniel's plate.

"Pizza!" Daniel said playfully. "How romantic." He smiled up at her. Her beauty was as radiant as ever.

She sat down across from him and looked at him seductively. She spoke in the sexiest voice she could manage, "If you want, we can skip dinner and get on with dessert."

"You made dessert too? Oh, Roxy, you didn't have to go to all that trouble." This Daniel spoke without the playful tone. He picked up his pizza. "Smells good, Rox. Got anything to drink?"

Roxanna stared at him. She realized that he was seriously not getting it. "Yeah," she said sharply. She stood up. "Sure." She walked swiftly back to the kitchen.

Daniel was now certain that Roxanna had more in mind than just dinner. He tried frantically to think of a polite way to leave. He could just run away while she was in the kitchen, but that would hurt her feelings deeply. It would also be cowardly, and Daniel was no coward. He could tell her it had gotten too late, and that he needed to get home before 9:30, but that would be a lie. Daniel never lied. He could scarf down his pizza and induce vomiting, but that was totally ridiculous. Finally he thought that, perhaps, he could just tell her the truth. It's not like he'd been hiding it from her. It had just never come up before. Though, it had ended his last romantic relationship, and if he brought it up now and was wrong about Roxanna's intentions, they would both be embarrassed. Daniel decided that he would just have to risk it, unless some miracle got him out of it.

At that second, Roxanna walked into the room with a large pitcher of lemonade. "Here we go, Dan...yeeek!" She tripped. In the dark it was impossible to tell how, but she did, and, as she fell, lemonade drenched Daniel where he sat.

"Oh, yuck!" Daniel said in amusement. He looked at Roxy, who was lying on the floor and rubbing her right elbow. "Are you okay, Rox?"

"I've been better," she replied unhappily.

Feeling that he had gotten out of the situation, Daniel lost his discomfort and allowed himself to laugh. "Some romantic evening, huh? I'm completely wet and sticky. How will I explain this to my parents? Oh, this feels so gross."

Roxanna was struck with sudden inspiration. "Oh, Daniel, I'm so sorry! You can't go home like that! You can go take a shower in my dad's room to get the stickiness off."

"But," Daniel felt his fears returning, "I'll just have to put my sticky clothes back on again. What's the point?"

"No you won't. You still have an extra pair of pants and a T-shirt in the equipment shed out back from the last time you and Tom came over to swim this summer!"

"What if they don't fit?"

"Daniel, it was only five months ago. I doubt you've grown that much. Now go on. There's a towel in there already, and I'll go get your clothes from out back."

"But..."

"No buts, Daniel. Just go get clean."

"But I don't even know how to get to your father's room."

"Oh. Hold on." Roxanna stood up and went to turn on the living room lights. Then, after her eyes had adjusted, she pointed to a hallway. "Second door to the right." She laughed. "I assume you can tell the bathroom from the closet."

"Oh, all right. Hey, do you need some help cleaning up the lemonade?"

"No. I can manage. Go on, before you're too sticky to move."

Daniel gave her one last, pathetic look, then went into the hallway. Roxanna's heart started to beat a bit faster. This was going well. Lemonade with pizza had been a bad idea anyway, but the point had been to skip dinner.

Now to follow Carey's advice. If all else fails, get naked. Carey had broken up with Daniel before testing her theory about men on him, but then, most guys hadn't require as much work as Daniel had. Carey had given up on him and decided that he was a homosexual. Roxanna hoped very much that Carey had been wrong.

Daniel was scared. He had a sneaking suspicion that Roxy was going to intentionally walk in on him. He loved her so much, and he was so afraid that she would not understand. Carey was the genesis of his fear. She had wanted terribly to bed him. When he told her how he felt about it, she had gone nearly insane with rage, called him a liar, and then broken up with him. It was probably just as well. Daniel had already decided that his relationship with Carey was not going to work, and later he found out that she had been sleeping with two other guys during the time she was still dating him. Daniel knew that Carey still wanted him, even if only vicariously through someone else.

That's why the friendship between Carey and Roxanna made him uncomfortable. He feared the encouragement of his seduction that might come from Carey. If Roxanna tried any of Carey's tricks, since he found her infinitely more attractive than Carey, he feared he would not be able to resist.

On the other hand, he could just be paranoid. Maybe Roxy was just being hospitable by her insistence that he take a shower in her father's bathroom. Daniel felt, out of love for her, that it was his obligation to trust her. He sat down on her father's bed and removed his shoes and socks. He then walked into the bathroom and closed the door. He breathed a sigh of relief at the sight of a lock on the doorknob. "Thank You, God." He twisted the lock, then he removed the rest of his clothing and tossed it into a corner. He pulled back the barely transparent, plastic shower curtain and looked over the spotless, gray tiles covering the walls and floor of the shower. The shower was so big. It was like a closet. Daniel turned on the water and reached out to touch it with his hand as it shot out of the shower-head. When it started to get warm, he got in. The water continued to get warmer, and Daniel, now totally relaxed after locking the door, allowed himself to get lost in the hypnotic massage of the hot water hitting him on the back and chest, as he turned, and flowing all over his once sticky body.

Roxanna was shaking slightly as she entered her father's room. She walked, barefoot, over to the bathroom door and noticed Daniel's shoes and socks lying next to her father's bed. Her heart began racing. Soon she and Daniel would be in that bed together.

Roxanna looked at the doorknob. If all else fails, get naked, and if that doesn't do it, he's definitely gay. That's what Carey had said. *She should know; the slut.*

Roxy wondered if Daniel had locked the door. She then smiled, knowing that he probably had, as she considered the fact that the lock on this particular door had not worked since she was four years old. She reached out and held the knob. She paused, trying to keep her courage, then turned it.

The door opened silently as Roxanna walked in. Steam surrounded her as she stood in front of the shower. She could see Daniel's blurry image through the curtain. She couldn't make out any details but, since he had not moved when she had come in, she assumed he had his eyes closed. He always tended to close his eyes when he was relaxed or in thought. He also closed his eyes whenever he kissed her. She wondered if he would close them as they made love—or when he came.

Roxy pulled back the curtain with one sharp motion. She gasped with satisfaction and amazement at the sight of him.

"Roxy!" Daniel had been knocked out of his trance by the sound of the shower curtain being pulled back. He stared at her, disbelieving. She really had been out to get him. He thought about covering himself, but decided there was no point, as she had already seen what he would have been attempting to hide. And, he noticed, she was still staring at it with unblinking eyes. He forced himself to relax. *Please, God, give me strength,* he prayed before speaking. "What are you doing here?"

Roxanna took her gaze from his god-like phallus and stared into his dark, brown eyes. She said nothing as she unzipped the back of her crimson, silk gown and let it fall to the floor around her ankles.

Daniel's eyes widened. He felt a surge of excitement soar through him, as his most masculine organ granted her a standing ovation. She stood before him like a goddess. He had never seen anything shine with such radiant beauty as she in her purest of appearances. In his eyes, her body was perfect. Her breasts were just right—not too big, but in no way small. Her skin was as flawless as her sculpture-perfect shape. Daniel studied her sensual form, and all he could think was, *perfect, perfect, perfect.*

She stepped into the wet heat of the shower, and, as she moved, Daniel grew harder, and the heat that surrounded him grew ever more stimulating. He stepped back against the wall as she moved forward. She reached out to caress his muscular chest. Daniel's already impressive erection grew taller and stiffer still at the feel of her soft, feminine touch. He could not resist her. He felt lost in her beauty. He reached to cradle her face in his hands. He then kissed her lightly. He pulled his face back and said, "I love you." He kissed her again, and through that kiss, he let flow all of his emotions. The taste of her mouth intoxicated him, as if it were a drug. The familiar flavors seemed different somehow. So potent. He wanted her more than life.

As she took his passionate kiss, Roxanna's body burned for Daniel's. She found the uncharted territory of his muscular buttocks and latched on tightly with her hands. As he put his arms around her waist, she pulled herself close to him. His embrace became stronger, as she pressed herself firmly against his burning manhood. She could no longer wait. She needed to feel the force of his penetration. She pulled away from his passionate embrace. "Make me scream," she said to him with fire in her eyes.

Daniel stared at her with desperate desire. "How loud?" He picked her up and pressed her against the shower's only other bare wall. He kissed her again, harder still. She moaned with anticipation, her legs wrapped around his back. Daniel felt her nipples hard against his chest. The moist, hungry mouth of her fertile flower hovered eagerly just centimeters above his own impassioned organ. He began to slide her down the wall. One centimeter. Two. He could feel the heat of her forbidden fruit calling for him to slide her down the final distance.

She moaned again, the tension of her body against his screaming for insertion. She felt herself begin to slide. She braced herself for Daniel's tempered mass, but then, suddenly, he was no longer pressing against her. She felt only his hands around her waist as she slid all the way down to the floor. Then, not even his hands were on her.

Before she could determine what was going on, she heard a sharp squeak, as a shower knob was turned violently. In an instant, she found herself screaming, as ice-cold water hit every inch of her body like the wrath of an angry god. When she finally jumped out of the shower and opened her eyes, she saw Daniel facing the frigid onslaught deliberately. He seemed determined to freeze himself to death. She stared at him in silent shock. What had happened?

Finally, he spoke. "No!" he shouted sternly. "I cannot do this! Roxy…," speaking her name threatened to reignite his fire. "No! I will not!" This he shouted more it seemed for his own ears than for hers.

Roxanna wondered briefly if he had gone mad. "Daniel, are y—?"

He cut her off without even looking at her, "Get out."

Roxanna stared in disbelief. Her eyes filled with tears, as she grabbed a towel and ran out of the bathroom. What had she done wrong?

Daniel left the bathroom a few minutes later with a towel wrapped around his waist, feeling more in control of himself. He found the clothes from out back lying on the bed. He was grateful that she had left them for him, but uncertain about what it could mean. Had she forgiven him? No. How could she? She hadn't the slightest idea what was going on. Daniel paused to consider his situation. He had to talk to her, if she would listen. He dropped his towel and quickly got dressed. When he finished dressing, he was garbed in a pair of cut-off blue jeans and a rainbow colored, striped, long-sleeved shirt. He knew he looked completely ridiculous, but there was nothing to be done for it. He left Mr. Stillwaters' bedroom, miserably bracing himself to face whatever came next.

Daniel found Roxanna sitting on the sofa in the living room. She was staring at the burnt out candle on the floor, and tears still fell from her violet-tinted eyes. Without looking, she knew that he had entered the room, so she did not jump when he put his hand on her shoulder. "What did I do wrong?" She asked in a strained voice.

Daniel felt a pain in the deepest part of his soul when she asked this of him. He was in agony at having let her feel responsible for what had happened. A tear came to his own eye. "Nothing. Nothing. It's…" He paused, deciding. "It's me, Rox."

Daniel walked around the couch to sit by his beloved. After he had seated himself, she spoke again, "You?" She sniffled before going on. "What do you mean? Are…" She hesitated, fearing his answer to the question she needed to ask. "Are you, you know, gay?"

Daniel could not restrain a small chuckle at this. "Roxanna," he looked right into her reddened, teary eyes, "you know I'm not gay." He smiled at her.

Even in her present state of hurt, Roxanna could not resist his broad, glowing smile. She smiled involuntarily and looked away. "I guess you're right." She looked back at him, noticed the wet trail that a tear had made from his right eye, and asked, "So what *is* wrong, Daniel? Don't you want me?"

"Yes!" Again, Daniel hurt for what he must have done to her, how he had hurt her. More tears fell from both his eyes, but there was no weakness in his speech, "I want you terribly! I love you, Roxanna. I love you as though love was a myth before I found you."

Roxanna felt a surge of warmth, as if Daniel's words were a thick blanket, protecting her from the cold hurt of his sexual rejection. "I love you the same way, Daniel. I've saved myself for you. I wanted it to be so special. I just wanted you to want me the same way.

"I do. I do, Roxanna. And I want it to be special too, but even more so. I've been saving myself too," he smiled lovingly, "for my wife. My plans have been for my wife to, someday, be you."

Though new tears fell from her eyes, Roxanna had now forgotten her sorrow almost completely. "Oh, Daniel...I don't know what to say. You've been waiting for marriage? But if you plan to be with me then, why not be with me now? I'm the same woman now as I'll be when I take your name."

"Yes, but, there is another factor. There is only One to whom I am more loyal, and love more, than you. God—Jesus Christ. I will do nothing to betray him. It's God who has told us not to commit adultery. According to Jim, sex with anyone who is not your wife or husband is adultery. I wanted to, Roxy. I wanted to so bad. I almost did. I love you so much. Just, please, be understanding. Let me express my love to you through my words, my hugs and kisses, my loyalty. Please, forgive me. I never, never wanted to hurt you." Another tear fell from his left eye.

Roxanna was completely at a loss. She would never have expected this in even her craziest of nightmares. She knew not whether to be further endeared to Daniel for his devotion to God, or frightened of him. No one was *really* that loyal to God. People prayed and went to church, but even the ones who believed it all weren't *that* sincere. Most people, even Reverend Jordan, accepted their human failings and went on with their lives. It was impossible to truly live one's life completely for an invisible god who existed beyond time and space; a god who could just as easily forsake you to Hell as he could admit you into Heaven. And to come that close to making love! There couldn't have been more than a fraction of a centimeter between the parts that made them man and woman. No one could have stopped after as passionate an embrace as they had shared. No one. If she had been in the shower with the Pope, she surely would have scored.

After thinking it all over, Roxanna spoke, "Roxanna Mason. The wife of a Methodist minister huh? That'll work."

Daniel sounded both surprised and lowly. He didn't feel that he deserved her forgiveness for hurting her, "You...you forgive me?"

"How could I begrudge you your loyalty to God? How could I begrudge you anything at all? You're so good. Too good. It scares me a little. Maybe Carey dumped you for it, but I love you, Daniel. I truly do, and I can only ask that you not begrudge me, because I love you more than God a thousand times over."

"I don't. I'm not here to judge you, only to love you. That, I would do even if you became the most Satanic pagan who ever lived."

Roxy looked at him in disbelief. "You're not even judgmental! You're not human at all, are you? Are you a fallen angel, sent to Earth for redemption? Are you the next Christ? Do you at least *see* angels?"

Daniel smiled at her humor. "No. I'm not a fallen angel, and I'm not the next Christ. I've never even seen an angel. I'm just a normal guy who has chosen and practiced allegiance to my God."

"Good. I think. No, I can deal with that for sure." Roxy wiped the tears away from her face, sniffled, and said, "So will you hug me at least? You can keep your clothes on, if you want to."

He laughed. "I love you, Roxy." Daniel leaned over and hugged her. As Roxanna hugged him back, she wondered, was she in love with a saint, or a madman?

***

Daniel got home that night at 10:37. When he walked through the door, he found his father still up, while his mother had already gone to bed. Daniel noticed that his father looked unsettled. "Hi, Dad. What's up?"

"Nothing, Son. Just...nothing. So how was your day?"

"Oh, it was pretty good."

"That's good. How about that car?"

"Oh, it's great. Top condition. He's being forced to sell it you know. His neighbors think it's too old."

"Yeah, money makes people crazy. Oh, well. Poverty can make ya' crazy just as well." A haunted look fell over Robert Mason, as he considered just that. He did his best to shake it off. "How's Roxy doin'?"

"She's doing all right."

"What happened at her house? Hope you impressed her ol' man."

"Oh, well… We… She made dinner and stuff. I think the night went well."

"What happened to your clothes, Son?"

"Oh, well…" Daniel was holding the clothes that he had left home in, and he was wearing the extras that he had put on at Roxy's. "Roxanna spilled lemonade on me."

"On purpose?" Robert Mason asked with a mischievous smile.

"Uh, she tripped. And fell."

"Hm." Mr. Mason considered that. "Your mother spilled vodka on me once."

"Then what happened?" Daniel asked, wondering if the circumstance had been the same.

"I married 'er." Mr. Mason's expression changed from that of amusement to that of sad contemplation.

"Oh," Daniel said simply. "Good night." He went over to hug his father.

Mr. Mason returned the hug. "Good night, Son. Sleep well."

"I'll try." With that, Daniel went to his room to get ready for bed.

He turned on the light in his bedroom, closed the door behind him, and noticed an envelope on the floor, right next to his bed. He dropped his wet clothes in the laundry basket and opened the envelope. He found a letter of acceptance from yet another college. This raised the total number to five. Daniel smiled. He started walking to the bathroom, but was stopped by the ringing of the phone. Daniel turned around, went to the phone, and answered, "Hello?"

"Shut up! Don't you try to make nice with me, Daniel!" It was Brenda, and she was mad.

"Brenda, I—"

"Don't try to cover it up for him, Daniel! It won't work! And don't try to act innocent either. I get so sick of your act! Just tell me where he is! I know you've been with him all night! So don't even try to lie! Who does Trevor think he is!? He acts like he can just go off and do whatever he wants without coming to me first! I had plans tonight! He never called me to see if it was okay for him to go someplace or anything! So fess up! Where were you tonight!?"

"Actually, Brenda, I've been over at Roxy's house."

"Oh yeah, I'm sure you have! Fine! Just lie for your precious friend! I'll remember this the next time you need help from me!"

"Brenda, I'm not—"

She slammed the phone down before he could finish.

Daniel thought that he would hate to be Trevor whenever she caught up with him. A call from Brenda was all anyone needed to ruin a good mood.

Daniel sat down on his bed and dialed Roxanna's number. The phone rang five times, and he almost hung up before she finally answered groggily, "Hello?"

"Roxy, did I wake you up?"

"Yeah. Crying always makes me tired."

"I'm sorry. I was just calling to say good night."

"Oh."

"I'll let you get back to sleep though. Good night, Roxy."

"Good night, Daniel. Love you."

"Love you too."

Roxanna hung up, and so did Daniel. Everything was back to normal; perhaps better than normal. At least, he hoped it was.

As an afterthought, he dialed Trevor's number. No one answered. Trevor and Tom must have still been out. Daniel had wanted to see if Trevor was willing to help clean the church basement on Tuesday, but he supposed he could ask him tomorrow.

Daniel stood up and walked to the bathroom. He kicked off his shoes and pulled off his socks. He then brushed his teeth and washed his face. As he left the bathroom, he removed his colorful shirt and his shorts, and he switched off the lights. Since he was wearing no underwear, he decided not to put any on. His testicles ached anyway. He fell down to his bed, pulled back the covers, and slid beneath them.

As he waited for sleep to claim him, he prayed silently. He thanked God for giving him the last-minute strength to resist temptation. He thanked Him for strengthening his relationship with Roxy. He asked Him to be with Trevor whenever Brenda found him. He thanked Him for leading him to the car. Then, as his thoughts lost their focus, Daniel was consumed by peaceful slumber.

IV

It was now Sunday, and church had just ended. Nightfire United Methodist Church was the only Methodist church in Nightfire, Texas. The one fault that anyone ever saw in Daniel Mason was his membership there. Nightfire was small. In the entire town, there were only ten Christian churches of any denomination and one synagogue. Most of the churches were Catholic. There was one Catholic church right next door to Nightfire U.M.C. by the name of Saint Paul. The competition between the two churches was highly unchristian, as so many things about churches could be.

Reverend Jim Jordan was a very brave and very strong man. He always regarded sneers and jeers from the good Christians of other sects with kindness. Not everyone else in Nightfire disliked Methodists—just enough people to make it noticeable.

Though the church was small, it had been standing for many years. In fact, it was the only one of Nightfire's original churches left standing. There had been an incident nearly one-hundred-forty-seven years before in which all of the other churches had been destroyed. There were too few records remaining on the events of 1850 for most people to learn exactly how it had happened, and the few people who did know never spoke about it publicly.

Reverend Jordan was now almost forty-three years old. He had been in Nightfire since 1982, and he was well loved by the entire congregation, aside from some of the over-seventy crowd.

On this particular Sunday morning, Jim's sermon had been about the patience of Job. As Daniel had listened, he had wondered briefly if he would have been capable of forgiving God, had he been Job. Job had been a good and righteous man, and yet, for the sake of a bet, God had allowed Satan to take everything from him. Job had cursed the day he was born until God's point had been made, but Job had never given in and cursed God. Daniel decided that, if he had possessed the strength to get out of that shower situation the night before, he would probably be even stronger than Job if used in such a way.

The congregation flooded out through the big double doors of the sanctuary. Reverend Jordan was standing in the doorway, trying to shake everyone's hand as they passed him. This was no easy task, but Jim felt that it was important to let the people know that he appreciated their attendance. Daniel, Nic, Tom, and Trevor lingered last in line as always. They liked Jim, even though he was a middle-aged preacher, because he was easy to relate to. He always shot straight with them, never pretended that he was a saint, never condemned them for their required teen-aged mistakes. Jim had always said that youth ministry was one of his strong points.

The four young men watched as Jim finished talking to Ned Tyler, the last of God's older sheep to walk out the doors. Ned was one of Nightfire's oldest residents. He was now ninety-eight years old, but he was still known for the accomplishments of his youth. His pictures still hung on the walls of the school where he had been a legendary athlete. In fact, Nightfire High's mascot had been named in his honor. Though he was old now, nothing about his personality had changed. "Now you be sure to come over to see me an' Amy tonight." The old man smiled mischievously when he mentioned his scandalously young, fifty-three-year-old wife. "She can cook anything, I tell ya. When we send her off to do the dishes, you can come downtown with me. I'll get some beer in ya, an' we can ogle the youngster girls." Ned playfully punched Jim on the shoulder and cackled like the dirty, old man that he was.

"Thanks for the offer, Ned," Jim replied sincerely, "but I'm afraid it would be bad for the image of the church if I were seen drinking and ogling young girls downtown. Especially if I'm with you."

Ned cackled proudly at this.

"I will take you up on your offer for dinner though, and, if Amy has no objections, I'll have a few cold ones with you there."

Ned smiled widely. "That's the way! Yessir, I always say to the fellas at the bar that yer the only human preacher I ever met. Well, see ya at six, Jimmy!" Ned left, cackling all the way.

Jim waved, smiling as Ned walked off. Trevor, of all people, was scandalized. "Jim? You're gonna go get wasted with crazy old Ned? I thought you weren't supposed to drink!"

Jim smiled, as he turned to answer Trevor who, he noticed, was very red-eyed and smelled of marijuana. "I never said I was going to get wasted, Trevor. I said I'd have a few beers with the man, that's all. And no, I'm not supposed to drink. At least, not according to the Methodist doctrine, but even Christ had a drink with his friends from time to time. I only follow the rules that I believe in. You know I'm only a Methodist because they're the *closest* to what I believe. So far, there is no perfect branch of Christianity."

Trevor seemed deep in thought over Jim's words. "Oh," he said, before drifting back into thought. "Yeah."

At this point, Jim decided that it was time to say something about Trevor's scent. "You smell like pot. Stoned? In my church?"

At this, Tom started giggling uncontrollably. Nic and Daniel looked at Tom, then at Trevor. Nic shook his head and smiled. "Oh boy."

Daniel too was amused by this revelation. "So that's what you guys were up to last night." He chuckled.

Trevor was terrified. "Oh, uh, we just... It was just... I don't do this all the time, just once in a while. Just last night... I don't... I won't go to Hell for this, will I? Are you gonna tell my—?"

"No, Trevor. I won't tell your parents." He looked over at Tom, who was still giggling furiously. "Nor will I tell your mother, Tom. I don't have a problem with it, as long as you aren't doing it all the time. And don't be so afraid of my judgments, Trevor. We're all human. We all make mistakes. It's not like *I've* never smoked out before."

Trevor was relieved and suddenly sober—the terror at being caught by the preacher having flushed out his buzz. "Thank God," he said with more breath than voice. Tom, who was not sobered at all, laughed at him mercilessly.

"And I'm certain that you won't go to Hell for this," Jim reassured him.

Daniel was amazed. "I never even noticed. I thought you guys were just tired from staying out all night. So did you see the ghost at the Witch's Tree?"

Nic answered for them, "Yeah, that's who sold 'em the weed." Everyone laughed at this; even Trevor.

Still giggling slightly, because he found stoned people generally amusing, Jim asked Daniel, "So did you ask them about Tuesday, Daniel?"

"Oh yeah. I asked them this morning, but we've still only got Nic and Tom."

Nic spoke up, "I can draft Bert. Then we'll have five."

"Oh, that should be fun," Trevor said sarcastically.

"That will be great, Nic," Jim said. "What about Roxy? And you, Trevor?"

"I don't want to," Trevor said. "I'll hopefully be too busy being single again."

Jim grinned. "You broke up with Brenda?"

"No, but I'm hoping she's gonna dump me."

"Okay. You'll have to tell me the story behind that remark." Jim laughed, then looked back to Daniel. "And Roxy?"

"I haven't asked her yet. She had kind of a bad night, so I'll just ask her later." Daniel made no eye contact when he said this.

"Good," Jim said. "That should be enough. When you boys get a good look at this basement, you'll have no reason to fear Hell."

At that second, Brenda Calahan walked through the doors. "So, there you are! I've been looking all over for you, Trevor!"

Everyone stared at Brenda with a hint of fear in their eyes. Trevor nearly wet himself. "Hi, Brenda." He mustered up some courage. "I went out with Tom last night."

"Oh, did you!? And what made you think that was all right with me?"

Tom laughed at her and drew her wrathful attention.

"What're you laughin' at, you short, crusty, little bastard!? I'll give you somethin' to laugh about when I knock your head down into your neck!"

Tom still laughed, especially at the visual image she had just given him.

Brenda had no tolerance for Tom. She groaned horribly and walked briskly towards him. "This is none of your business, blondey! Shut the f—" She looked at the preacher. "Just shut up!" She shoved Tom hard on the chest, and he fell back, landing hard on his rear end. He stopped laughing. Before anyone could react to this, Brenda spun around and slapped Trevor with all the arm power she could manage. "Don't you ever try to ditch me again, boy!"

Trevor fell to the ground in a daze. He held the left side of his face in agony, as it turned red in the shape of Brenda's hand. Daniel's muscles tensed, and he readied to tell Brenda how he felt about people slapping and shoving his friends, but then Jim spoke. "Get out, young lady," he said in his strictest of voices. His controlled anger had reddened his face. "I do not appreciate anyone coming into this church with such violent intentions. I want you to leave, and come back when you can control yourself."

Brenda looked at Jim in shock. She was not used to being told no, and she did not deal with it well. "Fine. All y'all Methodists're gonna burn in Hell anyway. Get up, Trevor. You're coming home with me today! Let's go!" She stormed out through the doorway.

Trevor looked up at his friends and across at Tom, who was sitting on the floor. "Thanks, Jim," he said, still in shock. "I think I might as well go with her though. This might be the part where she dumps me."

"God willing," Jim said. "I should use this to make fun of Jack Scott, the priest next door at Saint Paul. She just walked over here after listening to one of his sermons, and this is what she did!" Jim laughed, knowing that Jack's sermon, no matter what it had been about, had most likely managed to have no effect on Brenda whatsoever.

Daniel offered his hand to Trevor, who took it. He pulled Trevor up and wished him luck. Then, as Trevor walked out to catch up with Brenda, it was not anger at her that Daniel felt, but sadness for Trevor.

Tom giggled once, still holding his chest and sitting on the floor. He then assessed the situation, "What a bitch."

Jim smiled and said truthfully, "That's an understatement if I ever heard one."

V

Daniel's alarm clock screamed its welcome to Tuesday morning at exactly 7:00 A.M. Daniel woke up sluggishly. He had just been torn out of a dream from his childhood. It was a recurring dream that had violated his sleep off and on for years. In this dream, he always found himself alone in a field. He would always hear a rustling in the tall grass behind him and, as he realized what was coming, he would begin to run. He would run to a hill and, as he tried to make his way to the top, his shoes would become incredibly heavy. He would turn around to see a hungry wolf, fangs bared, running towards him with great speed. Knowing that he had no chance of outrunning the beast, Daniel would turn to face it, tears streaming down his puffy, six-year-old face. The wolf would then leap into the air and pounce on him, and Daniel would fall to the ground beneath it. He would stare into its horrible, scarred, and hungry face as it lunged at his throat with its powerful jaws. Daniel always managed to grab the wolf around the throat before it could sink its teeth into his own tender neck. With strength previously unknown to him, Daniel would hold the wolf at bay, all the while squeezing harder with his little hands. He would squeeze and squeeze, until his strength threatened to leave him. With the last of his will, Daniel would tighten his grip and scream out in defiance. Then, defeated, the wolf would vanish into thin air. Needless to say, Daniel was not sad to be awake; though, whenever he had that dream, he woke up exhausted—feeling as if he had just been through a vigorous workout.

Daniel sat up, turned off the alarm, wiped the sweat from his brow, and opened his eyes. The dream always felt so real that Daniel felt the need to look beneath his bed before putting his feet on the floor. It was not as serious a fear as when he had actually been a six-year-old, but it was still a precaution he felt it didn't hurt to take. This is not to say that he was unshaken by the nightmare. Daniel jumped at the instant the phone rang. He pulled himself together quickly enough to answer it after the second ring. "Hello?"

"Hey, Daniel," the voice of Trevor answered him. "It's Trevor. Did I wake you up, man?"

"No," Daniel answered him sleepily. "I just got up a second ago. What's up?"

"Well, you know how Brenda decided to forgive me for going out with Tom and all."

"Yes. You poor soul."

"Well, I was wondering if you still wanted me to help out at the church this afternoon. You know, give me a good, religious reason not to go to her house after school."

"Trevor, why don't you just tell her no?"

"Are you mad!? You saw what she did at the church on Sunday! She might kill me. I think I'll just have to slowly distance myself from her. Maybe get her interested in someone else.

Someone I don't like. Someone like Bert. You know. Come on, Daniel. Just go along with this."

"Oh, don't worry, Trevor. We could really use the help." With a hint of amusement in his tone, he added, "Nic got your good friend Bert to agree to help."

"Joy."

"But Roxy can't go. She slept in on Sunday, and her father came home before she could clean up. He figured out that I'd been over there and grounded her for a month."

"What a jerk!"

"I don't know. He means well. He's just watching out for his daughter."

"Oh. How do you do that? Everyone has a good side with you. Bet I can stump you though. Brenda."

"I'll have to get back to you on that one, Trevor." Daniel laughed. "Anyway, just meet me and Tom at the car after school. We're going straight to the church."

"Okay. See you at school, Daniel. Thanks."

"No prob."

"Bye."

"Bye." After hanging up the phone, Daniel stood up, stretched, and walked over to the closet. He picked out his clothing for the day and went into the bathroom. Daniel got ready for school, as he did every weekday. He prepared himself mentally for a day like any other, blissfully unaware that this was a day that would forever change the course of his life.

***

After school that day, Daniel waited at his car for his friends to arrive. As he waited, he puzzled over the fact that he was always the first of his group to leave the building after the bell had rung, wondering what could possibly take a person so long to get out of there.

After exactly thirteen minutes, Trevor and Tom came walking out of the building. By the time they reached the car, another two Minutes had passed, and Daniel could see Roxanna just leaving the building. Daniel smiled warmly and greeted his friends. "Hey, guys."

Trevor, who had lit a cigarette the moment he stepped outside, removed it from his mouth and asked, "How do you always get out here so fast, damn it?"

Daniel responded with his own question, "What always takes you guys so *long* to get out here?"

Tom gave Daniel a sexy smile and said, "I'll tell you what takes us so long," as he reached over and squeezed the right side of Trevor's rear end. At this, Trevor, without expression and without even looking in Tom's direction, reached out and shoved him away. Tom flew backwards in an exaggerated stumble and started laughing. Daniel laughed too.

Roxanna Stillwaters walked up to the trio. "Hi, boys. Is Tom fagging out again?"

"Yes. The child needs a woman—badly," Trevor said insistently.

"Hey! No woman at all is better than *your* woman!" Tom retorted.

Trevor glared at Tom with eyes that pierced like daggers.

Daniel, unable to hold back, began laughing out loud, as Tom bit his lower lip, lowered his head slightly, and looked up at Trevor with big, sad, blue eyes.

"Oh," Trevor started with a smile, "go get laid!" Trevor then joined Daniel in laughter, and Tom looked dejected in a rather amusing sort of way.

"You're so mean!" Roxy whined sympathetically. She stepped behind Tom and wrapped her arms around his shoulders. "Tom's sweet."

Tom smiled and stuck his tongue out jokingly at his two male friends, who had stopped laughing, but were still smiling.

"Trevor was just playing, Rox," Daniel explained.

Of course, Roxy had known this. "You know, Tom," she began, still with her arms around him, "I was talking with some of my friends in gym today. A lot of them think you're pretty cute. Especially Robin Winters."

At this, Tom became uncomfortable and started to blush. "Good," he said. "She should. My eyes arc to die for." He squirmed out of Roxanna's grip and ran over to Trevor. "At least," he wrapped an arm around Trevor's waist, "that's what Trevor tells me."

Trevor wasted no time removing the younger boy's arm from his waist. He then asked simply, "What in the hell did you eat for lunch today?"

Suddenly the words *faggot soufflé* popped into Tom's head. He began to laugh hysterically. Daniel, Trevor, and Roxanna had no idea what was so funny, but this was not the first time Tom had started laughing insanely at nothing at all. They all chuckled at him, except for Trevor, who was mildly frightened. Tom laughed his way to the right side of the car, opened the door, and got in the front seat, where he continued to laugh as his mind built on his odd, random thought.

"So, does this mean we're leaving?" Trevor asked. His tone suggested that he was telling Daniel it was time to leave, rather than asking him.

"Yeah, we'll leave in a second," Daniel answered him. Daniel then kissed Roxanna gently on the lips. "You coming?"

"No," she said. "Grounded. Remember?"

"We'll try not to have too much fun without you then."

"I'm sure," Roxanna replied sarcastically. She turned around and waved, as she walked off to wait for her father to pick her up. "Call me when you get home!" she called over her shoulder.

"Okay!" Daniel answered. He watched her walk away. She was so beautiful. He found himself amazed, not for the first time, that he had been able to refuse her bed. *Someday,* he thought, *when we're married. It will be so perfect.*

"Hey!"

"Huh?" Daniel turned dreamily to face Trevor.

"You awake, man?" Trevor asked.

"Yeah. Just thinking." Daniel stared off after Roxy, in one last second of thought, then spoke again, "Ready to go?"

Trevor simply nodded, lit another cigarette, and got in the car.

As Daniel himself got in the car, he found himself worried for Trevor's health. He smoked those cancer sticks like a dragon.

Daniel worried for the day it might catch up with him. He knew Trevor wouldn't be happy about it, but Daniel would have to tell him eventually that he was concerned. As a friend, he saw it as his unpleasant responsibility.

Daniel turned the ignition, the engine faltered, almost started, then died. He tried it again. The same thing happened. On the third attempt, the engine started, sounding as if it might explode. Daniel put it in drive and left the school parking lot. As soon as he was in the slow-moving school zone traffic, the car died.

"Good ol' *Clunk*," Tom stated sarcastically.

"Come on…" Daniel pleaded with his car, as he once again tried to start it. It started roughly, smoke gushed out of the exhaust pipe, and the car moved forward with a violent jolt. After that, the car ran smoothly.

As they drove, Trevor spoke from the back seat, "Saturday is only four days away. Do you think *Clunk* will make it that long?"

"Yes. She has to," Daniel answered honestly.

"I can drive you around 'til Saturday if it doesn't," Trevor offered. "Assuming *Clunk* gets us back here, after we clean the church, so that I can pick up my car."

"Don't worry, Trevor," Daniel responded. "*Clunk* will make it to Saturday. I have faith. And anything's possible with enough faith."

"I don't know, Daniel." Trevor suggested. "Some things might be too screwed up for even God to fix." He laughed, as he reached out the window and patted the top of the old station wagon affectionately.

"So what happens to *Clunk* on Saturday?" Tom asked with a touch of sadness in his voice.

"I don't know," Daniel answered. "I'll have to cross that bridge when I come to it." There was also a touch of sadness in Daniel's voice. *Clunk* had taken him everywhere for years, and soon she'd be replaced. "Let's look on the bright side though, Tom. On Saturday, I'll have my dream car, and we'll drive all over town in it, all night long."

"Yeah, we'll party all night. And we can get Daniel stoned," Trevor suggested.

Tom Giggled.

"I don't think so, Trevor." Daniel smiled.

"Stick-in-the-mud."

"Shut up, Trevor." Daniel knew that his friends would never truly pressure him into doing anything he didn't want to do. It was good to have friends whom you could count on to never hurt you, and to always accept you as you were. Daniel thought to himself, as he drove, that he would never trade his friends for anything in the world.

At just that moment, Daniel noticed that *Clunk* was running dangerously low on gas. Knowing that he would have to stop at the gas station, he took one hand off of the wheel at a stop light and felt for his wallet. He was startled to realize that it was not in his pocket. Either it had been lost at school, or he had left it at home. "Guys, we're gonna have to stop by my house real quick."

"What's wrong?" both of his companions asked in unison.

"We're almost out of gas, and it looks like I left my wallet at home this morning."

"Uh-oh. Do you think we'll make it to your house?" Trevor asked.

"Oh, yeah. I'm pretty sure. I just don't know if we can make it to the gas station after that."

"Hey, I'd help you out here if I had any money, but Brenda took it."

"Don't worry about it, Trevor. We'll make it." Daniel smiled reassuringly.

A few minutes later, they pulled into the driveway of Daniel's house. Daniel was puzzled to see his father's car parked there in front of him. Neither Trevor nor Tom mentioned it, so Daniel decided not to voice his concern. He got out of the car without turning it off, for fear that it wouldn't start again. "I'll be right back," he said to his friends. Daniel then made his way into the house to get his wallet.

Daniel entered the house and went straight to his room. He found his wallet lying on his dresser. He opened it to make sure it had money in it, which it did, and then he left his room and headed for the front door. A sound stopped him. He heard his father cough. The sound had come from the kitchen, so, wondering why his father was even home, Daniel followed the sound.

Robert Mason was sitting at the kitchen table, staring at a pile of bills and an unopened bottle of beer. He looked as if he had forgotten the world around him. His eyes were glazed over and wide open, staring blankly. His breathing was slow, as if he were asleep. He didn't even notice Daniel entering the room.

Daniel was both very concerned and very puzzled by the scene before him. He had never, as far as he could remember, known his father to drink. And he still didn't know why his father was home in the first place. He spoke cautiously, "Dad?"

Robert jumped slightly with surprise, then turned around. "Daniel?" He turned back to his bills. "Oh, God. I didn't… I thought you were going to the church. I… Oh, my God." He put his hands on his face and let out a long sigh of despair.

"Dad, what... What's wrong? What's going on? Are you okay?"

"Oh, Daniel," Robert looked at the bottle in his hand. He looked at Daniel, and a sick expression came over his face. He looked back at the bottle as if it were an old enemy, and he had just remembered a treachery of its past. "I don't… I never drink. My God, I don't even know why I got this out of the refrigerator. We only keep these for your uncle, you know…" He drifted off, back into painful thought. A terrible, strained look came over his face. As far as Daniel knew, this was a look totally alien to his father. And then, red faced, Daniel's father shed a tear. According to the twisted cringe on Robert Mason's face, Daniel could tell that the act of shedding tears was physically painful for him.

"Dad, please, what happened?"

"Oh, Daniel," Robert put the bottle down and slid it to the other end of the table, "I've messed things up for us so bad. For months I've been deep in debt. I work so hard, just to make ends meet. It's never enough. I… I made a few investments that went bad…" Another tear rolled down his tense face, and from that moment, they came as a steady stream, accompanied by sniffing, but not sobbing.

Daniel was very uncomfortable. He had never seen his father cry. He had never wanted to see his father cry. He had no idea what to say in this situation. The silence became maddening, but then Robert continued. "I tried to talk to your mother about it. And she… God! Do you know what she said to me?"

Daniel just looked down, away from his father's tortured gaze.

"She said," Robert continued, "that if I were a real man, I wouldn't have to ask her for her family's help. She said that if I couldn't get us out of this situation myself, she would leave me to my debt and go *live* with her family in Boston. That woman, she can be so cold. I have nowhere to turn. You shouldn't have to suffer for my mistakes, Son. Oh, Jesus, what will we do? Why can't I fix this?" Robert fell again into contemplative silence.

"Dad," Daniel spoke nervously and paused briefly before going on, "I'm just wondering. Um, why…? What…?" He struggled to choose between all of the questions that were flooding his mind, before finally settling on, "How come you're not at work?"

Robert laughed bitterly. The tears had stopped, but he still sounded stuffy. "I'm sorry, Son. I didn't mean to make you worry. Your mother called to let me know she was packing her bags. She didn't even call my line. She called my boss. Told him she was leaving me. Asked him to relay the message. I guess she thought I wasn't humiliated enough already. He was understanding. He told me I'd probably be better off without her anyway. He could tell that I was upset, though, so he told me to take the rest of the day off."

Daniel had a look of total panic on his face, yet he managed to stay calm in spite of it. "So," he asked, "where's Mom now?"

"Oh, she's in the bedroom, packing. I know you hate me, Son, for what I've done."

Daniel's expression suddenly changed from panic to shocked disbelief. He did not hate his father at all.

Robert went on, "You can try to go with her, keep a roof over your head. She might take you, but I'm afraid the chance is slim. She doesn't believe in giving hand-outs. She sure as hell believes in taking them though."

"Dad," Daniel was nearly shouting with his adamant protest, "you know I don't hate you! I love you! You did what you could. You did what you had to do. Everything's gonna work itself out. Just have faith."

"Son, there aren't enough miracles left in the world for me." Robert's head sank down to rest in his folded arms on the table.

Daniel walked out of the kitchen and back to his room. He was not angry in any way—just determined to help. He got his check book out of his dresser, opened it to the back to make sure how much he had, picked up a pen, and went back to the kitchen.

His father's head was still down when Daniel returned. He didn't stir when Daniel started scanning the many overdue bills and cut-off notices on the table, taking a mental tally. When he was finished, he asked his father, "Dad? Are these all the bills you can't pay?"

"Yes, well," Robert raised his head and looked at the bills, without looking at his son, "all except for these three." He put his hand on the three closest to him.

Daniel opened his check book and purposely wrote his father a check for fifty dollars more than the bills required. He tore the check out of the book and held it out to his father. "Here, Dad. Everything will work itself out."

"Son, no!" Robert had never intended to ask for Daniel's money, and he had no intention of taking it now. "That's your money. I won't take your money."

"Dad, it's not my money. The check is written out to you. If you go put this in your account, you'll have enough to cover all of these bills."

"No! Son, that's all the money you have! All the money you've saved up for your car! Son, what about your car?"

"I saved up for it once. I can save up for it again. This is more important."

"Son, I don't deserve your help."

"Yes you do! You've never done wrong by me! Never. You always stand up for me when it matters. You would do this for me, if it came down to it. Dad, please take the money. There's no other way. I won't tell Mom, if you don't. You have my word. This stays between us."

"Oh, my son." Robert again started to cry. These were not purely tears of regret, but neither were they purely tears of pride. They were the tears of a thousand different emotions flowing all at once. Robert stood and went to Daniel. He hugged him tightly. "Oh, my son. What did I ever do to deserve you. I love you so much. Thank you."

"Dad, please, don't thank me. I didn't do anything you wouldn't have done yourself for me."

Robert released Daniel from his grip. "I'll pay you back, Son, as soon as I'm able. I wish I was a rich man. I'd buy you any car you wanted."

"I'm not asking you to pay me back."

"I don't care, Son. You will let me pay you back, or I can not let you help me. Promise me? Promise me." Robert smiled at his son.

Daniel smiled back at his father. "Okay. I promise."

Daniel returned to the car to find his friends frantic. "What took you so long!?" Trevor asked in near panic. "The car's been running all this time!"

"I know," Daniel answered, as he buckled his safety belt. "I had to talk to my dad."

"Your dad?" Trevor asked, as they pulled out of the drive-way. "Why isn't he at work?"

"His boss let him come home early," Daniel answered. "He's not fired or anything, if that's what you're wondering."

"Hey!" Tom interjected. "Doesn't this thing go faster than thirty miles an hour?"

"Yeah, but that's the speed limit," Daniel answered. "Besides, I want to coast as much as possible. And speeding won't really help our situation."

Ten minutes later, Daniel pulled the car up next to a gas pump at the nearest gas station. Before he could turn the ignition off, the car died. "Talk about cutting it close." Daniel looked up to the ceiling. "Thank you," he said. It was apparent to Daniel, on this day, that God watched over and took care of his sheep.

After using what little money was in his wallet to buy gas, Daniel started the car, and it didn't give him any trouble. He drove to the church, grateful that, though he would no longer be getting a new car anytime soon, he still had *Clunk*.

When Daniel, Tom and Trevor arrived at the church, they found Nic and Bert already hard at work helping Jim in the basement. "You were right, Jim," Trevor said, as he lit a cigarette and took in the apocalyptic mess that was the church basement. "I no longer fear Hell."

"Trevor! You made it after all! I'm so glad. We need all the help we can get," Jim said with great enthusiasm. "I suppose your generous sacrifice of time gives you permission to smoke in the church basement?"

"Oh! Sorry, Jim! Damn! I mean, darn!" Trevor dropped the cigarette on the floor and put it out with his foot.

Jim laughed. "I'm sorry, Trevor. I'll let you smoke down here once we get enough of this stuff put away. I only ask that you don't now, because most of the junk in this basement is highly flammable."

"Sorry we're late, Jim," Daniel offered. "We had a little car trouble, and I had to stop for gas money and talk to my dad."

"That's all right, Daniel. Just as long as you're here." Jim smiled at the three new arrivals. "And how are you, Tom? I'm glad you made it."

"I'm spiffy-good, Jimmypoo!"

"Glad to hear it, Tommydon," Jim responded with amusement.

"Dangit!"

Daniel looked around the basement. The floor was covered with papers and boxes. There were candles, banners, and old hymnals scattered all over. This would indeed be a long, hard day.

"Hey, where does this go?" Nic asked.

Jim turned around to see Nic and Bert carrying a medium-sized box full of pornographic magazines. All eyes were wide and staring at Jim, as he blushed and answered, "Oh, those, well, the trash of course."

"Whatsamatter, Preach?" Bert asked rudely. "Not gettin' any?"

Jim turned the other cheek. "Actually, Bert, I confiscated those at the last Confirmation class lock-in. Several boys were huddled together in one corner of the sanctuary, trying to look inconspicuous. None of them claimed responsibility, when I broke them up and found what was keeping their attention. I put them down here, in a box, and as you can tell, I haven't been down here again to throw them out."

The boys believed him, but they still laughed at him playfully. Jim could not deny the humor of the situation. "Oh, all right. Let's get to work. Nic, Bert, and I are enough people to handle the main room here, but we have three very messy storage rooms. Don't worry, they're small—each about the size of an average bathroom. If the rest of you would each take one, we'll be out of here faster. Just tidy them up, straighten out the shelves. Invent places for all the stuff on the floor to go. Just as long as it all *looks* neat."

Trevor entered one of the three large closets, and he looked around. There were all kinds of books scattered about. Hymnals, Bibles, theology books, church handbooks, photograph albums, and choir music. The one peculiarity that stuck out was a glass beaker sitting on one of the shelves. It was propped up in a corner, on top of a big, black book. There was a cork plugging the opening of the beaker. Trevor took a closer look at the little, glass container. There was some kind of red liquid inside it. He picked it up. It looked like blood, but why would there be a beaker full of blood in the church basement? Trevor wondered briefly just how strange the new Confirmation class was. He decided to ask about it later. For now, he had work to do. He placed the beaker back where he had found it and commenced cleaning up the dusty book closet.

Three hours passed quickly for everyone. Trevor was amazed, when he finally left the book closet, to see how much progress had been made in the main room. There was actually a floor. "Hey, Jim!" he called. "I'm finished in here. What do you want me to do now?"

"Smoke a cigarette," Jim called back over his shoulder. He, Nic, and Bert were still busily moving boxes, but all of the paper had seemingly vanished without a trace.

"Will do." Trevor lit a cigarette and inhaled deeply. It was hard to believe that he had gone three hours without craving one. He had just been too busy cleaning, and too busy wondering about the beaker. "Hey, Jim!"

"Yes, Trevor?"

"Could you come here for a second? I want to show you something."

"Hold on, Trevor. I'll be right there." Jim helped Nic lift a large, dusty box and place it on top of another large, dusty box. He then exhaled heavily and wiped the sweat from his brow. "You guys want to take a break?" he asked Nic and Bert.

"Yeah," they said in unison. Like Jim, they were also both covered in sweat and dust.

"Hey, we're done!" Tom called out. He had finished cleaning his closet an hour earlier and gone to help Daniel with his.

"Good!" Jim answered. "Take a breather."

Daniel and Tom walked out of the closet. They were sweaty and dirty, like everyone else. They joined Nic and Bert in following the reverend over to Trevor's closet, where Trevor stood in the doorway. "Now, what do you want to show me, Trevor?" Jim asked, as he arrived at the door.

"It's in here," Trevor answered. He went inside and pointed to a shelf. "What's this?"

Jim, along with the others, entered the closet to see what exactly Trevor was pointing at. When Jim saw what it was, his eyes went wide, and he let out a gasp. "My God! How could I have forgotten?" Jim made his way over to the shelf and picked up the beaker. "If it had been broken…" He dismissed the thought. "But it wasn't. Thank you for being careful, Trevor."

"What is it?" Trevor asked excitedly. "Why are you so freaked out about it?"

"It's the blood of Christ. Isn't it, Jim?" Tom asked.

"No. Actually, it's…" Jim looked at his young helpers thoughtfully. He knew that he had to be truthful, and he felt that he could trust them, so he finished his sentence honestly, "…werewolf blood."

"What?" the five boys all asked, more or less in unison.

"It's werewolf blood," Jim repeated, without a trace of humor in his voice.

The boys laughed.

"Werewolf blood?" Trevor asked incredulously. "Good one, Jim!"

"Yeah, that's a lamer story than the one about the Confirmation class!" Bert laughed at his own statement, but he laughed alone.

"Shut up, Bert," Nic said. "So, what is it really, Jim?"

"Oh, I wasn't joking. Not at all. This," he held out the beaker for all to see, "is the actual blood of an actual werewolf."

Daniel had been studying Jim's face. He could always tell when Jim meant business, and this was one of those times. "You're not joking, are you, Jim? That really is werewolf blood." When Daniel spoke, everyone became serious. Daniel had never been suckered in by lies. He didn't have a gullible bone in his body, as far as his friends were concerned. If he believed Jim, then it was definitely worth hearing the pastor out.

"Yes, Daniel. It is. I know this is hard to believe, but if you put it into perspective, it's really not that strange. After all, as Christians, we're asked to believe that Moses parted the Reed Sea, that the *virgin* Mary gave birth to God's son, that Jesus turned water into wine and rose from the dead. The Bible makes numerous references to demons, so why shouldn't we believe in werewolves. It would be rather hypocritical not to even consider the possibility, if you think about it."

"Well," Trevor asked, "if that is truly werewolf blood, why is it in a beaker, in a small church, in a small town, collecting dust?"

"I suppose I'm obligated to explain, now that you know it's here. The problem is that it's a very sensitive issue. You see, the mayor of this town put a hush order out on this shortly after it happened in the 1850's. The story, he feared, would prevent the town's growth. They even tried to take this beaker, but they lost that battle. This blood has been passed from one preacher to the next in this town for generations. I'll tell you boys the whole story, but you have to promise not to repeat what I tell you. The higher-ups in Nightfire all know the story, they know about the blood, and they like the fact that only a handful of citizens know the story. If you repeat this, I could end up in trouble. But to answer you more concisely, Trevor, the blood is here to keep the werewolves out of Nightfire."

To all the young men assembled, the basement seemed strangely darker at this moment, strangely colder. Every one of them, for the rest of the time they spent in that basement, on that evening, would feel an uncontrollable impulse to look over his shoulder to be sure there was nobody behind him.

"So what happened?" Daniel asked bravely.

"Do you all agree to keep quiet about this?" Jim asked.

They all nodded at him.

"All right, then. "I'll tell you the story; the very true story of what happened here in 1850. Even better, I'll read it to you. It's all recorded right here in this book, by the Nightfire preacher who was there." Jim picked up the black book that had been under the beaker. He then put the beaker back on its shelf. He turned to the back of the book, and then he said, "Ah, here we are. Take a look at this for yourself." He turned the book so that the boys could see the pages.

They were old, yellowed pages. Handwritten at the top of the first page was, "A Testimony of the Werewolf Plague of 1850." The authentic look of the pages sent chills down the spines of everyone assembled, including Jim, who had rarely looked at them since his arrival at the church years ago. The antique pages were covered in plastic, but still readable. As Jim began to read, the basement took on the atmosphere of a campfire sight, where a scout master, or someone's mischievous uncle, was just beginning to tell a frightening tale of the supernatural, something that was "absolutely true," a story that all of the boys knew would keep them up nights for weeks, but they had to hear it, just the same. And their attention was thus undivided.

VI

A Testimony of the Werewolf Plague of 1850

I, Reverend David Alexander Paul, being of sound mind and body, have been called to give my testimony pertaining to the demonic events of these past weeks. I take no pleasure in recalling all that has transpired, but this record must be passed on in order to ensure the future safety of Nightfire, Texas.

It all began in July, just over a month ago, in the new church building. Everything seemed normal, except for the stranger. As I was preaching, I noticed the man staring at me. His eyes seemed to cut through my flesh and chill my very soul. At the time, I could not place what it was about him that troubled me so. He seemed like a nice enough fellow. He was well groomed, dressed all in black except for his rather elegant looking white shirt, which he covered with a fine looking jacket. He wore his dark hair long, pulled back behind him like a tail on his head. He was, by all appearances, a very wealthy man and, after the service, he seemed to attract a great deal of attention to himself. Especially from the ladies.

He at first returned attention to only one lady: Miss Anabell Richards. She was a lovely, young girl of seventeen, the daughter of a local merchant named George Richards. George's wife had died five years earlier, so he and his Anabell had lived alone. They were such generous, kind people. Dear God, if only I had known then what I know now.

I went outside, where I found George and Anabell talking with the stranger. At Anabell's insistence, George had invited the stranger to supper. At this point, I joined in the conversation. I learned that the stranger's name was Sebastian Barnes. He claimed to be from a failed settlement in the unorganized territory somewhere along the Santa Fe Trail. He had come to Nightfire, Texas to start a new life, and was at present staying in the town's hotel. He claimed to be only twenty-seven, but there was something about him that made him seem like the product of a more antique time, and he had the speaking skills of a very well educated man. Perhaps this is what made him so seductive to everyone who spoke with him. No one could refuse his charm and kind manner. This is why Anabell died such a terrible death.

It was the night of the full moon, later that week. I was going for an evening walk before going to bed. Sebastian had just left Dan Parker's Saloon, where he had used his money to make friends of just about every man in Nightfire. I stopped to talk with him briefly. The way he was looking me over made me terribly uncomfortable. It frightened me. He wasn't looking at me in the way men usually looked at each other. He was looking at me with a very hungry glare in his eyes, as though I were a fatted calf—something to be devoured.

My first, uncomfortable thought was that he was the sort of man who took unnatural pleasure in the company of other men, and that he was looking at me with such desires in mind. But when Anabell Richards approached us, my discomfort and my theory were replaced by perplexity. Anabell, God rest her soul, told us that her father, God rest his soul, had developed a cough, and she was on her way to ask Doctor Hildebrandt for some medicine. Sebastian, who had dined with the Richards again earlier that evening, told her that he had a treatment for coughs that never failed. He then took her hand, looking at her in the way that a young man is expected to look at a beautiful, young lady, and insisted that she allow him to walk her home, where he promised to cure her father. The pair bid me good evening and walked away.

When they arrived at George's store, I watched them hesitate at the door. Sebastian started to speak to her, but they were too far off for me to hear. She looked away, as if embarrassed. He spoke again. She seemed to argue, but in the end she willingly walked away with him, arm in arm, into the woods.

I gasped, and Sebastian turned his head—staring directly at me. At first, I thought that it was impossible for him to have heard me from such a distance, neither did I see how he could possibly have recognized me. But then he offered me a menacing smile. It was a smile that said, "I know you're watching, and I find it amusing." And I thought, "How could I tell that he was smiling from such a great distance?" But I will swear to my merciful grave that I saw him smile exactly as I say. That was the last time that anyone saw Anabell alive.

The next morning, a group of school boys playing in the forest came across Anabell lying in the brush, or rather, what little there was left of her. The boys ran to tell the sheriff, who in turn told George Richards, who had reported that she went out to get him some medicine and never returned the night before.

George, after going to the forest with Sheriff John Thomas to identify the remains, came to me. He was holding the necklace that had been his late wife's. After her passing, Anabell had worn it at all times in her mother's memory. George told me that it was the only way, along with the few shreds of the clothing that Anabell had worn that night, that he was able to identify her without doubt. He insisted that I go to the undertaker's with him, so that I could see for myself what kind of demon had taken hold of her. George was at the edge of his sanity. I dared not argue with him.

Out of respect for Anabell, I will keep the details to myself. Suffice it to say, her remains were barely identifiable as human. I prayed over her, asked God to have mercy on her soul. George wept fiercely. I then escorted him home.

Once George was safely home, I went to speak with Sheriff Thomas. John and I had never been friends, but we respected each other. He had no love for, or belief in, God, and I had problems with his extreme ways of handling law-breakers. Our mutual respect for each other, however, came from our devotion to our causes.

When I told him about seeing Anabell going into the woods with Sebastian Barnes, John listened. He knew that I would never lie, and he himself had found Barnes' presence unsettling. He told me to go home and keep quiet. No need to tip the suspect off that he was caught. He then went over to the hotel to ask Sebastian for an alibi. I knew that, if Sebastian could not come up with a convincing alibi, John would just shoot him and be done with it. Kill the fear of having a sadistic murderer in town. That was John's way.

I went home, as John requested. I tried to work on my sermon for Sunday, but found myself far too distracted. I needed to know what was going on, and I had a very strong feeling that things were about to take an even darker turn, and, God forgive my premonition, I was right.

I told myself that I was just going out to clear my head, but deep down I suppose I knew where I was going all along. I ended up at the hotel a few minutes later. Harold Martin, who ran the hotel, explained to me, before I could ask, that the sheriff had come by looking for Sebastian Barnes. I asked what had come of it, and Harold told me that Mr. Barnes had left about twenty minutes before the sheriff even arrived, leaving instructions to tell anyone looking for him that he had gone to visit George Richards. Harold had sent the sheriff there. So that is where I went.

I arrived at The Richards Store, just in time to see the end of a conversation through the window. George Richards was standing behind the counter, looking frightened to his wit's end. The sheriff was waving a pistol around, as if wondering whom to shoot. And Sebastian Barnes was standing in front of him, looking calm and self-assured. I could not hear through the glass, but I could see lips moving. Sebastian started to talk to the sheriff very calmly. The sheriff held his gun aimed at Barnes. Sebastian reached up and put his hand on John's shoulder. John shuddered. He looked frightened, like a child facing the devil. Sebastian spoke to John with a sly grin. John lowered his pistol, looked to be deep in thought. When he finally raised his gun again, he turned it on George Richards and fired. George, with a look of terror forever frozen to his face, fell to the floor dead behind the counter.

I ran into the building. John looked at me with a pathetic, desperate expression on his sweat-drenched face. He holstered the gun and wiped the sweat from his mustache with his right hand. He then looked at me as if searching for words. His eyes seemed to beg for my forgiveness. I asked what had happened. Barnes spoke first. He looked at me with an almost amused grin and said, "When a man like George Richards brutally murders his own daughter, one should know that the town is going to Hell."

His words both puzzled and frightened me. I looked to John for answers. He said to me only, "We found evidence," all the while looking away from me. He then told Sebastian and me that it was best if we left and sent someone to take care of the body.

I felt ill. Something was terribly wrong. Sebastian looked at me and told me it was nice to know there was a preacher in town, because Satan could be found at the scene of every murder. He never stopped smiling.

I was left that day with nothing but my confusion. Something had transpired between John and Sebastian. I feared it was something unholy.

The following afternoon, sixty-seven-year-old Agetha Conner found me praying in the new church building. She needed to ask me if I believed in demons and Satan as an actual persona. I told her that lately I feared I did strongly. When I asked her what had brought the question to her mind with such urgency, she told me that she believed she had seen a demon. It was running out of the woods on the night of Anabell's demise, and it was howling horribly, like a wolf out of hell. My blood ran so cold I thought I would die. I told Agetha to pray about what she had seen. She died of a heart attack in church that Sunday. She was standing next to Sebastian Barnes, singing a hymn.

The better part of a month passed quickly after the Richards' deaths. In that time, I had grown far more troubled. Curious about Agetha's sighting, I had started asking people if they had seen or heard any wild animals on the night in question. Most people had only heard the howl. Others had seen and heard nothing. There were a few, however, who had actually seen something. Some of these claimed to have seen a demon, some claimed to have seen a ghostly shadow, or an unusual bear. But the most agreed upon description was that of a very large, shadow-like wolf. It had howled like one, after all. It was at this point that I re-evaluated my college-educated disbelief in were-wolves. And if werewolves weren't enough to worry about, every day I saw an Indian standing at the edge of a cliff, dressed in war paint. He just stood there, staring at the town from above. I feared a Comanche raid would soon bring more death to Nightfire, but for some reason I dared not shout "Indians about!" For some reason I found myself unable to mention the Indian to anyone. I wanted to pack my bags and leave town, but for some damned, unexplainable reason, I couldn't.

Sebastian Barnes had also kept himself busy that month. He had paid very special attention to several of the town's young la-dies. Many thought him a mere scoundrel, but others, like myself, had assessed the truth. Unlike me, many of them packed up and left town.

Other than pursuing the ladies, Sebastian pursued several seemingly close friendships with several of the town's men. He quickly became a very central figure here.

It wasn't until the night of the full moon of August that my greatest fears were confirmed. I had been thinking deeply about what had transpired at The Richards Store the month before, and I had finally reached a decision. It was obvious to me that, as is always the case when dealing with the devil, Barnes had made an offer of power that John couldn't refuse. My fear was that John was granted this power by becoming a werewolf himself. Like a fool, I decided to investigate.

That night, as the moon had just arrived in the night sky, I snuck over to the sheriff's house. Once there, I hid outside, where I could peek in through a window. I was terrified as John entered the room. He looked frightened as well, was the odd thing. He opened his front door, and from my windowsill perspective, I saw a shadow-like skin cover him. It was indescribable, like nothing I've ever seen, and I hope to God I never see it again. It did indeed look very wolf-like, but entirely out of proportion and, from the look of it, there was no physical texture to the beast that our sheriff had become. It wasn't hairy, as one might expect, but instead, it was just a shadow. And when it turned to face me, I saw its glowing, red, hungry eyes. The eyes were just as unearthly as the rest of him. No pupils, no corneas, just a devilish, red light. I knew that I was going to die. The beast left the house with great speed. I saw it turn round the corner of the house an instant later, speeding in my direction.

Paralyzed and mute with terror, I accepted my fate, and I didn't even notice the arrow sailing right past my ear, so close that I should have been able to hear it whistling through the air. The monster screamed in agony—a sound straight out of Hell. The shadow that had surrounded Sheriff John Thomas dispersed and, along with John, it died. I didn't realize that I had been saved, I didn't register the fact that the beast had been slain, until I felt a warm hand on my shoulder. Still scared mute, I opened my mouth in a silent scream and turned around. To my shock, I saw the Indian, covered in war paint, holding a bow. He had saved my life. He looked to be about thirty years old and, with a knife in his boot, a hatchet at his hip, and a sheath full of arrows strapped to his back, he seemed prepared for battle. I didn't know whether to thank him or to run. My decision was made for me. As he pulled me up, he said simply, "You will come with me." Getting my voice back, I started to ask why, but he covered my mouth, gave me a stern look, and led me away into the forest, at the edge of which we had been standing, and into the hills. He did not speak again until we reached the Indian camp sight. My complete disorientation was not helped at all by the way the other Indians cheered his return, and even regarded me with warm expressions. At this point, they told me, I collapsed.

I awoke the following morning to find myself in a tepee. The Indian who had rescued me was there with a woman and a small child. He introduced them as his wife and son. I asked him what was going on. He told me he would first tell me his tale, and then he would tell me what he needed from me. He introduced himself to me as Running Wolf. This is the name he had been given as a youth, before the massacre that would grant irony to his name. He then told me that to most he was known instead as the Tracker. As he told his tale, I learned that, as a boy, Running Wolf had been greatly esteemed in his own tribe for his inborn tracking skills and his great speed and agility. His tribe, however, had been dead for many years as he told me this tale.

To make his very long story short, when he was only seventeen, a werewolf had murdered his entire tribe. Though the braves fought a valiant fight, he alone survived. He alone managed to kill the Shadow Wolf, as his people had called it. It was with White Man's Magic that the demon was finally felled. None of the weapons of the tribe had affected the werewolf, so Running Wolf, and two of his peers, went to a nearby White Man's settlement to find a healer. They had all heard tales of a local preacher who had the magic of the White Man's God. The ability to heal. Running Wolf and his companions managed to sneak into town without being noticed. They found their way to the man they sought and tried to tell him of their plight. Unfortunately, he didn't speak their tongue. The man, who was not blinded by the town's general Indian prejudice, could see that the three young Indians were desperate and sought his help. He held up his hand and placed it on Running Wolf's forehead. From that moment forward, Running Wolf could understand the magic man's tongue, and the magic man could understand Running Wolf's tongue. The two of them spoke, and Running Wolf translated for his friends. The man agreed to help them. He prayed over a pail of water. He then took their weapons and submerged them. When he gave them back to the three youths, he told them that the weapons would now cut with the power of Christ.

The three returned to their village to find everyone dead—horribly mutilated. They decided to wait for night and avenge their dead. The werewolf came again, killing two of them before they knew what had hit them. Running Wolf was saved by his much admired speed and agility. He managed to slay the beast with his newly enchanted dagger.

At this point in his story, the Tracker paused to give me his opinion. "The werewolf is a punishment given to us by the White Man's God; therefore, the werewolf can be vanquished by the magic of the White Man's God alone."

Being a minister, of course, my view was slightly different. The werewolf is the spawn of Hell, and there is only one God; therefore, only the power of the one, true God can vanquish the forces of Hell. But I digress.

Running Wolf went on to tell me that he tried to return to the magic white man for further guidance, but found that he had been put to death by his own people for aiding the Indians. Running Wolf was alone. He decided that he was meant to hunt these Shadow Wolves, and slay them wherever he found them. He traveled the continent for years, without a tribe, doing just that. In that time, those whom he had helped came to know him and refer to him as the Tracker. He destroyed werewolves in many small settlements, Indian and White Man alike. He learned many secrets about fighting them off and preventing their return. He told me that the legendary silver bullets only worked when blessed by a holy man. He also told me that any weapon dipped in holy water would be able to penetrate the werewolf's shadowskin, bringing it certain death.

The Tracker told me that for the past three years he had been living with this tribe of Comanches, who had allowed him to become a part of their tribe after he had single-handedly slaughtered three werewolves that had been plaguing them.

Strangely, the three werewolves in question happened to have been Texas Rangers.

Running Wolf only agreed to stay because he had fallen in love with one of the tribe's young girls. He now had a wife and a three-year-old son, and was chief in all but name, for not one warrior among them was as mighty, wise and courageous as he.

It had been a long time since he had fought the Shadow Wolves, and he was almost out of the White Man's magic. He showed me a half empty canteen. It contained holy water that he had acquired during his many great hunts. I asked him if the holiness wore off of the weapons dipped in the holy water. He regarded the knife with which he had killed his first werewolf, as he explained. When the holy weapon hit the werewolf's blood, both forces were neutralized. The werewolf's life was taken, and the weapon's magic was tainted. He dipped his knife again every time he planned to use it on a werewolf.

I explained to him that I was a Methodist and had no access to genuine holy water. He told me that it really didn't matter. The healer from his youth had been a Methodist as well. I considered the overwhelming events of the past night, and after a few moments of thought, in which I again considered running, I agreed to help him.

He told me that all of the tribe's warriors' weapons would need to be tempered by the fire of White Man's God, and, without my asking, he gave me his word that none of Nightfire's innocents would be harmed by his people. I agreed to temper the water for him. He took me outside, where several children had gathered bowls of water from the nearby streams. I blessed the water in the name of Christ, and the Indians prepared their weapons. I asked to be led back to town, so that I could gather more help while they did their preparations for war. The Tracker led me home, and quickly vanished back into the forest.

I find myself running short of paper, so again I shall try to be brief. I returned to town, and I found that many people had been wounded, but not fatally. It was then that, for the first time, I really asked myself why Sebastian Barnes had given the sheriff the power of the werewolf. Why had he been seducing so many of the town's people, befriending them? What was his goal? I knew that he was repopulating Nightfire with werewolves, but why? How many had been left untouched? Sheriff Thomas was obviously not the only one who had been transformed the night before. The town must have been swarming with the beasts over the past night. If so, tonight would be even worse, assuming that no one was being killed.

I walked into the church building, and was grabbed violently, stripped completely naked and pushed to the floor, where my skin was inspected thoroughly. A group of surviving townspeople had already gathered in the church. They were all armed—men, women and children alike. Harold Martin had caught on earlier to the truth of what was happening in Nightfire and had prepared a mass of silver bullets. The people were satisfied that I was uninfected, so they allowed me to live and to get dressed. I told them where I had been and what I had learned. I told them that help was on the way. I was pleasantly surprised to hear no negative feelings about the Indians; especially after hearing Tracker's story about the healer. I quickly blessed all of the silver bullets in the name of Christ, and had them all dipped in home-made holy water just to be sure. We were ready to make our stand.

Tracker and his warriors arrived moments before moonrise. As we all held our weapons ready for the inevitable battle, Tracker pointed out a flaw in our identification system. "We have some of them in here with us," he said simply. I protested, telling him that everyone here had been stripped and searched for cuts where the werewolves could have penetrated their blood streams. My blood ran colder than ever when Tracker looked at one young lady in particular and said, "You only checked them on the outside."

At that moment, the light of the full moon came through the window of the church in full force, and we were jumped by a force of infiltrators. Women, all of them. Women I had known for years as friends and neighbors; fellow Christians. I helped the other pure humans to shoot them dead, one by one. Our bodies were slow to react, and combat was not my place. I thank God for those Indians, and for the hunters in our company. Those people killed with grace and skill, even in the unexpected situation. Though our number was decreased significantly, we managed to kill all of the werewolves inside the church. But then, one of the walls collapsed. None of us was hurt by this, but the sight before us made us all wish the wall had crushed us to death. There were so many of them! All sizes they came at us. Some were very, very small. Children. My God, why the children? How can a just god so freely damn the innocent? Forgive me, God, for my failure to accept this.

It was very fortunate for us that Tracker had possessed the foresight and experience enough to leave a large number of his

Indians hidden outside. The Comanche warriors materialized out of the background like rain from a storm cloud. They fell on the werewolves as the werewolves fell on us. There was also a large number of townspeople who were untainted, that had not known to gather in the church, who had joined the fight.

The battle raged violently and, though it seemed to last forever, it was actually brief. Our number had been greatly decreased, and so had theirs. There were so many bodies scattered about. Arrows poking out of the fallen devils, the limbs of the innocent tossed about like a scene one might expect to find in Hell. I had somehow managed, after my gun had been rendered useless, to step away from the fight. There was nothing for me to do now but pray.

I watched as the people of Nightfire mopped up the remaining werewolves. I was startled to feel a warm hand on my shoulder. I turned around to see the very face of evil smiling at me. It was Sebastian Barnes. He was somehow still in human form. "Forgive me, Father, for I have sinned," he said to me. I wondered if the feeling I kept getting (that I could know no greater fear than I had already known) would ever be right. I remember his every smooth word, "For six hundred years I have put up with the world of Man. My first sin is that I waited six hundred years before I decided to build my new world. My greatest sin is that I have failed. It would have been so beautiful. You could have been a part of it. We would have our own laws. No human court could judge us."

He screamed suddenly. His words had been cut off by a searing pain. Tracker stood behind him now, holding an empty canteen. Unfortunately, holy water is only fatal to a werewolf if it enters the blood stream, and Tracker was out of weapons. Sebastian had only been drenched. His shadowskin revealed itself around him without true shape. It went into a sort of seizure.

As Sebastian slowly gained control, he screamed out in defiance, "*Here is your evidence that I am of Hell!*" At the moment he contained himself, in the demonic form of the werewolf, he lashed out with his right arm and struck Tracker, ripping open the skin on his chest and knocking him to the ground. Tracker wailed in agony.

I looked behind me and found a pistol that someone had dropped. I grabbed it and aimed it at Sebastian. He distracted me by regaining his human form. He told me that Tracker would, within seconds, be one of his, and by the time I fired one shot, whichever werewolf I had spared would tear me apart.

I realized that I was without hope. I turned the gun on myself as I watched the Tracker become enveloped in a shadowskin. Then I heard a gunshot that was not my own. Tracker's shadowskin dissipated as he died. I realized what had happened and quickly turned the gun on Sebastian and pulled the trigger. I left him without a head.

After the werewolves had all been destroyed, one of the Indians, the one who had shot Tracker, approached me with a beaker. He told me that Tracker had told him to tell me, if he didn't make it. He had forgotten to tell me how to prevent a werewolf from ever coming to Nightfire again. The Indian explained that werewolves' senses were heightened to an extreme. They found the scent of their own dead unbearable, and they could smell it from several miles away. If a beaker of werewolf blood was kept in Nightfire, the town would be safe for as long as it remained. Any werewolf within scent range would stay clear of the town.

I thanked the Indian and took the beaker. I went to Sebastian's neck and let the blood flow into the now sacred glass tube. I later put a cork in it, because he also told me that the blood, if kept long enough, would develop a putrid stench that even humans could detect if it wasn't well contained.

Now I shall leave this God-forsaken town. I don't know where I will go, but I can't stay here. For some reason, most of the others have elected to stay and rebuild. Perhaps it's because of the safety Nightfire now has to offer—werewolves will be repelled, and the Comanches have agreed to leave this settlement alone. I leave them to it. I shall wait for my replacement to arrive, and then I will go where the Spirit moves me to go. I pray that this town is kept well. For all time this blood must be kept. I will relate the story recorded here to the minister who replaces me, and this tradition must be carried on. The blood can not be forgotten, or this may very well happen again.

Peace be with you,

Reverend David Alexander Paul

VII

The room was silent as Jim closed the book. Everyone was lost in his own thoughts. Jim eventually broke the silence, "So, what do you boys think?"

"I don't know what to think," Daniel answered. "I believe it, but I don't know what to think about it. Werewolves…" He shook his head in contemplation.

"Well, I think it's a load of sh—"

"Shut up, Bert!" Nic scolded. "Nobody cares what you think."

"I do," Jim corrected him. "Please, Bert. I wasn't asking you to believe it, just to listen to the explanation at hand. If you think I was lying, or that the papers were fabricated before I ever came here, you shouldn't feel as though you must be quiet."

Bert looked at Jim stupidly. He wasn't used to being stood up for; especially by the one he was about to ridicule.

Jim ended with a question, "Do you think I was lying, Bert?"

Bert answered honestly, "No. But I think maybe whoever wrote the paper did. Or they might have been confused, or insane."

"Even though I personally believe the story to be true," Jim said, "I see where that could surely be possible. And it is an intelligent theory."

"I don't know whether to believe it or not," Trevor interjected. "I've never really seen anything supernatural before, you know? But, well, I know strange things happen. I believe in the supernatural, but I don't know if I believe this particular story. There's no reason not to, but at the same time, there's not really any hard evidence. It could have happened."

"Well," Nic said, "I just don't believe in evil. I don't think God would allow such things as werewolves to exist in the world. I don't think there's any such thing as ghosts, werewolves, vampires, or the devil. If God is purely good, which he is, then evil just doesn't make sense."

"Without evil, good is an empty word," Daniel pointed out with a smile.

"Well, I don't know about that." Nic smiled back at Daniel, agreeing to disagree.

"I believe in ghosts," Tom offered solemnly. Everyone looked at him, held captive by his uncharacteristic tone. "When I was little, I spent the night at a friend's house. While he was asleep, I turned over on the bottom bunk and looked out the window, into the back yard. His dog had just died a week earlier, but I saw the dog sitting outside, looking at me. It was at the other end of the yard, in front of the flower bed.

"The next day, I was in the back yard with my friend, so I went to the spot where I had seen Shelly, his dog, and I asked him if that's where she was buried. He looked at me kind of funny and said that it was. I never stayed at his house again. So I have no trouble believing in anything else supernatural."

"Tom," Nic said with a chuckle, "you really are crazy, you know."

Tom did not return Nic's smile. He was hurt that Nic didn't believe him, but he knew of nothing that he could do about it.

"Well, what do you say we get this basement finished?" Jim asked. "We still have a few boxes in the main room to get put away. Then we can all go home and rest." He smiled as he stood up, put the book back on the shelf, and rested the beaker back on top of it. The boys murmured among themselves as they rose to leave the closet.

As Jim led the others out of the closet and soon found himself distracted by appointing people to boxes, Tom stayed behind. When all were gone, Tom crept over to the doorway. He peeked out to be sure no one noticed his absence. Everyone seemed busy.

Tom went over to the shelf where the blood rested. He felt a need to see for himself. Tom had always been the experimental type, and werewolf blood was just too good to pass up. He reached out and took the beaker from its place on the top of the book. He studied it. How could he prove to himself the accuracy of the story? It did not take Tom long to think of something. He remembered that, according to the story, the werewolf blood would become pungent with age. After almost a hundred and fifty years, the blood should be quite stinky. All he had to do was remove the cork, take a whiff, and put the cork back on. If the blood smelled worse than his late aunt Matilda had smelled when he was little, then the story had to be true. Tom snickered as he considered his smelly, dead aunt. Yes, all he had to do was pull the cork, but Tom found himself feeling nervous. In one final act of procrastination, he pushed his long, blonde bangs out of his eyes. He then thought to himself that this would be his only chance to smell old werewolf blood, and then he pulled the cork. "Ugh!" was all Tom could say as he fell to the floor. The breath had been pulled from him by the strength of the putrid stench. Tom didn't even realize that he was falling until the cold, cement floor slapped him on the right side of his face. Just before everything went dark, Tom thought to himself that he was feeling somewhat dizzy, and then he lost consciousness.

Daniel was placing a large box of he-didn't-know-what against the wall, near the closet where they had all just been. It suddenly occurred to him that he hadn't seen Tom since leaving the closet. Before he could ask anyone on the other side of the basement about it, he heard someone say, "Ugh!" from inside the closet, followed by the sound of glass breaking and something heavy hitting the floor. Daniel dropped the box and ran to the closet.

Tom was lying there alongside a puddle of blood. Daniel gasped, but was relieved when he realized that it was not his friend's blood on the floor, but the werewolf blood. Tom had probably dropped it, but that didn't explain why he was on the floor, "Tom! Tom, are you okay?" Daniel was frantic. The room smelled terribly sour, but, unknown to Daniel, this was only a fraction of the stench that Tom had inhaled. The smell had been diluted as it was spread out in the closet. Daniel ran over to his friend and turned him over onto his back. Tom's face was bruised, but he wasn't bleeding, and nothing appeared to be broken. He was breathing shallowly. Daniel held Tom in his lap on the floor, trying to wake him. "Help! Guys! Tom's hurt! In the closet with the blood! Hurry!"

Everyone heard Daniel's call and came running to the scene. Jim gasped. "My God!" he said hoarsely. He looked to Nic, Trevor, and Bert. "You three get Tom outside—fast. If you can't wake him up with some fresh air, call an ambulance." As they complied, Daniel helped them to lift Tom, so that they could drag him in a near standing position. "Daniel, help me clean this up."

As Tom was dragged out of the closet, Jim ran past to get some rags. He had never anticipated that the day would go like this. How could he have forgotten about the blood? How could he have not noticed Tom's absence?

While Jim was gone, Daniel decided to do what he could to clean up the mess. He bent over the spill and started carefully picking up the broken glass. Daniel's thoughts were with Tom. He wanted to go outside and be with him. He quickened his pace, picking up three pieces of glass at a time. It was not long before Daniel felt a sharp sting in his right index finger. He inhaled quickly through his teeth and looked at it. There was a bloody shard of glass hanging there in his finger. The blood that now dripped down the jagged piece of glass was a mixture of his own blood and the blood that had originally been spilled in 1850.

Daniel pulled the glass out of his finger. The cut was actually pretty small. He wiped it off with his other hand, and it looked much better. Only a small amount of blood trickled from the cut after that. Just enough to seal it shut. Daniel felt relieved to remember how old the blood on the floor was. No AIDS in 1850. He noticed that the blood on the floor was quickly drying up. The blood was so old that any diseases that it had carried had probably been neutralized. Besides, he hadn't gotten very much of it on him. Not enough to even consider. That's what he kept telling himself.

Jim came into the room with some rags. "Oh, my. That stuff sure dries up fast."

"Yeah. I picked up a lot of the glass while you were gone."

"Well, I suppose I'll take care of this later. They got Tom to wake up. He's doing fine from the looks of it. Says he has a bit of a headache though. Let's go on up. I think it's time to call it a day."

Outside of the church, standing on the front porch, Tom was feeling incredibly guilty after learning what had happened. "Jim's gonna hate me. I feel so stupid."

"Don't worry about it, Tom," said Nic. "You didn't pass out on purpose. If the stuff stank as bad as you say, how could you have known?"

"I shouldn't have been messing with it. That's all." Tom looked miserable. The right side of his face was purple and swollen and, aside from that, his entire posture was depressed. His hair hung down in his face, and he made no effort to remove it. He was slouching, looking only at his feet and, though no one could see them, his big, blue eyes had lost their trademark shine. "Now we could all be in trouble. Big trouble."

"Jim won't care, Tom. He won't toss you into Hell or anything," offered Trevor.

Tom responded quietly, "I wasn't talking about Jim."

"Oh, grow up!" Scolded Bert. "There ain't no werewolves!" He rolled his eyes and huffed disgustedly. "Moron."

Even though Tom had no respect for Bert, the words had hurt him. The pain was evident on Tom's face when he looked up. Bert's insults were just one more thing to pile onto Tom's troubled soul—on top of his guilt and shame.

Trevor, who loved Tom like a brother, turned red with rage at Bert's words. He moved so fast that Bert was on the ground before he even realized what had happened. Trevor lunged at Bert with his entire body, slamming him flat against the brick wall. Wasting no time, Trevor backed up slightly and released all of his rage, through the full force of his right fist, into Bert's gut.

Bert's face turned red, as he struggled for air.

"Shut the hell up!" With these words, Trevor summed up all of his feelings for Bert. As Bert sank slowly to the ground, wide-eyed and clutching his stomach, Trevor felt good—refreshed. When Bert started whimpering and shedding tears, Trevor began to laugh. He looked at Tom, patted him on the back, and said, "Don't let 'im get to you, Tom."

Nic looked down at Bert. "You were askin' for it, buddy."

Bert spoke through tears, "Le'me alone."

Nic turned his attention to Tom. "You know, Tom, I wouldn't worry about werewolves if I were you. It's just not worth the energy. Everything'll be fine, pal. You'll see."

Jim and Daniel walked through the doors. Jim looked at Tom. "How's your head, Tom?" There was nothing but concern in the pastor's voice. No anger at all.

"It still hurts, but not as bad." Tom looked back down to his feet. "I'm sorry, Jim. I didn't mean to—"

"Don't worry about it, Tom. The preacher who wrote that was probably just nuts, like Bert said," he lied. Jim then noticed Bert, who was huddled in a corner, clutching his stomach. "What's wrong with Bert?" he asked no one in particular.

"Oh, nothin' Jim," Trevor answered. "He's just resting. That's all."

"I see." Jim looked at Trevor suspiciously.

Trevor gave him a *what?* look.

Jim decided to let it go. "Anyway, I thank you all for your help, but I think it's time to call it a day. You've definitely all earned your rest, I'd say."

Daniel went to Tom and put his hand on his shoulder. "You okay?"

Tom smiled at Daniel. It was the first time he'd smiled since he had woken up. "Yeah, I'm all right."

Everyone said their good-byes. Daniel, Trevor, and Tom went off to Daniel's car, and when Bert finally got up, he limped away with Nic. Jim smiled, as he locked the church up and waved good-bye to the youths. He smiled for their benefit, as well as for his own, as he attempted to cover his terrible fear.

VIII

Daniel walked through the front door of his house. "Ah, lasagna! I could smell it baking half way down the block!"

Daniel's father looked up from his paper. "Daniel! How did you know what we had for dinner? It's been in the refrigerator for an hour now."

"Sure it has." Daniel laughed and went to the kitchen. He was relieved to see that his father was in a much better mood now, and his mother had apparently decided to stay. He saw her standing in the kitchen, cleaning the counter. "Hi, Mom."

Barbara Mason looked at her son with an accusing stare, said nothing, and kept right on cleaning.

Daniel ignored her unprecedented hostility as always and asked, "So when's dinner?"

"An hour and a half ago. You could have at least had the decency to be here when it was served. There's some left in the refrigerator, if you just need to start messing the kitchen up this late."

Daniel never could understand his mother. It wasn't that late, considering how late it could be when he got off work some nights. It was now barely 8:00. He had told his mother well in advance where he was planning to be that day. "Mom, I did tell you that I was going to help Jim at the church today, didn't I?" He thought it was possible that he had forgotten to let her know, although he did clearly remember telling her.

Mrs. Mason stopped cleaning and regarded her son coldly. "I know what you told me." She walked out of the kitchen stiffly, without another word.

Daniel, as always, had to pretend that she had a good reason for her strange behavior. He looked in the refrigerator and found a small portion of lasagna. He assumed it would still be hot, since he had smelled it from so far away. He picked up the small plate, and he touched the lasagna with his finger. It was stone cold. It felt as though it had been refrigerated for days. Daniel was thoroughly dismayed. He could have sworn that he had smelled it cooking. Even now, the smell of the meat seemed so strong, so magnetic.

Daniel felt a strange lustful hunger for the lasagna, not just a desire to eat it, but a need to *have* it in his mouth, a need for it to *be* devoured. Without thought, Daniel picked it up and put the entire portion in his mouth at once. He chewed only enough so that he could swallow it at all. By the time he realized what he had done, the food was gone. Stunned, Daniel decided that he didn't feel so good. He decided to go to bed early. He did so right after he called Roxanna, but he kept the conversation very brief

As Daniel slept, he was bombarded by nightmares. He tossed and turned all night, suffering one bad dream after another. The only nightmare that he would remember in the morning, however, was this:

He was floating in a black, endless void, and there he met the devil. The devil was just sitting there in the void, as if on a sturdy chair, watching Daniel tumble helplessly. He looked very much like the stereotypical Satan. He was unclothed, red skinned, hoofed, fork-tailed, and he had a fiendish pair of horns atop his head.

Daniel considered asking the devil to help him, to stop the endless tumbling, but he quickly realized the implications of reaching out to Satan. The Fallen One smile sadistically at the tumbling mortal. Daniel cried out, "God! Jesus! Please, deliver me!"

Satan laughed, and Daniel looked at him with question. The devil finally spoke, "You're mine now, little lamb, and there's nothing that God *can do about it. Only* I *can deliver you from your helplessness. Give me your hand."*

*As Satan reached out for him, Daniel screamed, "*No!*"*

Next door to the Masons' house was the house of Lillian Foster. Lillian was in her early forties, and she had lived alone in that house for as long as Daniel had been alive. She had always been a friend to all of her neighbors. She was a single, free-lance writer, but was in no way reclusive.

For all of her life, Lillian had kept a secret about herself from almost everyone. She had only told one man, Reverend Jim Jordan, though she never had attended, nor planned to attend, his church. He was the one friend whom she trusted completely, and he had a very strong belief in the supernatural, from what she could tell. Most people wouldn't have believed her, if she had told them that she could sometimes see the future, and that she had a slightly higher understanding of the world than most people did.

Lillian was secretly a very potent psychic and, at this moment, she was asleep. At this moment, she was dreaming. When she woke up, she would remember only flashes; images. She would remember watching Daniel Mason tumbling through a dark void in fear of the devil…

…a bloody battle that took place in Nightfire in 1850…

…the violent, merciless death of Roxanna Stillwaters…

…Daniel Mason being covered by a shadow and howling at the full moon…

…her friend Reverend Jordan—his frightened eyes deliberately keeping a dark secret from her…

When Lillian woke up at 3:34 that morning, she was covered with both tears and sweat. She knew that she was being called to do something, and she would spend the next several hours trying to piece her nightmares together and figure out what exactly they were calling her to do.

IX

It was 8:57 A.M., and Lillian had been awake since just after 3:30. She had puzzled over her nightmares for several hours, before coming to her decidedly ridiculous conclusion. Lillian knew deep down that it was not truly ridiculous so much as extraordinary, but she feared that if she told the wrong people the wrong things, she herself would be seen as ridiculous, or crazy.

She had decided that Daniel Mason, through no fault of his own, had become a werewolf. She had also decided that it was somehow connected to something that had happened in Nightfire's past, specifically in 1850. Her final realization had been that, if she said nothing, bad things would happen. But who would believe her? Daniel Mason was the nicest, most well rounded kid in town.

Even so, if she went straight to Daniel, she could end up getting hurt. Therefore, she decided that she would go talk to Barbara, Daniel's mother. She would explain everything: her psychic abilities, how she once used them to save Daniel when he was little. If Barbara was convinced of this, then she might be responsive to the rest of it.

Lillian watched the clock and the window all morning. She told herself that she would go to Barbara at 8:00. The time came, Robert left for work, Daniel left for school, and Lillian decided that she would go to Barbara at nine instead.

Now, at 8:57, Lillian realized that she was not going to go to Barbara at nine. She just couldn't make herself do it. She was too afraid of being called crazy. That's just the reason she had always chosen to keep her psychic gifts a secret. Only Jim knew about it.

Lillian felt a sudden burst of energy when she realized that she could talk to Jim about her visions. Though in her visions, his eyes were hiding something from her—something dark. Could he know about Daniel? She decided it didn't matter. In reality, Jim hadn't yet hidden anything from her, and she needed to talk to someone; someone who could help her decide what to do.

She stood up from the couch by the window and went out to her car. She then drove to Jim's church, where she hoped to find, if not answers, confidence.

Reverend Jim Jordan sat in a pew in the church's sanctuary. As he sat, staring at the large, golden cross in front of the pulpit, his mind drifted into turmoil. His thoughts were with the deep, dark secret that he had been entrusted with for so many years. The secret, and the responsibility, that now meant nothing.

The blood was gone.

The document from 1850 quoted Sebastian Barnes as having claimed to be at least six-hundred years old. If werewolves were so long-lived, it was entirely likely that Sebastian Barnes had a friend or two who had been waiting fourteen decades or so for an opportunity to avenge his death. It was only a matter of time before a werewolf, assuming they still existed, noticed that Nightfire was no longer off limits.

Jim hated himself for sharing that awful story with the boys. If any of them had really believed it, they must have been terrified, just as he was.

Jim briefly toyed with the idea of going to the mayor and telling him what had happened. He quickly dismissed the idea as pointless. The problem could not be solved so easily. What could the town government do about it anyway? Go out and get another beaker of werewolf blood? No. It was better not to get in trouble for something that could not be fixed and would probably go unnoticed anyway.

At least until another werewolf showed up in town. Jim contemplated his guilt over and over. If only there were some way to undo the whole thing.

"Something's troubling you."

The sudden interruption caused Jim to jump in his seat. He gasped and turned around to face his visitor. "Lillian, you scared the hell out of me." With his hand on his chest, he quickly caught his breath.

"I thought, being a preacher, that you weren't supposed to have any hell in you to begin with."

Jim muttered under his breath, "If only."

"What?"

"Nothing. Just… Nothing." Jim snapped out of his dark trance and smiled up at his old friend. "So what brings you by?"

Lillian looked at him tensely. "I need to talk."

"Of course. Sit down." Jim noticed how tense she seemed. He grew concerned. It usually took a lot to rattle Lillian Foster. "What's happened?"

Lillian sat down next to Jim. "Nothing yet."

"You've been dreaming again." At this point, Jim became tense as well. *God, what did she see?* he thought. *I can't take it if this has anything to do with that damned blood.*

"Well, it's kind of…" Lillian looked to the cross in front of them, as though she expected to see her next words written upon it for her. "…crazy...ish." She looked at Jim with frightened eyes.

Jim could tell that she needed reassurance. Whatever it was, she did not expect him to believe it. "Lillian," he assured her, "it can't be so crazy that you can't tell *me* about it. You've told me everything. I haven't called the men in white yet. Please, take your time, and tell me what's bothering you."

"Well, how should I say this?" Lillian bit her lower lip and considered for a moment before going on. "I feel that I'm being called to do something, but I'm not sure whether or not I can."

Jim, in all honesty, wanted nothing less at the moment than to ask his next question, but now there was no turning back. "What is it that you feel called to do?"

Lillian took a deep breath, turned her head to look Jim dead in the eyes, and asked, "Do you believe in werewolves?"

Jim's flesh turned white, and his mouth seemed suddenly and terribly dry. As he struggled to think of an answer, his every movement, down to his very heartbeat, seemed awkward. Finally, he spoke. "I…" he swallowed involuntarily, "…suppose I believe in the possibility. Why?" When the words had finished dragging out of his mouth, Jim thought to himself that the dries of his mouth was due only to the fact that all of the water in his body was now leaking from his forehead.

Lillian looked at Jim with a puzzled expression. *He knows something.* Even though she had seen it in her dream, she was taken by surprise to see him actually hiding something from her, maybe even lying. She decided to keep it to herself for the moment. "Let me tell you about what I remember from my dreams." She smiled nervously before going on, "The edited version. I dreamt of something terrible happening in the past. Here, in Nightfire. There were werewolves—countless werewolves. It was horrible. Men, women, children. So bloody. The townspeople and a group of Native Americans eventually killed them off. I don't know how that connects to the rest of the dream, but I *know* it does. You see, I saw…," *Daniel Mason.* Lillian decided that the edited version of her dream didn't include a name, "…a boy. A teenaged boy. He was spinning around helplessly in a void of blackness, and his only hope of regaining control was to reach out his hand to the devil. This part, I think, was symbolic."

Jim wiped his brow with a handkerchief that he had taken from his pocket. He then asked in a painfully hoarse voice, "What do you think it means?" He made a pathetic attempt at clearing his throat.

"I think that it means, well…" Lillian realized that she was no longer so unsure of herself, and Jim definitely knew something. "I think it means that one of Nightfire's young citizens has somehow become a werewolf, and it's somehow tied to something that happened here decades ago."

My God, Jim thought to himself in panic, *how could this be? Who could it be? Tom!*

"Who?" Lillian asked, as if Jim had just mumbled something aloud.

You bitch "Huh? I didn't say anything. You must be hearing ghosts again or something." Jim covered his sickly pale face with shame at how rude he had just sounded. How badly he was treating one of his best friends. He did hate it when she read his mind though. He never had decided whether it was comforting or unsettling to know that she usually couldn't control when it happened. "I'm sorry, Lil." He looked up at her apologetically. "I'm not feeling well. Not well at all. Please, go on."

Lillian contemplated her next words carefully. Should she tell him the rest? Why not? It might be enough to make him talk. "There's only one more thing." She shuddered as she recalled the images of Roxanna Stillwaters being torn apart. "Someone's going to die if nothing is done."

"Oh my God, no! Who?" Jim waited in terror for her answer, though not once did he fear that it might be he who died. His concern was only for others. For himself, he felt only contempt.

Lillian again looked to the cross, then she looked down and twiddled her fingers. "If I did know who was going to die, I wouldn't be able to warn her directly." *Her, damn, I've said too much.*

Her? "Why not?" Jim asked absently, as he considered her statement.

"A feeling. It would only worsen the situation if I went to this person."

"Her," Jim said with a corrective tone.

Lillian ignored the comment. "If I went to this person, I don't know what would happen exactly, only that it would be worse. I do have another person in mind though."

"Oh. Who?"

"Please, Jim. I'd rather not say right now. I'll tell you when it's important, or when the whole thing is over with. Promise. I just don't know if I can talk to the person. I feel like I'm being called to, but this person can be intimidating."

"I'm sure Moses felt the same way about the Pharaoh. You have a gift, Lillian. Use it. If you feel that you are being called to do a specific thing, do it. God gave you your gifts for a purpose. Follow your guts." Jim was pleasantly surprised to hear how easily the words came to him now, but he felt no better about what he had neglected to say.

"You're right, of course. I knew what needed to be done. I just needed some support. It always helps to hear it from someone else. I don't think I can go through whatever is coming alone. Now I just don't know *when* I should go to this person."

"Go first thing tomorrow. That way you can sleep on it—figure out what you're going to say."

"Yes, that sounds like a good idea. Thank you, Jim. I think I'll be going now."

Thank God. "So soon? We've just gotten started."

Lillian fixed her trusted friend with a genuinely hurt expression. "Jim, you're really upsetting me. You're relieved that I'm leaving. I feel very unwelcome, and frankly I'm surprised at you." Lillian stood up.

"Lil, I..."

"No, Jim. You're hiding something from me. I don't know what, but you know something. I'll warn you right now, Jim. We've been great friends for a lot of years, but if you hold out on me when things get critical, I'll never forgive you."

"Lillian, please don't talk like that."

"Goodbye, Jim." Lillian smiled with surprisingly honest affection. "I'll see you later." She left, and Jim guiltily fell over in the pew and released a massive sigh of relief.

As Mr. Krandall stood drawing on the chalk board, Daniel Mason sat at his desk, oblivious to what the algebra teacher was saying. Lunch was ready. Daniel could smell it. It was on the opposite side of the school building, and lunch was a full hour away, but he could smell the meat as if it were right on his desk. He craved it. He could pay attention to nothing else.

"Daniel?"

Daniel was still not quite with it. "Huh?"

"I asked you to tell us how you solved problem 17." Mr. Krandall sounded concerned.

"I didn't!" Daniel barked at the man without thought, as he tried to concentrate on the gripping smell of meat.

At this point, all eyes were on Daniel. He was behaving very uncharacteristically. "Mr. Mason, did you, or did you not, complete the assignment?"

The smell filled Daniel's nostrils like a melody. Meat. Blood. Death.

"Mr. Mason!"

Daniel was finally snapped out of his trance. "Yes! I mean, no. Er… What was the question?" Daniel's classmates were beginning to snicker, and he was beginning to blush. He was also starting to feel a little bit scared. What was wrong with him?

Mr. Krandall had become agitated, but due to Daniel's grades and past behavior, his voice carried more concern for his best student that scorn, "Mr. Mason, are you feeling all right? Do you need to go see the nurse?"

Daniel just stared blankly at the teacher. As he stared, he considered how satisfying it would be to tear off Krandall's head and drink from the crimson fountain that gushed from his neck. Daniel wondered at the possibilities of how delicious the math teacher's raw flesh would taste in his mouth.

"Mr. Mason?" Mr. Krandall repeated. "Nurse?"

Daniel came back to reality with a wide-eyed look of terror. "Yes! Sorry." Daniel got up from his desk and ran out of the room, terrified by his own sick train of thought. Where were these morbid, obsessive fantasies coming from?

Daniel thought to himself, as he ran through the hallway and out the back door of the school building, that he might be possessed. Maybe when that beaker had broken, the ghost of that werewolf had been released along with the blood. Maybe, since Daniel had been the one who stayed and cleaned up, he had been chosen as the spirit's host. One thought continuing to surface in his mind was that maybe the blood had actually infected him, but he refused to entertain the notion. The cut had been small, and God would never allow such a thing to happen to his faithful follower.

Whatever the problem, Daniel was certain that Jim could help. Daniel prayed as he ran to his car. He prayed very hard, as he drove straight to the church, where he hoped to find his reverend friend.

Daniel arrived at the church and ran to Jim's conference room. When he found it empty, he went to the sanctuary, where he found Jim lying on a pew with his hands over his face. He approached the minister cautiously, unable to determine whether or not Jim was awake. He finally asked, "Jim? You awake?"

Jim had to think about that. Then, having come to the realization that someone else had asked the question, he removed his hands from his face and sat up, springing like a mouse trap. "Who…?" he asked in surprise.

Daniel jumped, when the preacher sat up, and let out a startled gasp. When he regained his composure, he said, "Hi, Jim."

Jim laughed. "Hello, Daniel. I'm sorry about that. I was just, um, thinking. I wasn't asleep. Well, not yet." Jim shook his head and rubbed his eyes. "I wonder how long I've been like that. I had a stressful morning." He looked at his watch, then back up at Daniel with concern. "Daniel, shouldn't you be in school?"

Daniel looked down at his feet. His face was wearing the most pained expression Jim had ever seen on it. It was abundantly clear that something had shaken the boy.

"Sit down, Daniel. Tell me what's on your mind." Jim scooted over to make room for his young friend, and he patted the seat to punctuate the invitation.

Daniel sat down, folded his arms, and stared at the cross in front of the pulpit. He felt unable to make eye contact with Jim, mostly for fear of the thoughts it would bring. The hellish, hungry, perfectly evil thoughts. "Well…" Daniel had no idea how to begin. He feared that Jim would laugh at his fears, but, at the same time, he also feared that Jim would take him seriously. "I don't know." Daniel exhaled and looked down at his folded arms in an act of surrender.

Jim was very worried. He almost never saw Daniel down, and he absolutely never saw Daniel this down. He put his hand on Daniel's shoulder. Daniel quickly grew more tense. Jim, noticing this, removed his hand and tried to think of something to help Daniel talk. After a few moments of thought, he spoke, "It's all right, Daniel. Just take your time, but please don't choose to hold it in. You give me the impression that something has upset you pretty badly. What's goin' on, bud? Girl troubles?" Jim smiled. "Guy troubles?"

Daniel sat, his expression unchanged.

Jim frowned. He usually got a giggle out of the youth he counseled when he used the homosexual inference. Usually. Jim, now too concerned to let Daniel hold on to his silence, decided to go down the list. "How's your family doing?"

Daniel lifted his head and stared again at the golden cross. "I don't know. They could be better, I guess." Daniel sat in silence for a few seconds, tempted to talk about his family instead, tempted to forget his real problem and pretend that he was this upset over his parents' marital problems. He dismissed the thought quickly, when he allowed himself to remember his true, undeniable fears.

"Do you want to talk about it?" Jim asked in a comforting voice.

"No. That's not what I'm here for. Not them. It's something else." Daniel's face became even more strained as he spoke. His eyes were now fixed on his knees. "It's crazy. You'll think I'm insane."

Jim smiled. "Daniel, after hearing me talk last night? You can't top that for sounding crazy, my friend. I assure you, I've heard some pretty strange stories in my life, and I always take them with an open mind. You have my word that I won't think you're crazy. I know you too well, and I can tell that your feelings are very real."

Daniel took a deep breath before he spoke again. "I don't know. This sounds so crazy. I think…," Daniel paused, giving himself one last chance to reconsider, before he continued. "I think I might be possessed."

Jim found himself taken by surprise. Daniel now appeared to be holding back tears. Something awful had happened to make Daniel suffer such a complete and honest fear. If this statement had come from anyone else, Jim might not have been so quick to accept it as a real possibility. Jim thought carefully about what to say next. This was a doozy. No one had ever come to him with this particular problem before.

Jim thought hard in the brief moment of silence. This was by no means the *most* difficult one-on-one he'd ever had. The worst had been during the last trip he had made to Camp Bridgeport with his church's small youth group. Tom had come to him, frightened of Hell by his own erotic desires for a very openly homosexual male life guard whom he had befriended. Jim had really stumbled through that one. Tom had been honest with him, and Jim had left him even more confused than before. Jim had every fear that this talk would take the same direction. All he could do was try. "Daniel, who... Why? I mean, um, could you...?" *Bad start.* "What gives you cause to believe this?"

Daniel answered in a very shaky voice, "I just haven't been myself today. Or last night. I'm scared. I just...have this blood lust—this hunger for meat." At this point, Daniel began to grow excited, and his voice took on a passionate tone, "I feel a need to kill." He looked at Jim for the first time since he had been seated, and his hands rested at his sides and curled into fists. "I feel a thirst for blood, a hunger, a rage, a desire to tear through human flesh with my teeth and bare hands!" Daniel looked Jim dead in the eyes with a piercing stare, and he saw the fear there. He calmed. "Jim, I..." Daniel quickly put his hands up to cover his face, as tears began to flow. "Please help me," he managed to plead through the pain of his tears.

Jim looked at Daniel. It pained him to see his friend this way. He could feel tears of his own trying to break through to the surface of his eyes, but he had to hold together. The look in Daniel's eyes as he had speaking had not been his own. Jim was scared, but he had to be strong. He feared the answer to his next question. "Can you tell me..." He paused, looking for the words. "Who is it that you think is inside of you?"

Daniel, still crying, spoke into the palms of his hands, "If I tell you, you'll think I just got scared of that story you told us and fantasized the whole thing."

Jim's face went white. *Damn me for telling them that story.* "Daniel, what you are experiencing is very real to you. I honestly don't see you as the type to imagine or hallucinate something this vivid. Tell me who you believe is violating you."

Daniel looked at Jim, having regained his composure. "Sebastian Barnes. I think maybe his spirit was trapped with the blood. When the beaker broke, he escaped, and while I was alone in the closet cleaning the blood, that's when I think he did it. I'm so scared. What if he makes me hurt somebody? All I could think about in class was killing my teacher, devouring him." Daniel gave Jim a desperate, pleading look, as he said again, "I'm so scared."

Jim leaned over and hugged Daniel.

Daniel hugged him back fast and hard, tears again streaming down his face.

"I'm here for you, Daniel." Jim tried to be strong, but the sight of someone he loved so much going through so much pain proved to be too much for him. He found himself silently shedding tears of his own, as he hugged Daniel tightly and thought desperately. Could Lillian have been talking about Daniel? That would mean she had been wrong about the werewolf, at least partially. No one had *become* a werewolf, but someone *had* been possessed by one. Still, there was Tom. It was possible that Tom had received a small, undetected cut from the shattered beaker. The blood could have infected him. That would mean that both Daniel and Tom were in trouble. And dangerous. Daniel and Tom were the two youths at his church to whom Jim felt the closest. He had bonded with them both very strongly, and it pained him greatly to consider that they might both be suffering like this.

Jim's final thought, before speaking, was that Lillian could have been completely wrong. There was no werewolf in Nightfire, and no one was possessed by one either. Jim broke the hug, but kept a hand on his young friend's shoulder. "Daniel, are you going to be okay?"

Daniel sniffed and looked into Jim's caring eyes. "I hope so, but I don't know." He looked down. "I feel a little better, but I'm still scared. Real scared."

"I'm scared too," Jim replied. "Now, before I say this, I want you to understand that I take your belief very seriously. I just want to be sure before we go any further. You must confess that it is *possible* that you just have a bug. You could be sick, and that story I told you is playing havoc with your mind. All I'm saying is that you should sleep on this. Be sure. Pray. That might be all it takes, even if you *are* possessed. Tell me how you feel tomorrow. If you still think you're possessed and need my help, we'll take it from there. I'll call you. Okay?"

Daniel forced a smile onto his tear-streaked face. "Okay," he said. "I'll pray."

Jim stood up. "So will I. With all I've got."

Daniel kept his talk with Reverend Jordan in his thoughts for the rest of the day. He also spent his every spare second in prayer. That night, when Daniel went to bed, he felt emotionally drained. He even forgot to call Roxanna. He was reminded when the phone rang. "Hello?" He spoke in a voice that announced he had just woken up.

"Hi, Daniel. It's me," a pleasant voice rang into his ear.

Daniel smiled warmly, without opening his eyes. "Roxy. I'm sorry I didn't call. I laid down on my bed without any intention of falling asleep." Daniel found that, talking to Roxy, he could at least temporarily forget the traumas of his day.

"You goob," Roxy teased.

"Goob? I'm not a goob. Your daddy's a goob."

"Your momma!"

"Your granny!"

Roxy laughed at the tired voice Daniel was using. "Are you okay, Daniel? I heard you went home early from school today, and I've been worried ever since."

"Why didn't you call sooner?"

"I did, several times, but your mom's been on the phone most of the day."

"Probably swapping gossip with Beth Green, as usual."

"Who knows? So are you sick? Are you going to school tomorrow? I want to see you! Do you need anything?"

Daniel laughed. "Slow down, girl. Take a breath."

"Sorry."

"I'm just playing, Rox. And to answer your questions, yes, I think I am sick, and yes, I'm probably going to try to go to school tomorrow. I don't think I need anything right now, 'cept maybe a kiss. So, I'll definitely want to see you tomorrow."

"I can't wait. But now I guess I'll let you go, so you can sleep. Don't go to school if you still feel sick. I know you can be stubborn about things like that. Promise?" She waited for his answer for only a moment, then turned the question into a command when no answer came, "Promise!"

"Okay, okay! I promise." Daniel smiled. It was so good to talk to Roxy after such a long, hard day. She was so good to him and loved him so much. "I love you."

"I love you too. Now get some sleep. Night."

"Night." Daniel hung up the phone and drifted off to sleep.

He slept peacefully.

Next door, Lillian Foster had also gone to bed and fallen asleep, but her sleep was not at all a peaceful one. The final dream of her restless slumber was the only one she was destined to remember.

Lillian found herself walking outside, taking in the hellish sights of what had once been Nightfire, Texas. Most of the buildings in her neighborhood had been destroyed, and she saw body parts and bones draped across the landscape like weeds. "No!" She spoke only to herself, for there was no one else to hear, "How could this happen? How am I the only one to survive?"

She turned around to face the remains of her own house, and she became overwhelmed with terror at the sight of her own, dismembered head, staring at her with only half a face. She screamed with the realization that she was dead, torn apart, and now just a spirit, wandering around, lost. "No, no, no!"

She screamed defiantly, as hell-spawned demons rose from the ground; ungodly, unholy, hideous monsters, rising from Hell, beckoning her. "No!" she screamed out again. "Stay away from me!" She continued to scream as she ran, "Stay away!"

The dark spirits surrounded her, grabbed her, tore at the very fabric of her soul.

Lillian cried out, in complete agony, "How can this be!? How could this have happened!? God, save me!" She felt the indescribable pain of her jaw being torn from her face, and she could speak no more. She shrieked horribly, with all of her pain, as she was helplessly dragged lower and lower; closer to Hell.

And then it was over. She found herself standing in the wreckage of Nightfire once more, but she was now in the presence of a faceless man in a white suit.

He said to her, in a voice that had no sound, "A few may be saved, but only if you plant the seed." He put his hand on her shoulder, and there was a brilliant flash of light.

Lillian awoke at 5:00 A.M. *Today*, she decided at once, *I will talk to Barbara Mason.*

X

Lillian Foster sat by her window, staring at the coffee mug in her hands. She had just watched Robert and Daniel leave for work and school respectively. Now she sat, trying to find the strength to do what she felt called to do.

Usually, Lillian spent the early part of the day writing. Now, however, she found herself too distracted to write a single word. She knew that if she had been able to write, she would definitely have been using that gift to escape this situation—to ignore the calling and lose herself in her work. Eventually, if she handled it that way, everything would work itself out without her. Maybe.

Lillian looked at her watch. 8:10. Now or never. Lillian released a massive sigh. She then looked up, set down her coffee mug, and said, "God help me. I have no idea what I'm going to say." She then rose from the couch and walked, with blind determination, to the front door of her house. As she stepped out into the waiting daylight, she wasted not another moment on her doubts. The time had come, to act or not. She had chosen to play her part in whatever was to come, regardless of where might take her.

***

Lillian stood before the front door of the Masons' house. This was the moment of truth. She took a deep breath, and then she knocked. As she waited for an answer, she amused herself by studying the patterns in the cracked and chipped paint of the old, wooden door. When she felt a tingle on her spine, she knew that Barbara was looking at her through the peep-hole on the door.

The door opened. "Hello, Lillian. Come in," came Mrs. Mason's warm greeting.

Lillian had always felt that she could call Barbara Mason a friend, in spite of the fact that there was something very fake about her. Lillian knew that Barbara always put on a mask for non-family members, though she had never actually seen evidence of this aside from her own feelings. "Thank you," Lillian answered, as she walked through the doorway of the little house. "How's life?"

"Wonderful as always, of course," Barbara lied, as she closed the door behind them and led Lillian to the kitchen. Once in the kitchen, Barbara continued with her hostessly duties. "Please, sit down," she gestured towards a chair at the small kitchen table.

"Thank you," Lillian said, as she seated herself.

"How 'bout some coffee?" Barbara offered, already on her way towards the coffee machine.

Oh yeah. One more cup of coffee. That's what my nerves really need right now, Lillian thought to herself sarcastically just before saying, "Thank you. That sounds great." She smiled at Barbara.

Great. I wonder how long she plans to stay, Barbara Mason thought to herself, pouring the coffee for her uninvited guest. “Cream?” she asked pleasantly.

“Um, no thanks. I’ll take it black.”

As Barbara set Lillian’s cup down on the table, she spoke sternly, “Too much black coffee’ll make a lesbian out of you.”

Lillian almost laughed at the seemingly jocular comment, but then she looked right into Barbara’s face and saw the look of complete seriousness and scorn painted there. Lillian didn’t know how to, or even if she should, respond to the strange remark but, realizing that Barbara was intent on staring until she received a response, she finally said nervously, without looking Mrs. Mason in the eyes, “I... I don’t drink it that way very often.” This was, of course, a lie.

Lillian was now even more nervous over talking to Barbara about Daniel. How open minded would Barbara be? *Perhaps,* she thought, *I should take comfort in the fact that the woman whom I am going to ask to believe in psychics and werewolves already believes that black coffee can turn a straight woman into a lesbian.*

Barbara went back to the coffee machine, poured herself a steaming cup of black coffee, then put some cream in it and sat down at the kitchen table across from her neighbor.

To Lillian, the table seemed suddenly smaller.

Barbara fixed Lillian with a smile, looking as though the act had caused her physical pain, and asked, “So what brings you by?”

Lillian considered the question. This is why she had come—to talk to Barbara. She gave herself a split-second mental pep talk, then spoke, “Actually…” She stalled, for just another split-second. *Now or never, now or never, now or never.* "...I wanted to talk to you about Daniel." There. It was out. She looked Mrs. Mason dead in the eyes, and she saw nothing but rage and hatred there. Lillian looked away quickly, and she wondered if the hatred in Barbara's veiny eyes was directed at her, or—

"I knew it," came Barbara's cold response. "He's gone too far this time. That boy is nothing but trouble. I knew that one day he'd find a way to embarrass me by upsetting one of my neighbors."

Lillian couldn't believe what she was hearing. The shock almost caused her to spit out the coffee that she had just taken into her mouth. Daniel Mason was the most well liked eighteen-year old in Nightfire. Everyone knew him, and everyone loved him. Yet, his own mother seemed to have an entirely different opinion of him. Lillian tried to protest, "Barbara. Daniel? What are you talking about? He's a good kid."

"Good for nothing!" Barbara snapped. "I'm his mother, and mothers know. I know the kinds of things Daniel does with his criminal friends. He may be able to fool everybody else in town, but not me."

Lillian was genuinely concerned. How could she reason with this woman? Of course, on the bright side, Barbara seemed to *want* to think bad things about her son, so convincing her that he was a werewolf might not be too difficult.

Lillian asked herself for the thousandth time why she was even talking to Barbara about this in the first place. And for the thousandth time, she remembered the dream that she had suffered only a few hours before, and she knew, for whatever reason, that telling Barbara was the only way to answer that horrific vision. She did feel the need to calm her down first though. "Barbara, I don't know where this is coming from. Your son, and all…" She corrected herself when she remembered being introduced to Bert Jameson, "…most of his friends are the epitome of friendliness and politeness. And Daniel is such a young gentleman. To see him and Roxy together—"

"If Roxanna Stillwaters isn't pregnant, I don't know who is."

Lillian looked Mrs. Mason in the eyes, which was always a very brave thing to do. "Are you," she wanted to say *crazy,* "serious?" How could it be, she wondered, that she had never realized the extent of her neighbor's obvious madness.

"Of course I'm serious!" Barbara scolded, her eyes growing wider and even more bloodshot as she spoke. Her facial expression quickly changed from one of rage to one of pity. She spoke in one of the most condescending tones that Lillian had ever heard, "Lillian, you've never had any children of your own, and at your age you probably never will. So, I can't expect you to understand this. A mother knows. A mother knows her son, and a wise woman knows that all men are just alike. A mother also knows a pregnant woman when she sees one. Or a pregnant whore."

Lillian could not believe the words she was hearing. She was outraged, but she somehow managed to keep her fury from exploding outright. "Where do you…?" *To call Roxy a whore!* "I've watched Daniel grow up since he was just a baby. I've never known him to be anything but sweet and gentle, and Roxy is not a whore."

Barbara shook her head. "They're all whores, Lillian." She corrected her, as if she were just a naïve child. "I know about the abortion Carey had just two months ago. I learned of it from Beth Green, who has a cousin that works at the clinic. That's what she gets for opening her legs to the boy without a wedding ring."

Lillian didn't know whether to laugh or scream. Instead, she just tried to reason. "If you're suggesting that Daniel is the father of Carey's alleged, terminated child, your math is just a little off. Don't you realize how long ago they broke up? And how long Daniel and Roxy have been together?"

Barbara sighed, as if the patience she was spending to educate this poor, stupid woman was beginning to take its toll. "Lillian, just because he has another girlfriend now, that doesn't mean he doesn't still use his old ones for the only thing he wanted out of them in the first place. You suggest that men are capable of faithfulness. This is never true. I know that Daniel is still sleeping with Carey behind Roxanna's back. And Daniel is a man like any other. He has no reason to use protection. He has no reason to care if she gets pregnant or not. Men only care about themselves. To them it's just the pleasure of the moment. So, as long as they do not bear the pain of childbirth or abortion, they will not care. It's not the man's concern. And of course, being the mindless whore that she is, it was easy for Daniel to talk Carey into destroying the child, so that she might continue to be his whore, for whom he has no responsibility."

A wicked smile crossed Barbara Mason's face as she went on, "Daniel may think he has everyone fooled, but no son can fool his mother. And he can't keep everyone fooled about Roxy for long.

"In his plan, I'm sure she would soon be reduced to a *bedroom only* whore, when he grows tired of her mindless banter and the way she clings to him; when she begins to complain too much about his excessive smoking and drinking and whatever else he's into. But this one will be Daniel's undoing, and I will turn him away when he inevitably turns to me, begging for help because he can't support a wife and child. He will have created his own hell, and if I were to offer him any comfort from it, well, I just wouldn't be a good mother.

"He needs to learn responsibility. And Roxanna's father is not the type to let a thing like this go. He'll make either a husband or a cadaver out of my son, and Daniel better hope that it's a cadaver.

"Because he could not keep his pants on, he's going to be forced to marry one of his little whores, and he'll never find happiness. His life might as well have ended."

Lillian sat dumbfounded in her seat. *So, where do we go from here?* "Barbara," she smiled, disguising her disgust with friendliness, "have you seen Roxy lately? She's most certainly not pregnant." She took a sip of her coffee, subconsciously shielding herself from the possibly psychotic retaliation.

"I don't have to see her. I'm Daniel's mother, no matter how it shames me. I know what's going on. And she's starting to show. That will be Daniel's downfall. A good, Christian man like Marc Stillwaters would never allow her to have an abortion or to give him a bastard grandson! She's starting, ever so slightly, to show!" She paused and narrowed her eyes into an accusing stare. "Have *you* seen her lately?"

The question had a deeply sobering effect on Lillian. "Yes." Flashes of her visions screamed before her mind's eye. "I have." She was now forced to remember what she had gone to the Mason house for in the first place. She looked up, a somber expression on her face. "I need to tell you, I'm worried about Daniel, and whether Roxanna is pregnant or not has no bearing on the matter at hand. I'm afraid that he's in a deeper form of trouble, and I believe that it is no fault of his own. Would you help your son in such a circumstance?"

"No," Barbara answered. "I most likely would not. Trouble, whether one's own creation or not, is a part of life. If I helped him out of his every desperate situation, he would grow up to be weak and cowardly, always crawling to Mommy for help."

You witch! Lillian wanted nothing more than to do Barbara Mason physical harm. She had to wonder, *Why is it that I must tell her what I know, if she is not even willing to help?* She decided that there was some reason that she could not yet perceive. She had to have faith in her psychic intuitions, even if it looked bad for the moment. Silently, she said a quick prayer, *Please, God, open her ears to me.*

Then, as if in answer, Barbara spoke, "Of course, there could be an exception even to *my* rule. I can't know for certain until I know how, exactly, Daniel has upset you. Can I?" Barbara's cynical expression gave Lillian a silent invitation to speak her mind.

Lillian smiled in relief at having her prayer answered in the way she had wanted. "No." she agreed. "I suppose not." Her smile faded instantly, as the reality of the situation again filled her thoughts. She had kept her secrets for so many years, and now she was going to tell all to a woman whom she could never hope to trust. She took a nervous gulp of her coffee, which she noted was starting to get cold, and then she once again looked Barbara in the eyes and spoke, "First of all, let me assure you, Daniel hasn't done anything to upset me."

"If that is true," Barbara responded, "then you have won my curiosity." She glared at Lillian, as if listening to a child tell a lie.

Lillian knew she was being humored, but she had to take Barbara's attention in whatever form it happened to present itself. "Before I get to Daniel, I need you to know some things," she looked away, "about me." When she looked back at Barbara, she could tell that Barbara was waiting for some demented, dirty confession, but at least she looked interested. "Do you remember," she asked in an urgent tone, "when Daniel was three, and his father nearly ran over him with the car?"

Barbara gave Lillian a *just how stupid are you?* Look. "Yes, how could I forget? Robert had been drinking, and he was late for work. He couldn't see anything clearly, let alone Daniel playing a few feet behind the car. I remember how you came rushing over, and I thought that it was awfully early in the morning for you to be paying a visit. You told me that I needed to keep an extra eye on Daniel that morning. I remember thinking what an odd thing to rush over and tell me right after breakfast, but then I realized that Daniel was not in his chair at the table. I looked out the window, and I saw Robert struggling with his keys, trying to find the right one, and then I glanced to the rear of the car and saw Daniel playing with his toy cars in the driveway. When I heard the engine start I ran out the door with speed I'd not known I had. As Robert backed out drunkenly, squealing his tires, I ran past the rear of the car, grabbed our son, and fell with him to the grass on the other side of the driveway. Daniel started to cry, both from the shock and from the bruises he got from being snatched up so violently. Robert hit the brakes sluggishly, stopping right on top of one of Daniel's little cars. When Robert realized what had happened, and what had almost happened, he sobered instantly and never drank again." Barbara's expression seemed to soften ever so slightly, revealing a hint of sorrow. "And if not for your odd advice, my little boy might not have lived to see another day."

"So," Lillian spoke without thinking, "you *do* love your son."

Barbara looked both stricken and amazed by the rudeness of her guest. "Well of course I love him! He's my son!"

Lillian realized all too late what she had said. "I'm… I'm sorry, Barbara. I was just… I just meant to say that…" She gave up on explaining herself, when she noticed how foul she found the taste of her own foot. "Well, of course you love him." The statement seemed to soothe Mrs. Mason's temper, so Lillian went on. "I've often found myself curious; did you ever wonder, afterwards, why I told you what I told you on that day?" Lillian sipped her coffee, which was now far too cold for her to ever hope to finish, as she waited for Barbara's reply.

Barbara looked suddenly uncomfortable. She turned her head and sighed. "Well, it seemed fairly clear to me at the time that you had the curse."

Lillian shook her head, as though she had not heard correctly. "The curse?"

"The ability to see into the future." Barbara still looked away. "I said nothing to you about it at the time, for fear that you were consorting with devils, but after much contemplation, I decided that if you were an evil creature you would have had no compassion for my son." Barbara looked up at last, a somber expression on her face. "My grandmother had the curse too, you see."

Lillian found herself surprised to receive such acceptance from Barbara, who immediately went on:

"Most of the family thought she was mentally unstable, but I learned better when I was a little girl." She shook her head, as if tossing the thought from her mind. "But tell me, Lillian. You use this talent for good, so you must see it as a gift. How long have you had this gift?"

Lillian considered, temporarily forgetting her task. It felt good to talk about this; to get it all off her chest. "Oh, since I was a very little girl." She looked off at nothing, as she recalled. "My earliest psychic memory is from when I was about three or four years old. My parents and I had just moved into a brand new house, in a brand new neighborhood, on the other side of Dallas. I used to have these strange dreams. I was always in a forest, and I always encountered a different animal. The animals always seemed to be fleeing, trying to get away from something. And they were always trying to express their anger to me. They wanted me to know that they had lost their home. And every time that I would wake from one of those dreams, I could hear the animal from my dream sniffing and clawing at the foot of my bed. I would scream, and my father would come in. He always humored me of course. I would tell him that an animal from a nightmare was sniffing and clawing at the foot of my bed, and he would take a blanket and pretend to beat the creature away, all the while thinking it was just my imagination. It always frustrated me that nobody would believe me about that." Lillian paused, then looked up and smiled at Barbara. "The dreams did eventually stop, but I never forgot them. I sometimes wonder if that was the whole point.

"It wasn't until I turned twenty that I finally realized what was going on in the house of my childhood. I don't know why it took me so long. I suppose I knew all along, but didn't want to think about it. But, the truth seems so obvious in retrospect. We lived in a brand new house, in a brand new neighborhood. Before us, there was nothing but land and trees in that spot. So many creatures had lost their homes, and their lives, due to the development. They just wanted someone to hear them. They didn't want to go unrecognized. So they communicated with me, the psychic child. And I often wonder if they gave the same dreams to any other people in that neighborhood. Maybe if they had, and I had known it then, my parents could have been brought to believe me."

Lillian was now completely lost to her task. It was so seldom that she found herself with someone she could talk to about her secret side. And knowledge of others like her always made her feel less alone. "So," she began with a wistful smile, "tell me about your grandmother."

Barbara looked almost frightened, as if she had wanted to ignore the devil sitting in her lap, but it had just been pointed out. She looked down at her hands, which were resting on her knees, and she spoke in a softer, more cautious voice than was accustom to her nature, "My grandmother…" she paused, searching for the best way to begin, "…was a good woman." She looked up at Lillian, as if expecting dispute. When she found none, she continued, "I was raised on a small, basically failed farm in the middle of nowhere. It was the family farm, and it had been there for generations. We finally had to sell it in 1959, just after my grandmother hung herself in the barn at the age of ninety-three."

Lillian winced. Suddenly, realizing that she might not want to know what was in this can of worms she had just opened up, she remembered what she had come to talk about in the first place, and she hoped Mrs. Mason would leave her recollections of her grandmother at that. She soon found herself to be not as fortunate as she had hoped.

"I was five years old when Grandma returned to the farm," Barbara continued. "She had been away for about sixty years, having moved to the city to build a new life with her second husband. But by this time, her husband had passed away, and the family thought she was unable to care for herself properly. Though there were relatives in Boston who could have cared for her, we all decided that it was for the best that she return to the farm in Kentucky to live out her final days in peace.

"I won't bore you with all the details of the four years she was with us—just the major points of interest. You see, Grandma was always muttering things to herself. Most people thought she had lost her senses, but it was actually, as I came to learn, the opposite.

"After she had been with us for about a year, Mother had become pregnant again. We knew this was dangerous, because she was supposed to be past the age of child-bearing. I already had two older sisters and an older brother, and I was hoping for a younger sister of my own.

"One day, while I was sitting on the porch, however, my grandmother came outside and sat beside me. She looked at me with the most serious of faces, and she said that my new brother was going to be a changeling, and that I would have to help her drown him before he grew to the age of being a danger to others. She told me that I must stay clear of the men in my family, because they were good for nothing but hindrance to us all.

"Understand that, at this time, I was still convinced that Grandma was senile. So I just nodded my head until she went away. A few months later, my mother had her fifth child, and it was not a girl as I had wanted it to be. Instead, she gave birth to a severely deformed little boy. It seemed a tragedy that it was not too deformed to live, but my mother loved him anyway, and she named him Alexander. I was shocked. My grandmother had been right.

"At that moment, I resolved to stay close to Grandma. She had warned me to steer clear of the men in my family in order to keep me safe, but I did still trust my father, and my older brother David. That soon changed, as did everything else.

"One night, when I was supposed to be sleeping, I had been disturbed by the sound of people creeping in the hallway. I found myself frightened by it, so I decided to go into one of my siblings' rooms to sleep. David was not in his room, and Ruth, the youngest of my older sisters, was nowhere to be found either. I was just about to check my oldest sister's room, when I heard my father screaming from the master bedroom. I had never heard my father express such rage, even when he would beat David for slacking in his chores. I wondered if he had gone mad and killed the whole family, leaving me for last.

"Before I ran, terrified, back to my own room, I heard my mother sobbing, and I heard the sounds of him beating her. Furniture was crashing, and I was crying. I heard him cursing my mother for giving birth to Alexander. He called her the devil's whore. I was terribly shaken. I ran to my room and found my grandma waiting there for me. She told me she knew there was going to be trouble that night, and that it would only get worse.

"Two months later, I was the one who found my mother dead on the kitchen floor. She had cut open both of her wrists with a butcher knife.

"Two years passed arduously without my mother. My father would have killed Alexander right after we buried my mother, if not for my oldest sister Maria. She took care of little Alexander as if he were her own. The farm was losing a great deal of money at this point, and Father always insisted that it was a waste to feed Alexander, but Maria always found ways to feed him, and he lived innocently unaware of all our hardships.

"Grandma often reminded me that Alexander could not live for much longer, but that he must be allowed to live out his innocence. And she would still remind me to stay cautious of the men, because they were not to be trusted.

"One day, Maria had fallen asleep from exhaustion after spending the night up with Alexander, who was crying and incorrigible. As she slept, he snuck out. I don't know how long he had been on his own when my grandmother came into my room and told me that it was time for me to help her, because she was too old and weak to carry the body to the river by herself. This terrified me. I didn't want Alexander to be dead, but what I found even worse was to learn that he was not dead at all.

"I followed Grandma to the hen house, and I only went along because I trusted her completely. She hadn't steered me wrong yet. She opened the hen house door and found Alexander screaming inside. No chickens were clucking, because, one by one, he had broken all of their necks." Barbara paused to gather herself. It was obvious that these memories were painful, and she was having to choke back tears.

She continued, "He was screaming loudly and holding his head, crying, 'Hurt! Hurt!' Grandma picked up a big board that had come off of the old hen house, and she swung it with all of her might. Alexander fell to the ground after being swatted so hard. He was quiet, but not dead; just in shock.

"Grandma calmly covered him with a potato sack and tied him inside. She then told me that she needed me to help her take him down to the river. Being in a state of shock myself, I helped her without question.

"Maria was twenty-five years old, but that was not too old for Father to take her into the barn and beat her for her neglect. The family decided that Alexander had wandered off and drowned in the river, even though they had no evidence other than that it was the most likely thing to have happened. Maria was most devastated of all, but she somehow managed to stay strong, unlike Mother had done.

"I cried that night when I finally found myself able. My grandma came into my room and comforted me. She explained that it was for the good of everyone involved. She said that Alexander would have grown up, the pain in his head would have gotten worse, and he would have eventually started to kill people.

She had such a soothing presence about her, and I found myself easily able to accept her explanation.

"Another year passed, and nothing else seemed wrong to me. David and Ruth were more frequently not in their rooms at night. When I asked about it, they told me that Father had asked them to do secret chores while everyone was asleep, and I was not to tell anyone about it. I wasn't even to let Father know that I knew about it. They explained that if he knew that they had told me, he would beat us all. So I stayed quiet and just wondered what secret chores they had to do so late at night.

"I finally found out. One night that year, I was woken by Father screaming for David to get his shotgun. A raccoon had gotten into the house. When he found David absent from his room, he started to scream and cuss, and he called us all out of our rooms. He quickly found that Ruth wasn't in the house either. He continued to scream and ask where they were.

"I was only nine at the time, and very naïve. I got his attention and whispered to him, as if he were so silly to have forgotten. I explained what they had told me, in a voice small enough to not let Maria or Grandma hear the secret that I thought my father already knew. His face went pale as he rose from his listening position. He swore, set down his shotgun, and told Maria to keep me inside.

"We watched from the porch, as he marched towards the barn and swung open the doors. We heard him shouting awfully at them, and I could make out the words 'stand up.'

"When they did so, we could see them. Maria gasped sharply in complete disbelief, and then I noticed that Ruth and David weren't wearing any clothes. At the time, I couldn't help but giggle at this, but Maria covered my mouth. My amusement faded, as I saw Father beat them both in front of the barn, until they were on the ground, unable to get up. Then he marched back to the house. When Maria asked him what he was going to do, he answered simply, 'God's work, darlin'. Stay out of this now.' He then readied his double barrel shotgun and started out the door. In a state of hysteria, Maria tried to stop him, but he backhanded her so hard that she lost consciousness.

"Grandma told me that Father needed to be alone with Ruth and David, and she convinced me to help her tend to Maria. I looked up one more time, and I saw that Father had stood Ruth and David up again, and then, as I looked away, I heard them pleading and crying, and then I heard gunshots. When I looked again, my brother and sister were dead. He was only eighteen years old, and she only two years older."

Shit! This was the only thought continuing to run through Lillian Foster's mind at this point in Barbara's story.

"The next day," Barbara continued, "I had to help my father dig two graves. He explained to me, through a drunken, mental fog, that David and Ruth had been wicked, and God always punishes the wicked. He told me that my mother had been wicked, and that's why she had given birth to a monstrosity.

"All the while, we thought that Maria was too sick from shock to get out of bed and help dig, but I found out from her later that she was just pretending, so that Father would leave her in the house alone. When he and I were safely out of sight, she got out of bed and started looking for the keys to Father's truck. Grandma, having the gift of knowing, had already found them, and she brought them to Maria and told her to hurry.

"It was as the sun was setting that we finished putting the dirt on top of my murdered siblings. Father carried me back to the house, where Grandma was waiting. She walked me to my room, and she again told me to always be wary of the men in my life. She even warned me that my own son could be the death of me. Then she kissed me on the forehead and said good-bye.

"The police arrived with Maria twenty minutes later. She brought them inside to my father, who cursed her and, when they started to question him, went for his gun, claiming that they had no right to be on his property. Fortunately, the police were in control of the situation. He was drunk and sluggish, so it was easy for them to restrain and hand-cuff him.

"At this point, one of the officers went with Maria to the scene of the crime. He found Ruth and David's blood all over the barn doors. Unfortunately, this was not the only horrible thing that he found."

Barbara paused. She seemed to be struggling to hold back her emotions. She closed her eyes for a moment, then let out a long breath, opened her eyes, and went on, "Inside the barn, Maria and the policeman found my grandmother, hung by the neck, swinging from the rafters, dead. No one could figure out how she had managed this feat, and I could never understand *why* she did it. Maybe it was something she saw. Perhaps a future she wanted nothing to do with." Barbara shook her head slowly, her now teary eyes staring intently at nothing.

Lillian didn't know how to respond to her neighbor's tale. She found herself marveling that she had known Barbara for nearly twenty years, but had never *really* known her. And she found herself thinking that she had liked it better that way.

After a few moments, she found the silence too uncomfortable. "So, what happened then? I mean, what happened to you and your sister? What did they do with your father?" Barbara's silence filled Lillian with paranoia. Had she come across as too nosy?

Thankfully, the awkward silence was broken before her worries could grow. "Well," Barbara answered, still staring into the air with unfocused eyes, "they exhumed the bodies, and my father went to prison for life. He died there—ten years ago next month. Maria and I went to live in Boston at the insistence of our very wealthy aunt; my mother's sister.

"Aunt Gretchin, along with the rest of the family in Boston, helped us to get on our feet and start a new life. Maria became like a mother to me and, finally away from the farm, I began to realize and resent what a sheltered life I had lived." She smiled, looking now at her guest's worried face. "But I think I turned out all right. I met Robert while I was working in a little gift shop that my aunt owned. He was so charming, and a college man. He swept me off my feet.

"When we got married, he wanted to move back to his home state. And we've been here ever since, happy as can be." Barbara repeated the unnatural, strained-looking smile that she had worn earlier.

Lillian saw that the smile hid a lie, but she knew better than to point this out.

Barbara noticed the puzzled look on Lillian's face and decided to turn the focus of the conversation towards Lillian. "So, Lillian, now that we have established that I won't hold your 'gift' against you, why don't you tell me what brings you here?" She smiled again. "I know you didn't come by just to drag up bad memories."

No, she hadn't. Lillian found herself still nervous; perhaps more nervous than before. She had never even suspected that Barbara had been through so much. She seemed more than ready to accept that her son might be the death of her, but did Lillian really want to be the bearer of such news—the next tragedy of Barbara's life? But it was not Barbara's death she had seen. At least, not in detail. That had been Roxy. But she had seen a possible future in which the entire town, herself included, was slaughtered. That was what she had come here to prevent. Somehow.

She looked down, away from Barbara's gaze. "This might be difficult for you to hear." She looked up. "And even more difficult for you to believe."

"Lillian, please go on," Barbara urged. "I have already assured you that I have great respect for people who use the cur… 'gift' for helping others. You already know that I believe you. Tell me, what is Daniel into that you think I should help him?"

"Well," Lillian realized that she could procrastinate no longer. With this realization, she found herself suddenly eager to tell Barbara. The sooner she spoke her mind, the sooner this situation would be over and done with. "I don't know how this happened, but I know that it has. My visions told me only what I needed to know. Everyone in Nightfire is in danger—mortal danger. But no one is in as much danger as your son. I don't know how you can help exactly, but my intuitions suggested strongly that I go to you in answer to my dark visions."

She paused and chewed her lip, as she tried to sort through the information in her head to find an appropriate starting place. When she had it, she looked Barbara Mason in the eyes and spoke to the anticipation she found there. "It all, somehow, has something to do with a tragedy that happened in Nightfire, in 1850. Do you know anything about Nightfire's history? Because I've lived here nearly twenty years, and I've never heard a hint of history that would suggest that the things I saw actually happened, but I know they did."

Barbara, wishing Lillian would just get to the point, shook her head. "I haven't heard anything significant about the town's history. Nothing to make me concerned."

"Well, I saw some pretty terrible things about the past. I saw countless people slain by werewolves."

Barbara chuckled shortly. "Are you sure you know the difference between visions and nightmares?"

Lillian was stricken by that remark. Her face showed it. "I know the difference," she said simply. She sat silent for a number of seconds, trying to get past her frustration at being asked that, then she went on, "I wouldn't be here if I didn't believe, beyond the shadow of a doubt, that Daniel was in great danger."

Barbara was starting to get agitated. "So what are you trying to tell me; that I need to go out and buy some silver bullets, because my son is going to be slain by a werewolf?"

"No," Lillian closed her eyes in forced patience, then opened them and said, "I'm saying that Daniel *is* a werewolf."

There was not a hint of life on Barbara Mason's face. All amusement was gone.

Lillian saw that her time was running out. "And I also saw that, as this situation puts the rest of us in *mortal* danger, Daniel's very soul is on the line. He needs help, and I don't know how we can help him."

Mrs. Mason stood up abruptly, a look of deadly hatred upon her face. She sneered as she spoke, "Get out of my house." She - pointed furiously towards the front door.

"But, Barb—"

"No! Get out!" Barbara had lost her composure completely. "How dare you come into my home, convince me of your gifts, and make me open up about my past, just so that you can make a mockery of my grandmother!? *How dare you!?* It's people like you who make the true psychics into jokes! How dare you come in here with your absurd lies about werewolves! What do you really want from Daniel? Just what in God's name are you trying to accomplish?"

Lillian stared up at Barbara. She was visibly shaken. It had felt so good to open up to someone. It had been so nice to think that Barbara could respect her, and it hurt so much to be rejected in the end, after all it had taken to get there. Lillian's eyes began to tear up, as she set down her coffee mug. "I was just trying to help," she spoke in a small, pathetic voice.

When she felt the first tear begin to escape her, she quickly stood up and walked out of the house. She was relieved to find that this action stopped her eager tears from flowing.

When she returned to her own house, she locked the door and stood there in the entryway. She held her arms, as if she were freezing, and she wondered why she had been put through that. Why had she been led to spill everything before Barbara Mason?

How would she ever face her neighbors again? *God works in mysterious ways.* This was the only thought she found comfort in. Surely things would work themselves out, and she may even learn how telling Barbara had fit into God's plan. She had to have faith that it did, and that's all there was to it.

"Excuse me, Helen. Someone's on the other line," Beth Green, an overweight, fifty-year-old woman who rarely left the phone, interrupted her boring conversation with Helen Don to see if whoever was calling on the other line had anything interesting to say. She clicked over. "Hello."

Barbara Mason responded to the greeting, "Hello, Beth."

"Oh, Barbara," Relief filled Beth Green's unnecessarily loud voice. Barbara was always good for swapping gossip. "How good it is to hear from you! I'm stuck on the phone with Helen Don."

"Oh, how is Helen?"

"Oh, she's fine, but unfortunately as boring and whiny as ever. She's so timid and never has anything interesting to say about anybody. She only calls when she needs advice about her son. You'd think a woman who's been widowed as long as she has would be so much stronger. I honestly don't think it's any wonder that her son is so very strange."

"Tom?"

"Yes, Tom. Do you mean you haven't noticed? How strange; especially since he spends so much time with your son."

"So what is wrong with Helen's son this time?"

"Oh, this time? She's just concerned, because she thinks he's been fighting. He evidently came home the other night with a big bruise on his face, and he's missed school two days in a row. He says he doesn't want to go to school looking like a freak. She thinks he's hiding from someone. I know it's a bore to hear about, and I've been stuck hearing about it for twenty minutes. Hold on. I'll get rid of her."

She clicked over. "Helen, are you there?"

"Yes," came her weak-sounding reply.

"I'm sorry. That's Barbara Mason. I've been waiting for her call, and I can't ask her to call back. Don't worry about Tom now. He'll be all right."

"Well, can we talk later?"

"Yes, I'll call you later. Bye."

She clicked over again. "So, what's up, Barbara?"

Barbara's voice was filled with fury, "Well, you just won't believe what my neighbor just did to me!"

Beth began to tingle with anticipation. "Which neighbor is that?"

"Lillian Foster," she spoke as though there was no fouler name in the entire universe.

"Ah, yes! The one who's having an affair with Reverend Jordan. What did she do?"

As Barbara hatefully related the story, leaving nothing of Lillian's claims out, Beth Green began to turn white.

"Isn't that the most absurd, idiotic thing you've ever heard of? My son, a werewolf? I can't believe the nerve of that woman!" Barbara waited for a response, but none came. "Beth? Are you there?"

"Yes," Beth spoke as in a daze. "That's some nerve." There was no emotion in her voice, no hint whatsoever of the giddiness that she usually felt at receiving juicy tidbits about Nightfire's residents. "I'm sorry, Barbara. Can I call you back another time? I suddenly have a headache."

Moments later, the phone rang at the home of Elizabeth Krandall, a retired historian, and wife of the notorious "homework barbarian," algebra teacher Ted Krandall. She put down the book she was reading and answered the phone. She was surprised to hear the voice of Beth Green.

The two women had little in common, but they had once shared a very interesting conversation at the library. Beth had uncovered something sinister about Nightfire's history and had wanted to know if Elizabeth could verify it. It had been three years earlier, and Beth had just inherited a truckload of junk from the attic of her newly deceased aunt. She had found an ancestor's diary from the 1800s. At first, she had dismissed it as fiction, but upon bragging to Anthony Paul, a local writer, about her discovery, she had learned that it might not have been a work of fiction after all.

Anthony had been in possession of an ancestor's diary as well, and his was an ancestor mentioned in the diary that Beth had found: Reverend David Paul. Anthony had also had a copy of a document, written by David Paul, warning future generations about werewolves, and revealing that a vial of werewolf blood was to be kept in the Methodist church. Going down the grapevine, they had learned that, while most people found the story absurd, several others had heard the story from their parents, and grandparents, and great-grandparents, and so on.

Elizabeth had naturally been intrigued when Beth had told her all in the library, so she had agreed to research the dates specified in the diaries. To her shock and thrilled fascination, she had found that, while the town histories stored in the library had told of what had happened before and after those dates, they had said nothing at all about the dates she was looking for, and the microfiche newspaper files, dating back to several years before the incident, included a copy of every newspaper from 1850, except for those dates. There had been some evidence of the natural aftermath of the stories in later editions: rebuilding, new preachers, new sheriff, much smaller population. For everyone concerned in the present day, this had been proof enough. Werewolves did exist, and they had nearly destroyed Nightfire, Texas in August of 1850.

Nothing had ever come of this knowledge, however. While it had been fascinating, it really hadn't changed anything in the everyday lives of those who had uncovered it.

Elizabeth now wondered if Beth Green was calling about that, because they really never spoke otherwise. "Bethany, how have you been?"

Beth sounded frightened, an emotion that she had quite possibly never shown anybody. "Liz, something's come up. It's about the werewolves."

Elizabeth suddenly realized the implications—the werewolves, plus a frightened Beth Green—and found herself beginning to shiver with death-cold anticipation. She found herself not knowing if she really wanted to know but, at the same time, she felt that she just had to know. "What?" she asked in a voice that startled her with the sound of near panic that it carried.

"Lillian Foster knows all about it. She went to Barbara Mason this morning to warn her."

Elizabeth spoke cautiously, "Warn her?"

"Yes. She's been having psychic visions. Visions of both the past and future. She told her that Daniel has somehow become a werewolf, and that we're all in mortal danger."

"But, what about the blood? Isn't that supposed to keep them away?"

Impatience was beginning to enter Beth's frightened voice, "Maybe it wore off! It is very old after all. Or maybe the story was never passed on to Reverend Jordan. The blood could have been lost! We have to call everyone who knows the truth and tell them to get out of Nightfire."

No matter the circumstance, this solution seemed extreme to Elizabeth Krandall. "Beth, I don't know what to do. I think we should wait."

"Wait for what!?"

"We need to wait for some sort of sign that there is another werewolf in Nightfire."

"But that may never come until it's too late! In 1850 everything was done covertly. No one knew until the very day that Hell rose to consume them!"

"But that's because they didn't know what they were looking for last time. We do. If someone dies, in a way that looks suspicious, then we should think about leaving."

"Liz! That someone could so easily be one of us! I don't want to die! None of us does, I'm sure! You're not taking this seriously!"

"Don't even think that, Beth. I'll tell you right now that I think this is true. And I'll tell you in confidence, Daniel was behaving very strangely in class yesterday. He went home sick. Ted is very concerned about him. He's such a consistent student. Consistently well-behaved and healthy. But, for now, we're safe, and maybe things will work themselves out before that changes, in which case we would be fools for having left."

"Better than being fools for having stayed."

"Beth, the next full moon isn't until," she paused and looked at her calendar, "the twenty-third. We're safe until then. But if someone dies suspiciously or disappears without a trace, then we talk evacuation."

"But the twenty-third is only seven days away!"

"That's plenty of time for you to warn everyone who might believe you."

"Yes, I suppose you're right. I don't really have anywhere to go anyway. I've got to call everyone and let them know."

And she did. She called everyone who had been involved in uncovering and keeping this secret three years earlier. Everyone except for Anthony Paul, who had gotten married and moved out of state in the middle of 1995. But she did, without fail, manage to call and convince everyone else on the list.

The seed was planted.

Daniel Mason knocked on the front door of Tom's house. Daniel had woken up feeling very refreshed. In school, he found himself thinking about eating people only twice, and he had convinced himself that it hadn't been the same as yesterday, because this time he had probably only been suffering from the morbid memory of his original dark fantasy. That's what he kept telling himself. Over, and over, and over. He hoped to convince himself any minute now.

The door opened. Tom's mother stood in the doorway with a worried expression painted on her face as always. She smiled, but still looked worried. She was a tall and very skinny woman. She was in her late thirties, had long, badly kept, dark blonde hair, and the newest clothes she owned were at least five years old. She worked as a waitress at a diner to keep food on the table, and she made just barely enough to get by. Daniel wondered how people failed to understand why she always looked worried. "Hi, Daniel."

Daniel looked Mrs. Don in the eyes, and for the first time ever, he found himself wanting her. He thought about how satisfying it would be to just shove her onto the floor, tear off her clothing just enough to get it out of his way, and go at it like an animal.

Daniel shook his head and started to feel afraid again, but then he told himself that he was just being affected by the cold weather.

"Are you okay, Daniel?"

Daniel tried to think of something to say. "Um, yeah. I just… I dunno. It's cold." He found himself starting to blush at the realization of how odd he must appear. He looked away from Mrs. Don and held up some text books. "I brought Tom his makeup work," he said, as he quickly walked past her and into the small house. He hated how rude he felt.

A cold hand landed on his shoulder.

"Daniel?"

His jaw tightened, as he stopped for her.

"Do you know anything about Tom's face? His bruise, I mean. Did someone hurt him?"

Daniel was relieved to find that he was no longer feeling sexual urges for his friend's mother. He turned around and smiled at her. She had asked him in such a frightened, timid voice. It was as if she thought they were hiding the truth from her, to keep her from worrying, so, of course, she worried anyway. "No," he spoke in a reassuring tone. "He fell on his face, and it wasn't anybody else's doing. Don't worry. If anyone was trying to hurt Tom, he wouldn't have anything to worry about. He's got too many friends. He just feels like a freak with his face all bruised up." Daniel chuckled, as he held up the Phantom of the Opera mask in his left hand. "That's why I brought him this."

She laughed out loud at the mask, visibly relieved. She knew that Daniel wouldn't lie to her. "You're a good friend, Daniel." She looked at her watch. "Oh, shit!" She covered her mouth with embarrassment at having spoken that way in front of Daniel. "I'm sorry," she said.

Daniel just laughed at her playfully.

"I've got to go to work." She rushed to grab her purse and her apron, as she scurried out the door. She shouted over her shoulder as she left, "Tom! Daniel's here! I'm off to work!"

"Bye, Mom," came Tom's shouted response from his room.

Mrs. Don left, and Daniel went to Tom's room. He found Tom sitting on his bed, flipping through an old *Star Wars* comic book. "Hey, ugly!" Daniel teased. "I brought you some make-up work, and a miracle cure." He tossed the mask, so that it landed right beside Tom.

Tom put down the comic book and cackled with sheer glee. He held the mask up to his face and stood before Daniel. "Kiss me now, oh Angel of Music," Tom prissed playfully.

Daniel laughed at his weird friend, but then, as he continued to stare at Tom, his laughter stopped. His smile fell.

Kiss me now, oh Angel of Music.

Why did that suddenly tempt him so? He was no longer seeing Tom as a person at all. He was seeing flesh on bones. Meat. There was nothing sexual about the way he now found himself wanting Tom, but there was surely something very animalistic about it.

Kiss me now, oh Angel of Music.

Just to taste his tender lips, his neck, the blood that flowed through his healthy, young veins, the fresh, raw meat that clung to his bones. *Oh, Tom, say it again, and I will. I will.*

If only just to taste *you.*

"Hey, Daniel. What's with the fuck-me-eyes?" Tom removed the mask and looked at Daniel with amusement.

Daniel found himself slowly, perhaps not even perceptibly, moving closer to Tom. *I want to, Tom. Say it again. Tell me to do it, and I will. But how will I explain it? What if thinks I'm gay? But then, who knows about Tom's sexuality anyway? I wouldn't have to explain it, because soon he'll be dead. Once I taste his lips, how can I possibly stop there? How could I not kiss him deeper then, taking in the full taste and fragrance of his tender face? How could I resist the opportunity to take a big, bloody bite out of him?*

Smack! Daniel was knocked out of his trance to find Tom giggling at him. Daniel shook his head and rubbed his face. *What was I thinking?* "What's so funny?" He forced a smile onto his face, trying to catch up to wherever Tom had gone while he had been off in his own, sick little world.

"What'd'ya mean, 'What's so funny?' I just smacked you in the blank-assed face with this Phantom mask, and you didn't even blink 'til I started laughing!" Tom laughed some more, but his laughter was just as much a mask as the one he now held in his hand.

What Daniel hadn't noticed, as he had been moving closer to Tom, was that Tom had been moving slowly closer to him as well, all the while remembering the words of Tanner Jones, the life guard at summer camp, and the empty cabin.

It's cold in here, but we can keep each other warm…

There's nothing wrong with a kiss between friends, Tom…

Don't worry, Tom. It isn't sex if we're just using our hands…

Whatever one called it, they had both gotten off, and it had all started with a glance.

Let's just keep this between us. We could get kicked out of camp, if anyone found out.

And Tom had never experienced greater guilt, or greater confusion. What he had done had been wrong in the eyes of the camp, in the eyes of the church, and in the eyes of God. Tom had felt like the most wicked sinner who had ever walked the planet. This part of the memory had been what had triggered the mask-slap to Daniel's face, and the laughter; trying to make it seem as if that intense moment had never bee; trying to cover up the fact that he had wanted Daniel to kiss him, that he had seen desire in

Daniel's eyes. It was all just too weird for Tom. And that was saying a lot.

"Oh, man," Daniel moaned into the palms of his hands. "I've been pretty out of it for the past couple of days. Ever since…" Daniel's thoughts trailed off. "Hey, Tom. Have you been feeling okay, I mean other than your face, since you sniffed that blood?"

Tom smiled. "Yeah. I'm just afraid to show my dang face. That's all. Why?"

Daniel didn't meet Tom's inquisitive gaze. "I don't know. I just, I probably just caught a bug. I'm coming down with a virus or something. I'm just hoping you aren't coming down with it too." Yes, that had to be the truth. He was having twisted thoughts, because he had inhaled some kind of contagious old dust when he had been cleaning out the basement. He couldn't be possessed. He had given himself to God. He followed the Commandments. God would never *allow* him to be possessed.

"No. I don't think I'm coming down with anything," Tom answered, no longer looking at Daniel.

"Oh, good." Daniel and Tom both drifted into silent thought. Daniel found himself thinking determinedly that he had a virus. He was now looking forward to telling Jim that nothing was wrong. Nothing at all. God would never allow his servant to fall to a demon. That's what he kept telling himself. Over, and over, and over.

"Hey, Daniel," Tom broke the silence, and Daniel met his thoughtful gaze, as Tom asked, "Is it a sin to lie to yourself?"

***

When Daniel got home, his mother seemed colder than normal. She didn't even speak to him to gripe about his appearance, or about taking too long to take Tom his home-work. She just glared at him and walked past him to shut herself in her room. The phone started to ring in the very next instant, and Daniel answered it.

It was Jim. "Daniel, how are you?"

"I'm fine, Jim. How are you?"

"Concerned. You don't sound fine."

"Oh, I honestly think I'm just coming down with a virus. I had to take Tom his school work, and it just took a lot out of me. Just a virus."

"Are you sure? You seemed pretty upset about it yesterday morning. Too upset, and not nearly sick. Are you sure it's just a virus?"

Daniel didn't want to think about that. "No, I think I've just been having waking nightmares…" *Is it a sin to lie to yourself?* "…as a result of the virus. I think I'll be okay after I get a little more rest. Thanks for hearing me out though. I know I sounded pretty crazy."

Daniel was failing to convince Jim of his certainty. "No, Daniel, you didn't. Crazy, supernatural things aren't restricted to Biblical times, they still happen today. I want you to feel that you can always come to me, Daniel, no matter how crazy things get. I hope you feel better soon, my friend. I'll let you go, so that you can get some rest."

"Thanks. I appreciate it, Jim."

Daniel clutched the phone to his chest after Jim hung up, and he closed his eyes in prayer, as he tried to erase the doubt Jim had planted in his heart; as he tried again to convince himself that it was only a virus; as he tried to forget what dark possibilities he himself kept thinking of.

Is it a sin to lie to yourself?

XI

A week passed, and Daniel believed himself to be back to normal. Whatever had entered his body, demon or virus, seemed to have left him. At least, that's what he kept telling himself. On this particular afternoon, however, Daniel was not allowing himself to dwell on his worries; for, on this particular afternoon, he planned to be far too busy enjoying the company of his beloved Roxanna Stillwaters. Daniel loved the times when he could just go straight from school to spending the rest of the day with Roxy.

He hadn't seen much of her in the past several days. Though her father had relented and allowed her grounding to end early, their schedules had just continued to conflict. So, today he had arranged to keep everyone away from their usual hangout at the covered picnic area on top of the hill in the park. He intended to make the most of this long awaited opportunity to be alone with Roxy. He hadn't even been able to see her over the three day weekend in honor of Martin Luther King Jr.'s birthday, but now they were at long last going to be together. Now they would be alone and, after that night at Roxy's house almost two weeks earlier, he knew that he had nothing to worry about; nothing to fear. They had come to an understanding about the sex thing, and they were both happy and looking forward to a long, wonderful future together.

Daniel leaned against his car, as Roxy approached. She wasn't carrying any books, which meant no homework. That was good, because no homework meant no rush. "You look funny without books in your arms," Daniel teased her. "When was the surgery?"

"Ha ha. At least I never looked as funny as you, Bug Head."

"Ouch!" Daniel put a hand over his heart and allowed a wounded expression to show on his face. "You hurt my feelings."

"I'm sorry." She smiled and leaned against him on the car. "I'll kiss it make it better."

Daniel got a look of mock outrage on his face. "Kiss *what*?"

"Shut up." She kissed him gently on the lips, then stood back and gave him some room to breathe. "So," she asked, "what's the plan?"

"I thought we could go to Hilltop and just hang out and talk, then maybe go get something to eat at Mr. Greasy. Unless you can think of something else you'd rather do."

"Sounds like a plan to me. What else is there to do in Nightfire anyway?"

"Ask Trevor and Tom. They never seem short on ideas," Daniel commented playfully.

"Yes," Roxy spoke as if she had taken the remark seriously, "but I was thinking we'd keep our activities legal."

Daniel feigned disappointment. "Oh, all right." He perked up then. "So, are you ready to go?"

"Actually, I wanted to see Tom before we left." A mischievous grin crossed her face.

"Hey, I know that look. What're you up to?"

She continued to smile wickedly. "You'll see. There he is now."

Tom walked quickly and cautiously towards Daniel and Roxanna. As he walked, he kept looking over his shoulder, as if he expected to be followed.

Daniel noted that Tom's face had healed well. All that remained of the massive bruise was a series of thin scratches on his right cheek, and those would vanish soon enough, leaving no hint that the accident had ever even happened.

When Tom was close enough to be heard speaking softly, he said, in a disgruntled sort of way, "Hello, dang it."

Daniel laughed at his friend's funky disposition. "What's wrong, Tom?"

Roxanna smiled and addressed Tom, "Did you talk to Robin Winters?"

"Yes. You are the spawn of Hell. But I shall allow you to live anyway, because I grow weary of impaling mortals with iron rods. I am also out of iron rods."

Roxanna giddily ignored Tom's odd comments. "So, what did she say?"

Tom spoke in a somewhat agitated tone, "She asked me to be her boyfriend."

Roxy gasped, as her hands flew over her mouth, then she spoke excitedly, "Oh, how junior high! That is so cute!"

At this point, both Daniel and Tom were looking at Roxanna as if she were an alien from another dimension.

"So what'd you say?"

Tom noted the speed at which Roxy's hands were flapping and decided to answer before they flopped off of her wrists. "I said yes, dang it, but it wasn't my fault. They pressured me into it. And then they all started acting like you. I was scared shitless, much like now."

Roxy had stopped listening after hearing the word "yes." "Oh my god! Tom, you finally have a girlfriend! Aren't you excited?"

"If I were any more excited, I might grin." He looked to Daniel. "Sir, please contain your woman, before it has an aneurysm."

Daniel laughed, and Roxy suddenly realized how he and Tom were looking at her. She laughed and slapped Tom playfully on the arm. "Oh shut up! You know you're excited." She smiled at Tom knowingly, and Tom decided that she was insane. He offered her a smile of his own, but his smile was the kind that just said *whatever.*

"So, Tom," Daniel asked, "now what are you going to do?"

"Hide until I can think of a way to dump her without being shredded by all of her screwy friends."

Roxy's face suggested that she couldn't decide whether she was appalled or amused. "Tom, you can't do that! Why would you tell her that you'd be her boyfriend just to turn right around and break up with her?"

"Status, baby." He winked at her and made a smacking sound with his cheek. "Now I'm the man." He started walking like a chicken and circling Roxy. "Most people know me as Thomas Raymond Don, but you can call me Studly Dudley. Love'em and leave'em, that's what I always say. Now I'm cool like Bert." He stopped and looked Roxy over. "And if you're a good, little girl, I'll let you give me a picture of yourself for my wallet, 'cause I wanna be a stud, like Bert."

Daniel and Roxy both found Tom's comments terribly amusing, and Tom hoped that it had been enough of a display, so that Roxy would stop harassing him. He really had been pressured into saying yes. He had been cornered at his locker by Robin Winters and her friends demanding answers, all because Roxy had gone and put ideas into people's heads.

The truth was that Tom wasn't attracted to Robin Winters at all, and he couldn't find a way out at the time of the ambush. If he had said no, it would have given her gossipy friends cause to ask him why and quite possibly destroy him, and Tom really didn't want that. If Robin had gone to him in private, he could have said no, because he most likely wouldn't have been attacked by countless angry high school girls for having said it, and Robin alone probably wouldn't have demanded angrily to know why he wasn't attracted to her. "So, anyway," he turned to Daniel with a rapid change of subject, hoping that it would force Roxy to accept his oddness as answer enough for the time being, "can I have a ride home?"

"Sure," Daniel answered with an affectionate smile. "What happened to Trevor? I thought he was your ride today."

"He's at home, boinking his Satanic girlfriend so that she won't dismember him."

"Oh. Poor Trev." Daniel got his keys out of his jacket pocket and went to the driver's side of the car to unlock it.

"Do you think Robin will want you to skip school with *her*?" It was as if Roxy had heard nothing of Tom's comments on the matter of Robin Winters.

Tom's reply came through a clinched jaw and teetered uncertainly between annoyance and anger, "Doesn't matter. I'm dumping her." He didn't even turn to look at Roxy when he spoke to her. He wanted this topic dead.

Daniel, who had gotten in and started the car, remarkably on the first attempt, reached over and unlocked the passenger side door. As Tom opened it and climbed into the back seat, Roxy's uninvited protests followed him, "Tom, you can't do that! Don't you *want* a girlfriend?"

"No," he said sharply, as he rolled his eyes and buckled his seat belt.

"Don't you get lonely?" she asked, as she got into her seat and closed the door. She turned around to look at Tom, who had not answered, but was only glaring at her with eyes that seemed to wish her a thousand hellish curses. It started to dawn on her. "You're serious, aren't you?"

Tom rolled his big, blue eyes and sighed disgustedly.

"Tom, why don't you want a girlfriend?"

Having found an answer for her, Tom somehow managed to speak in a less than hateful, and almost playful tone, "'Cause I don't wanna be whipped like Trevor and Daniel!"

"Amen, brother!" Daniel shouted playfully.

Roxy turned on him instantly. "Shut up, Daniel! You know you're not whipped!"

The smile instantly and purposely left Daniel's face, as he played the part. He turned around and looked down at his knees, pouting. "Yes ma'am. Won't happen again."

Roxy turned back to Tom and didn't realize that she'd been zinged by Daniel until she saw the smug grin beaming on young Tom's face. She turned right back around, laughing at herself, and slapped Daniel facetiously. "Oh shut up!" She folded her arms, as Daniel backed out of his parking space laughing out loud along with Tom. Roxy tried to look genuinely pissed off, but failed, as a rebellious smile curled her lips. "Y'all suck," she said in a final, failed attempt to escape her undeniable defeat, as Daniel drove *Clunk* out of the school parking lot and on to Tom's house.

After dropping Tom off at home, Daniel drove to the park and settled *Clunk* at the bottom of the hill. As soon as he got out, he saw Roxy bolt out of her side of the car and run up the hill. He laughed and instantly took off after her. She let him catch her, once she had reached the covered picnic area at the top. He growled and wrapped his arms around her from behind. The feel of his warm breath on her neck aroused Roxy instantly, and, not for the first time, she wished that she hadn't been so agreeable to his insistence that they wait until marriage. This thought only intensified as she felt his lips press against her neck, claiming his prize. "Gotcha," he said in triumph. He rested his head on her shoulder and smelled her golden hair, as he struggled, and failed, to catch his breath gracefully.

"Down, boy. You're panting."

Daniel released her and stood up straight. Roxy turned to face him. "Don't I always pant when I'm around you?" he asked.

She smiled. "Not nearly enough."

Daniel let himself sink into her eyes, still uncertain exactly what color they were. It really didn't matter to him. They were gorgeous regardless. "It's so good to be alone with you." He couldn't stop gazing into her eyes.

She sat down on the cement wall and patted the spot beside her. Daniel gladly sat down as instructed. "So," Roxy asked, "don't you think Tom and Robin make a cute couple? Maybe we could double date with them some time. Won't that be fun?"

"Roxy…" Daniel spoke sternly, preparing to argue with her on Tom's behalf, but then thought better of it and shook his head with a smile. "You're crazy."

"That's what you love about me."

"Yeah. I know." He leaned over and kissed her gently on the lips.

Not a second passed before Roxanna started talking again. "And isn't it cute how shy he is about the whole thing? I mean, can you imagine being seventeen years old and never having had a girlfriend? I feel so good that I was able to help him."

Daniel considered how Tom must feel about Roxy's "help." He decided not to say anything about it to Roxy. He didn't want to argue on this afternoon alone with her. He did decide, however, that he would have to try to help his young friend out of the predicament, before it drove them all insane. He had his own suspicions about Tom and girls, but he would never speculate out loud on the matter. "I'd've probably been better off if I'd've skipped everyone before you. They never lasted anyway."

"That's because you don't put out," Roxy teased.

"Nothin' wrong with being pure."

"Sometimes I think you're too pure." She smiled, and he considered the sinful thoughts that he had been having lately, wishing silently that he could agree with her. He considered talking to her about it. He hadn't really considered it a secret. It was just that he had spent so much effort trying to forget the issue that he hadn't thought to tell anyone how he had been feeling; not since he had talked to Jim over a week ago. He wrapped his arms around Roxy, and they leaned against each other as they sat there. "Hey, Roxy."

"Yes?"

"Can we leave Tom at home tonight?" He sounded like a little boy, asking an adult for something he thought he might not get.

She smiled. "Yes. I'm sorry."

They both drifted into thought, enjoying the silence and the unquestionable beauty of each other. As they lost track of time, the sun began to set, and the horizon glowed with a heavenly multitude of radiant colors that each of them saw as the perfect backdrop for the other.

Daniel kissed Roxanna on the cheek. He smiled brightly at her. "I love you."

She stared longingly into his dark, brown eyes, again aroused by both the masculine sound of his voice and the words that he spoke with it. "Prove it then," she said in a subdued tone, wanting far more than the kiss she knew he would give her in answer to her request.

He leaned over and gave her a more lingering kiss, but still it was an innocent one. She savored it just as well for all that it was. She allowed herself to become excited, as she felt the sharp prickling of his stubble against her and felt the wet smoothness of his flawless lips on her own. She burned for him with an intensity matched only by the distant setting sun.

Daniel sat back, startled. He felt strange. He felt a burning lust for her—a powerful lust that he had never known before. He could smell the yearning, the passionate, lecherous desire emanating off of her like a heat wave. He was frightened by the fact that he felt little control in response. He kissed her again, passionately this time, answering the eager calling of the smells that filled his flaring nostrils and battered the part of his mind normally reserved for judgment with their titillating aroma.

Roxanna took his deep, impassioned kiss with flaring eagerness. As they continued to embrace, she slowly lowered onto her back, and she found Daniel shifting position wordlessly, until he was on top of her, pressing her uncomfortably against the top of the small, cement wall with all the might of his passion. She reached down with her right hand and felt the rock-hard testament of his desires pressed tight within his blue jeans, as she clumsily attempted to unbuckle his belt.

Daniel ended the kiss abruptly, feeling her fingers' gentle stroke as they found their way to his belt buckle. He looked down at her, sweat dripping from his face, and thought that something was not right. For maybe half a second, he tried to think of what it could be, but then he decided to act now and think later. He sat up just enough to remove his jacket, then his shirt.

Roxy's anticipation grew hotter, as she watched all of his sculpted muscles at work in the simple, erotic act of pulling his shirt off over his head. She found herself moistening, ready to admit him, as he again pressed against her, his naked nipples poking her chest, his heart beating against her own. She found herself suddenly uncomfortable, as he kissed her again, more forcefully than before. It was as if he wanted to swallow her tongue and push his own through the back of her skull. She squealed softly and pushed him away. She lay there, staring into his eyes. He looked puzzled, as if he had no idea what she was doing. She dismissed it with a smile.

Daniel looked at her, still with the nagging feeling that something was not right. He dismissed it, and ripped open her blouse. He then pulled her bra up over her breasts, ignoring her pained yelp, leaned over and began caressing her left nipple with his tongue. He felt Roxy grab onto his head and pull his face into her breast as he continued to do what he was doing. She finally managed to unbutton and unzip his pants, and she slipped her hand in and found her prize.

As Roxy's hand slipped into his underwear, and the evening air hit his throbbing flesh, Daniel realized that he couldn't take any more of this foreplay. He had to *be* inside of her. All of his instincts were commanding this of him, as they were bombarded by the screaming scents of Roxanna's sexuality. He could wait no longer. It had to be done. He forcefully knocked her off of the uncomfortable wall and onto the grassy ground outside of the covered picnic area.

"Shit," was all Roxy could think to say as she fell. Before she could collect her thoughts, Daniel had pounced on her and started to unbutton her pants. Roxy had tried to get into it until this point, but this was just not how it was supposed to go. She really didn't want to be one of those girls who lost her virginity while rolling through the dirt and grass of some secluded park. She pushed Daniel off of her and spoke breathlessly, as she sat up, "Daniel. We can't do this."

He glared at her furiously.

"We agreed to wait until we were married."

His murderous gaze began to frighten her. What had gotten into him? It was as if he were someone else. She spoke timidly, "Remember?"

Daniel looked at her, struggling to make any sense at all out of the sounds coming from her mouth. What was wrong with her? This had to be done. He pushed her harshly back to the ground and violently yanked off her pants.

At this point, she started screaming, "No! Stop It! Daniel, what's wrong with you?!"

He yanked down her panties, easily overpowering her futile struggling. He let go of her with one hand to reach back and get his own pants out of his way. As he did this, she somehow managed to struggle out of his one handed grip.

Roxy scurried away from him and grabbed her clothes. She tried to cover herself by holding them in front of her, as Daniel turned to glare at her with those now terrifying, dark eyes. She was trembling, tears were streaming down her face. She screamed a mad and desperate cry of hurt and rage at his betrayal, *"What's wrong with you!?"*

The intense pitch of Roxy's desperate cry, mixed with the unexplained fading of his need to have her and the onset of a new, more unfamiliar feeling, called Daniel's uncontrollable lust to an abrupt halt and left him sitting dazed on the ground. As soon as his lost-looking eyes focused on Roxy in all of her terror, and he realized that she was looking at him, his mind snapped back on, and he was overcome with guilt and self hatred.

The sunlight had almost completely faded, the full moon was beginning to rise, and Daniel's entire body was beginning to tingle. He noted that it was the same sensation as regaining circulation to a foot that had fallen asleep, except that he felt it everywhere at once. He looked up at Roxy, tears filling his eyes, and decided to ignore the strange feeling, though he found this a difficult task at best, as it was growing more intense by the second.

Though she stood trembling in fear of him, Roxy found the remorse in his eyes and dared to take a nervous step forward.

Daniel noticed this and could barely speak through his sorrow, as he saw how much he had hurt her once again; this time more so than before. "It's okay." He choked up completely and could barely whisper his next words. "I won't hurt you."

In her mind, Roxanna knew that she could no longer trust Daniel. Something was very wrong with him. But in her heart, she wanted to believe him when he promised not to hurt her. She wanted to believe that he was still the perfect man that she had believed him to be before. She watched tears fall silently from Daniel's tormented eyes, and decided to listen to her heart.

She slid back into her pants, wasting no time with her undergarments as she tossed them aside. She held her torn blouse closed and approached him cautiously. She stood there, holding his wounded gaze with her own for a half second that seemed an eternity, before she finally sat down beside him. She looked away and asked quietly, "What's going on?"

Daniel considered the question. He tried to concentrate, to weigh the pros and cons of telling her everything, but the tingling sensation grew more intense and painful as the night grew darker and the moon rose higher, so he just spoke. He spoke as much to let her know, as he did to try to keep his mind from the painful tingling that had really grown into more of a stinging, like ants biting every piece of his flesh. "I think I'm possessed."

"Possessed?" There was no hint of disbelief or mocking in her voice. She realized that if he had offered a more "believable" explanation she would never have believed him at all.

Daniel went on, as he sat in a tight fetal position, rocking slightly back and forth, trying to block out the stinging. "I haven't been myself since last Tuesday. After Tom fell in the church basement. There was this story Jim told us, about this beaker full of blood down there, but he asked us not to repeat it. Anyway, Tom broke the beaker when he fell. I cut myself on the glass, and I think that's when it happened."

Daniel still refused to voice his fear that he had actually become a werewolf by mixing its blood with his own. That fear was far too horrible for him to even allow himself to think on it consciously. Whenever the thought came to him, he immediately suppressed it by thinking that God would never allow that to happen to his faithful follower.

Daniel realized that he was making little sense, and the needle prick stinging he felt all over his body wouldn't allow him to even look Roxy in the eyes anymore. "I've just been so scared. I've been feeling bloodthirsty. I can't control myself when I'm around meat. My sex drive is out of control. I've been trying to convince myself that it was over, but it's not. It's not." He looked to Roxy, desperately afraid.

She found the courage to reach out and put a hand on his shoulder. It was clear by the expression on her tear-streaked face that she didn't know what to think of him; that she was still afraid of him. He wanted to comfort her. He *needed* to comfort her. "I never wanted to hurt you, Rox. Please…" He didn't know what he wanted to ask of her. "I think you should stay away from me for a while. Jim said he would try to help me if this didn't get any better."

He looked at her pleadingly, and he found a more potent look of horror than he had ever seen instantly spread across her face, at the lightning-swift moment before she let go a mad, soul piercing scream. His eyes widened, and he stood up with a speed matching her own, as she jumped up and stood there rigidly, trembling, covering her mouth with both hands. "What? What is it!?"

She pointed with her right index finger, as her entire body continued to shake violently. "What's that! *What is that!!?*"

Suddenly the pain overtook Daniel, and he fell to the ground, hugging himself tightly. He saw a shadow. Roxy was pointing at it, and it was coming from him, but it moved as though it were alive. He now realized that the shadow was coming out of his body, enveloping him. He decided that this was the demon that had possessed him, and now it was going to destroy him. As Daniel resigned himself to death, he closed his eyes and prayed that God would at least have mercy on Roxy.

As soon as he had been completely consumed by the shadow, however, he opened his eyes and realized that he was not dead. What startled him most was that he could feel through the shadow as if it were an extension of himself. He smelled and heard now in a way that made his past week's experience seem like cipher in comparison. He saw in the same way, more clearly than ever before. He saw Roxanna, standing there, terrified of him. Paralyzed. He realized what had happened, and he recoiled, but the shadow did not follow his will. At the instant Daniel gave into rebellious thoughts, the shadow was an entity with a will all its own, and it was hungry. It was not a thinking or sentient entity, but rather it was one that acted only on instinct, and its instincts said *Eat*!

Daniel felt the hunger of his extended being and tried to move it away from Roxy, but it did him absolutely no good. The shadow's will was stronger; for now he was inside of it, rather than it being inside of him.

Roxy stood, terrified. Her eyes were wide and dry, as she stared at the monstrous Hell-spawn that had apparently devoured Daniel. No sound escaped her mouth, as she stared, completely lost to an explanation. The thing seemed taller, as a result of her terror, than it actually was. In truth it stood only slightly taller than Daniel had. As it stood silhouetted against the illustrious, white light of the moon, she found herself enthralled by its sleek, nightmarish form. It was completely black, except for two glowing, red eyes, and it had a wolf-like shape, though it was not nearly exact. It had two very large points on either side of its head, and Roxanna thought perhaps those were its ears. Its torso was very wide, and its legs had a human quality to them, while the arms were more ape-like; big and long. At the end of its arms were a series of very long, talon-like fingers. The monster appeared to have no substance, it was simply blackness, a shadow, but as it moved, walking on its hands and feet as an ape would and making sounds as its limbs moved through the grass, she knew that it had substance.

I'm moving! Why am I moving? I refuse to go forward anymore! God! Help me! Daniel was out of control. He was unable to scream out loud, but his soul was in agony. He now knew what had happened to him. He felt deep remorse for not admitting it to himself earlier and killing himself. In a hopeless panic, he realized that he could not stop himself from approaching Roxanna, and, most painful of all his new sensations, he felt the raging hunger of the newborn beast he had become. He continued to move towards her.

He looked at Roxy through his strange, new eyes. She looked insane. She was frozen with fear. Fear of him. Daniel's heart broke, as he looked into her beautiful eyes, knowing that the terrible fear he found there was directed at him, even though no one in the world could love her more than he did. Daniel cried out with his will, *I won't hurt her! I can't be this thing! God, please! Please! I'll do anything! Save me! Please! I have faith! Please don't let me hurt Roxy! Please! Jesus! Please! Please make her run!*

He watched her miserably. He was now close enough to strike her, and yet she still refused to run. She just stood there sobbing, too afraid to move or even to cry out for help.

Daniel intended to stand stubbornly still, but despite his determination he felt his shadowy new arm rise up, intent on the kill. *No!* Daniel could feel the arm, and he struggled with all of his might to lower it, but it did not obey his will. *No! Not Roxy! Anyone but her! It can be someone else. Just not her! We'll go find someone on the other side of town. Please!*

At that moment, Daniel found himself in control of his new body. Though the hunger was terrible, he was able to lower his deadly, clawed arm. For a few brief seconds, he was honestly intent on killing another.

Roxy was beyond horrified, as she waited for the monster before her to do what it would do. At the instant she had seen the thing's arm raised above her, she had known that she was going to die. She had seen her life running through her mind like a movie. She had remembered every moment leading up to this one: the moment of her death.

She had remembered her mother's funeral. She had remembered how stiff the corpse had been when they had found her in the snow after a two day search. What had been left of her corpse anyway. The men at the ski lodge had said that the bear had left more of her than they usually found in those situations. As she remembered, she had speculated, staring at the devilish claws raised above her own head, that maybe it hadn't been a bear after all that had killed her mother. Maybe it had been one of these things. The thing that got Daniel.

Daniel.

She had remembered her dreams. She had hoped they would marry right out of college. June 2001. They would buy a little house and a dog, raise two sons and a daughter. Daniel would be a preacher, and everyone in his church would love him and his beautiful family.

But now that would never be. She had thought, *Now I'm going to die, and this is all that my life has been.* But then, the monster's arm was down, and at that second, something happened within her. Roxanna's paralysis was broken. She was going to live! She suddenly became aware of the cold sweat that had drenched her entire body. She blinked, and when she opened her eyes, she saw the monster turning around. It was going to leave! Roxanna waited until it had turned around completely, and then she ran. She ran as fast as she could, and she dared not look back.

Daniel could hear Roxanna running and panting. He could even hear the pounding of her terrified heart. Relief washed over him. He relaxed. *Now no one has to die. No one.* He meant the words with every fiber of his being. He now knew how to manipulate the shadow body, and he had no intention of killing anyone, ever. Not until he killed himself for the good of the world.

Daniel's relaxation broke instantly, as he felt himself spun around by the shadow's will. He was bounding forward, chasing after Roxanna. The hunger of the beast *would* be satisfied, whether Daniel consented or not. *No! No!* Daniel tried to stop himself. He willed his hellish new form to stop, and in return found only that he could no longer feel the extended body at all. *It* had taken control. *Jesus please! I'll give my own life if you'll let Roxanna escape! Please, God, please!*

Daniel wept, and he knew that there was nothing he could do. He watched through the beast's eyes, as it carried him after Roxy. She was nowhere in sight. She had run off. Daniel hoped that she had escaped, and that he would find someone else before he found her. Then he heard a yelp.

Roxanna tripped over a root protruding from the ground near a large tree. She felt a cold panic fill her chest as she fell, because, at the same moment, she knew that the situation had changed. She could feel the monster searching for her. She wanted to cry when she hit the ground, skinning her palms on several small, jagged, rocks in the dirt, though she barely registered the pain. It was the extreme frustration and terrifying uncertainty she was feeling that made her want to cry.

She sat up, noted the blood on her hands, then ignored it and got back to her feet. She started running but found that she had twisted her ankle. She couldn't run very fast. Roxanna wished there were someone with her; someone who could help her. She thought to herself that she could pray, but she dismissed the notion and kept going forward. If anyone was going to save her, it would be Roxanna Gayle Stillwaters, not God. Besides, if there was a God at all, it wasn't as if he ever listened to people's prayers anyway.

Please God! Please! I'll do anything. Anything! Just save her! Daniel's pleading continued, but Roxy was now in his sights. She was bleeding. He could smell the blood. The hunger pains intensified. *God, no! Please, God no!*

Daniel felt his head fly back, as he unleashed a hellish howl. It was so loud, he thought, that the entire town had probably heard it. He knew for certain that Roxy had heard it, for she had stopped dead in her tracks.

Roxy didn't know what to do. It had sounded so close. Her body threatened to freeze up again, but she knew that would mean her death. She started to move forward again, and the monster leapt. No sooner had Roxy taken three steps, than the monster had leapt over her head and landed suddenly and silently in front of her. Roxanna stopped, perplexed. Her eyes widened with the realization of what now stood in front of her. She started to scream a scream that would have rivaled the creature's own monstrous howl, but her shriek was cut off as merely a peep, along with her head, when the monster's sharp claws sliced through her neck as easily as they might have passed through water.

No! Daniel felt his soul die, as he stared at the fountain of blood that gushed before him. Roxy was dead, and he alone was responsible for her death. Daniel wanted it to be over. He wanted to die. He wanted to close his eyes, but for some reason he dared not even try.

The nightmare grew suddenly worse than he could have ever imagined in even the worst of his boyhood nightmares, as he found himself lunging forward towards Roxy's still rolling head. *No! I refuse to move!* But Daniel knew his resistance was futile. He had become a werewolf, and now he must do as werewolves do.

He found himself staring into Roxy's eyes. They looked so alive to him, so afraid, and still so very beautiful. He could see the color of her eyes so clearly now; now that they were never again to look upon him, filled with love, as they had only minutes before.

Daniel was startled then, as he saw her mouth move, and he was filled with terror. It looked as if she were trying to scream, but she had been cut off from her vocal cords.

Just as Daniel found himself thinking that he had seen more horror in the past few moments than he had ever dreamed possible, it grew even worse. He tried to pull away from Roxy's still-screaming head, but the instincts of the werewolf that he had become would not allow it. He felt his monstrous jaws part, and Daniel felt himself die again, as they took the head between them and began to gnash it down.

Daniel wanted to choke on the taste of her hair, her bones, her flesh, her blood, but he could not. The consumption of her head had only begun to satisfy his burning, animal hunger. The same fate awaited the rest of Roxanna's body, and when he was done, not a drop of blood remained.

Daniel stood frozen. The shadow seemed to be temporarily at ease, though the hunger was still burning within him. Daniel was overcome with grief, and not a shred of evidence existed that any of the past few minutes had even happened as he remembered them. All he had wanted was a quiet evening alone with her. He had loved her. He believed with his whole heart that he could never love another in the same way. For the first time, Daniel felt true guilt for denying her the physical passion she had wanted from him. He knew that he could have given her all that she had wanted from him, and it would have been so perfect, so meaningful. But his loyalty was first and always to God. If not for that, he could have given her everything, but now he would never get the chance. For the first time, he found himself questioning his religious loyalties. But his only hope for Roxy now was in God. He prayed that she would find peace and joy in Heaven, with God. But then Daniel caught something in the corner of his preternatural eye.

It was Roxy.

Roxy stood, looking sad and confused, and she gave no sign of noticing the werewolf at all. Daniel stood tall with his eagerness. Perhaps this had all been a dream. Just a terrible dream, and he was still here with Roxy. He reached out his arm to caress her, but then he saw the werewolf arm, and he put it down, a chill running the length of his spine. *I am still a werewolf. Why doesn't she notice me? Why didn't she flinch when I moved?*

Daniel stared hard at the love he had thought lost only moments before. He thought to himself that it was possible he had killed someone else, someone who looked like Roxy, because there she stood. She was so quiet, and she looked so lost. She looked as beautiful as always, but she also looked so pale. It struck him then that he could see right through her.

Daniel shivered with the realization. Never before had Daniel seen or heard a ghost, as far as he could remember. He had never even believed in them. Daniel had believed that everyone went immediately either to Heaven or to Hell. There had been no room for ghosts in that belief. He waved a dark hand in front of her, but still she did not react. She seemed completely blind to him. *I want to go to her. I want her to see me as she knew me, not as this monster that I've become.*

Daniel presently noticed the chill of the wind, and he found himself human again. He didn't understand what had happened, but neither did he care enough to ponder the matter. He looked around urgently. Roxanna was no longer in the same spot. She had vanished completely.

"No."

Daniel wanted to shout. He wanted to shout so loud that even the moon would hear his sorrow, but he found himself overpowered by grief, and all he could manage was to fall to the ground and whimper her name between violent sobs that shook both his body and his soul, "Roxy."

Time passed, the night grew colder, and Daniel remained sitting at the spot where Roxy had died. He didn't notice the cold, he didn't notice the darkness, and he didn't notice the time that had passed. He didn't notice anything as he sat there, trying to convince himself that none of it had happened—until he felt the hunger; the inhuman need to do it all again. It was a painful sensation, but the pain was a price Daniel found himself willing to pay. "I won't do it again. Jesus, help me. I won't do it again." He had made his decision, but it was of absolutely no consequence.

He felt a slight tingle, as the shadow again enveloped him. He looked at the world through the werewolf's eyes, and again he saw Roxy standing before him, not seeing him. Why hadn't she gone on?

Roxy, why are you still here? I'll stay here with you forever if I must. I won't leave you to wander.

And then Daniel felt himself turn away from her, and he knew that there was nothing he could do. He started to run, and though he did not know where he was going, he did know why he was going. All he could think of was Roxy, standing there without salvation, and a new thought crept to the surface of his conscious mind. *Maybe there is no Heaven.*

Daniel soon found himself at the edge of the park, where only one, small house stood. It was the home of Abigail Johnson. Abigail was seventy-nine years old, and for the past fifty-three of those years, she had been a Sunday school teacher at Saint Paul. She had never been part of any public scandals, and as far as anyone who knew her was concerned, she was as close to sainthood as anyone could get without actually being a saint.

Abigail sat alone in her living room, reading the newspaper. Her husband had died in a boating accident in 1976. He had been drinking heavily, a problem no one had even been aware that he had until the accident, and he fell overboard and drowned while fishing, early one Sunday morning.

At the funeral, everyone had admired Abigail's strength. She hadn't let one tear fall in public, though everyone had known that she must have been crying herself to sleep every night. Truth to tell, no one had seemed more upset at the funeral than Mr. Johnson's twenty-two-year-old secretary. She had sobbed nonstop, and the following month, she had moved out of Nightfire altogether.

Abigail's life had been a very humble one since then. She had little to look forward to in life other than Sunday mornings, but sometimes she would allow herself to think back on one particular Sunday morning that she had spent on a boat before church. She would allow herself to think about her husband's funeral, and how everyone had said she was so strong. She would think back on these things, and she would smile.

As she read the paper, she heard a noise coming from outside. Someone was prowling around in the back. She had a sudden sense of danger. She put the paper down, and went out onto her back porch. She grabbed a flashlight and shined it straight ahead of her. "Who's there?" she asked. "Haven'tcha got anything better to do than to frighten old ladies?"

She heard a sound, and she quickly turned the flashlight to the left. Her hearing wasn't very good, and she couldn't quite tell from which direction the sound was coming. Her light found nothing out of the ordinary to her left, as it had found nothing out of the ordinary directly in front of her.

She heard the sound again. There was something groaning in the darkness. Abigail suddenly heard a high pitched howl, and she was so startled that she dropped her flashlight. "Oh, damn it all." She bent down and picked it up. The howl repeated itself. She aimed the flashlight to her right, and that's when she saw it. It turned to face her, all howling ceased, and it started to wag its little tail.

"Well, aren't you just the cutest, little puppy I've ever seen?" Abigail approached the very young golden retriever pup that seemed to have gotten itself caught underneath a large root. The root came out of the ground, rose slightly over it, and then went back down into it. Abigail knelt down and petted the pup gently on the head. It whimpered, as it happily licked her hands. It looked at her with eyes that said *Will you free me?*

"Now, how did you get yourself into this? Quite a pickle. Let's see." She looked at the root. "No way am I going to cut through that root to get you out. I don't want to damage the tree." She reached down and grabbed the puppy's front paws. "This will only hurt for a second now, pup." She yanked, the pup yelped, she yanked again, the pup yelped again, she yanked again, and the pup came loose.

She breathed a sigh of relief, and the puppy jumped up on her and started licking her face affectionately. She laughed and patted it on the head. She heard the puppy's stomach growl, and for the first time she realized how skinny it was. "Oh, you poor dear. You must be starving. I suppose that means you're lost. I'm sorry. I haven't got anything here for runaways to eat," she said as she stood. "You just think of that the next time you wander off. You'd better be about finding your way home now, pup. It's a cold night, and I'd hate for you to spend it outside." She turned to go inside, and the puppy scampered after her.

When she opened the door, the pup ran in before her. "Oh, no you don't," she said gently. She picked the puppy up and set it down outside. "You go home now." She waved it away, then nudged it off of the porch. "Shoo now. Shoo."

The pup looked up at her uncertainly as she pushed it away. It tucked its tail between its legs and gazed at her with sad, brown eyes.

"None of that now. This isn't an animal shelter." She closed the door and locked it.

The puppy sat down and looked at the ground, as it pouted and thought about life. The pup had been abandoned in the park by people who had thought that they were doing the right thing. He hadn't minded so much that they couldn't afford to feed him, because he could always find something to eat around the apartment. Here, it was just about the same, food-wise, but here he was all alone. No one to play with. No one to love him and call him *Goodboy* or *Heresamson*. The pup was now beginning to realize that people didn't understand the way that puppies saw things. And he was beginning to understand the cold, hard reality that most people didn't love as freely or as easily as puppies did.

The puppy looked back at the door. He then decided that he had to explain things to the lady. He had to make her understand.

He scampered up to the door and started scratching it with his paws. He started to yip at the door. This was the only way that the puppy could say, *Please come back. I'm Goodboy. I'm Heresamson. I love you. You saved me. Don't you love me too? Please come back. I love you.*

Suddenly the pup stopped his yipping. He sensed something, but, whatever it was, it had no scent. He knew this because, upon sensing it, he had tried very hard to find its scent on the wind. This scentless danger frightened him. *Bad.* The pup started to growl quietly at the dangerous presence he felt. He didn't want it to find his new friend.

A shadow soon fell over the pup, and as he looked up, he growled bravely and backed up underneath a rocking chair. When Heresamson found the source of the shadow, he was puzzled to find another, more ominous shadow, with red eyes. *Bad Dog! Bad Dog!* Heresamson continued to growl at the thing. The bad dog, however, disregarded Heresamson's warning. As it stepped up onto the old, wooden porch, Heresamson came out from underneath the chair and started barking the most threatening, squeaky-pup barks he could manage. *Go away! This is not your place!*

The werewolf looked down at the daring pup, as it continued to bark, and unleashed a howl that shook the walls of the house with its volume and shattered the nearest windows, and he aimed this howl right at the pup. As its fur was blown back by the force of the howl, the pup backed timidly back under the rocking chair, scared out of its wits, and urinated on itself, just before going into a state of shock.

Inside, Abigail had just reseated herself in her plush recliner, when she heard the howl and the shattering of glass. She reached over in terror to pick up the phone, as she hunched down below the top of the chair, so that whomever was there wouldn't see her. She dialed the number timidly, almost forgetting it half way through.

"Hello?" came the groggy reply.

"Elizabeth!" Abigail whispered in a panic. "Elizabeth, someone's just shattered my back windows. I think they might have broken in."

"Abigail? Are… Are you all right? Hold on. I'll be right over. Why don't you call the police?"

"Policemen make me nervous. Please, hurry. I'm so afraid."

"All right. Just hang tight, and I'll—" Elizabeth Krandall was stricken silent when she heard the terrible sounds coming from the other end of the phone.

There was a crash, as the monster burst through the wall at the back of the house. Daniel didn't know why it hadn't bothered with eating the puppy, though he suspected it was because the beast had a preference for human meat; not that he was bothered by the puppy's good fortune. He was just glad that someone had been spared. It was one less soul to torture his conscience. Daniel himself was now in a state of absolute shock. He had long since lost the strength to carry on his futile battle of wills with the werewolf entity he was attached to. It seemed, no matter how much he pleaded, that he was now just a passenger in his own body, going along for the ride and the horrible, if hauntingly satisfying, sensations.

The werewolf surveyed the living room as he entered it. Daniel could hear a mouse scampering somewhere in another room. Aside from that, the house was silent, save for the heavy thumping of an old woman's weak heart.

There was someone hiding on the other side of that recliner in front of the television. Daniel could smell it.

Daniel decided to make one more attempt at taking control of the beast. He waved his arm with his own will experimentally, finding the limb obedient once more. He chose to take a step forward, and he found that he could. He swiveled his werewolf head from side to side, continuing to survey the room. He then decided to leave, and this is where he found that he had no control. The new body would not follow his mental command to leave. It *would* feed. Daniel continued to will himself to leave, and the shadow body continued to walk forward, towards the chair. Now just behind the chair, he looked down and saw an old woman huddled there, holding the phone. Without preamble, the monster unleashed yet another of its hellish howls.

The woman looked up, gasped, and lost her grip on the phone. She was trembling as she slid all the way down to the floor. She couldn't seem to figure out whether she wanted to put her hands to her ears or to her chest, for both were in great pain. Abigail tried to scoot away, though she never once took her eyes away from the devil towering above her. "Demon from Hell," she croaked out, making the sign of the cross over her pounding heart. "I expel you in the name of Christ."

To Daniel's horror, the werewolf was unaffected by Abigail's Christian curse. It easily knocked the recliner between them to the side and continued to glare at her with its devilish red eyes.

Abigail began to sob. "You can't do this to me," she blurted out pathetically.

The monster leaned over and growled, as it parted its hellish, black jaws.

Abigail looked death in the face, through heaving sobs, and she screamed out in one last, desperate act of defiance, "I'm a Sunday school teacher!"

The werewolf pounced, and Abigail Johnson, Sunday school teacher though she had been, was gone within a matter of seconds.

A Sunday school teacher! Daniel stood horrified, still tasting her obviously sainted flesh and blood on his tongue. *My God! Where are you? Is there a Heaven at all? Please, God, let me know that there is, and that Roxy will be in it.*

Daniel suddenly realized that if he had seen Roxanna's spirit, then he should be able to see the spirit of the Sunday school teacher as well. He looked around frantically until he found her. Surely, if there was a Heaven at all, little old Sunday school teachers all had a place there.

When he found her, she was standing near the kitchen, and she was holding hands with a man in a fishing hat—another spirit. The man, who looked to be in his late fifties, was smiling at her and speaking to her, though Daniel could not hear his words. A soothing light surrounded him, and he seemed to glow with it inside and out. However, Abigail herself looked miserable.

It seemed to Daniel that whatever the man was saying, it was only further upsetting the old lady. She shook her head, and the man let go of her hands, as he backed away from her. A hideous, red light then surrounded her from the ground. "No, Thomas! Take me with you!"

Daniel was startled to find that suddenly he could hear her, as she tried to escape the red light and go to the man. The man stood stone-faced, as a legion of monstrous, disfigured, wounded-looking hands reached out of the red light and pulled the old lady inside. She screamed until she was completely inside the unseen source of the light, and nothing could be seen of her.

The light then faded and was gone.

The man looked sad. He shook his head, looking at the place where the old lady had just been, as the soothing light grew around him from above. The man then startled Daniel, as he looked over and stared him right in the eyes.

Can he see me? Daniel wondered.

The man continued to look Daniel in the eyes, as he smiled and said, "God has already forgiven you, my friend." The man then turned to look, one last time, at the spot where the woman had been taken by the red light. He shook his head, one last time, and went fully into the soothing light, with a peacefulness equaled in its potency only by the horror of the old woman's descent.

The beautiful light faded then and was gone.

Daniel now found himself perfectly lost. God seemed deaf to his cries. God had just sent a little old Sunday school teacher to Hell right before his eyes. God had left Roxy to linger in some sort of limbo. Daniel was beginning to wonder if he had wasted his faith on God completely. And yet, God was Daniel's only hope for salvation.

Daniel wanted to scream. He wanted to die. He was traumatically confused about both life and death, and he was in agony over the loss of his beloved Roxanna Stillwaters and the guilt that he alone carried for her death. There was no one Daniel could go to now. If he sought out any of his friends, it would mean their certain death.

For the first time of his own free will, Daniel threw back his demonic head and let loose a passionate howl that carried all of his rage and sorrow out into the cold, dark, uncaring night. And when it was done, Daniel ran forward, crashing through the front of the house. He ran without a destination. He ran, with the lone hope that something, be it of Heaven, Earth, or Hell, would strike him down and end the pain and confusion that he seemed powerless to escape on his own.

After the final howl and the crash that followed, Elizabeth Krandall hung up the phone wordlessly. Terror had crept into her heart, and she knew that there was no point in wondering whether or not her old friend Abigail was all right. Just as there was no point at all in calling the police. Beth Green had been right. They should have left already. Lillian Foster had tried to warn Barbara Mason an entire week before, and now, having not acted immediately, they were all in mortal danger. Elizabeth looked out her window and stared at the full moon. She suddenly realized how relatively close to her Abigail had lived.

"What's wrong, Liz?" Ted Krandall asked, with honest con cern for his paling wife.

"Get up and pack our bags, Ted."

"What?" Ted was silently questioning his wife's sanity. "Why, Liz? It's the middle of the night."

"We have to get out of Nightfire. Now!" Elizabeth realized that she sounded crazy. She also knew that, if she told her husband the truth, he wouldn't budge, and he'd have found her a psychiatrist by the end of the next day. "Ted, do you trust me?"

Ted realized that something very serious was hidden behind that question. He considered his answer carefully. "Yes," he said at last. "Of course I do."

"Then please don't ask me any questions. I promise to tell you everything as soon as we get back into town."

"When do we get back into town?"

"Um, Monday. We're just going away for the weekend."

"Can't it wait 'til after school? Tomorrow's a test day, and I hate to let substitutes handle tests."

Elizabeth thought for a moment. *No. We have to leave right now. But, then again, it's out there right now. If we go out there, it might notice us, where it wouldn't have before. I'm so screwed up!* "All right. We'll wait until after school, but we have to leave *immediately* after school, do you hear me?" *We have to leave before the sun goes down.*

"All right, all right. Liz, will you please tell me what's going on?"

"Do you promise that we can leave right after school tomorrow?" *If we're still alive tomorrow that is.*

"Yes. I thought I just did."

"Good. Then I promise to tell you everything. On Monday." She kissed her husband on the forehead and got up out of bed. "I'm going to use the phone." She grabbed the cordless phone by the bed and walked out of the room.

Ted was left to do all that he could do, given the circumstances. He scratched his head, shrugged his shoulders, and rolled over to try and get some sleep, before the aliens picked his wife up again for her nightly check-up.

Liz called Beth Green right away. "Beth, this is Elizabeth."

"Elizabeth Krandall? Do you have any idea what time it is?"

"It's 11:45. Beth, Lillian was right!"

"What? How do you know?"

"I was on the phone with Abigail Johnson when the werewolf attacked her."

Beth went pale. "What? When?"

"Just a couple of minutes ago." Elizabeth found herself shedding unexpected tears, as she recalled the incident. "It was awful. Ted and I are leaving right after he gets home tomorrow."

"How do you know it was a werewolf? Couldn't it have been a stray dog, or a coyote or something?"

"No!" Elizabeth's tone made clear that she had no patience for discussing the matter. "It was absolutely something right out of Hell. I heard its howl, and it was unlike anything I've ever heard in all my life, in all my travels. This was a sound that nothing of this world could have produced. I would swear before God. It was the cry of a monster from Hell!"

"I believe you, Liz. What should we do now?"

"Tomorrow morning, as soon as the moon has been replaced by the sun, call everyone who knows the story, and tell them to get out of town immediately. Tell them what happened. And if they don't believe you, tell them to pay Abigail Johnson a visit. I'm going to call the police as soon as I'm off the phone with you, and I'm going to tell them exactly what I heard. The story should spread like wildfire. Hopefully, enough people will have sense enough to leave town for a few days, while the moon is still full."

"But shouldn't we be safe after tonight?" Beth asked. "The moon is only full one night each month, isn't it?"

"Yes, but if you study your ancestor's journal closely, you'll see that the night of the last attack in 1850 fell on the day *after* the full moon. The werewolves changed two nights in a row, even when the moon was waning. I researched the dates with relentless scrutiny, remember. That was something that stood out to me. We have no idea how many nights in a row these things can change. It's imperative that you get the word out first thing tomorrow and then get out of town."

"All right. And what should I do until then?"

Elizabeth considered that for a moment, and then she said simply, "Pray."

Thirty-five-year-old Davin Adams walked up the rickety, old, iron stairs of the ninety-eight-year-old apartment building in downtown Nightfire, where he lived with his younger brother. Davin had just finished washing the blood off of his knife in gutter water downstairs. He hated killing. Every time he did it, he prayed that he would never have to do it again, but he had to do whatever it took to keep his life, as well as everyone else's life that he cared for, afloat.

He and his brother James had moved to Nightfire from Spring, Texas early in 1996. They had been forced to put their mother in a nursing home just before they had moved. A nursing home they couldn't afford. When the bank foreclosed on their house, Davin had lied to his mother about it all. He had told her that the house would be waiting for her when she got better, which everyone knew she never would; not unless they found a cure for old age. He told her that he and James had gotten good jobs in another city and were going to have to move away. She had been very happy to hear that they were doing well for themselves. Davin had then put his brother James, who wouldn't go without his damned chicken, in the van and driven away. After driving for a few hours, they had decided to camp out in Nightfire, mostly because they had nearly run out of both gas and money.

In Nightfire, they had been able to get a crappy, low rent apartment. However, they had not been able to get good jobs, because they hadn't been able to afford decent clothes. It also hadn't help that James was only one I.Q. point away from Down syndrome, and he had a bad habit of scaring everybody away. Especially with that damned chicken.

Davin had eventually found a way to make money, though, so that their mother could stay in a nice place, and they could stay at least out of a cardboard box. Unfortunately, he and his brother had needed to do some illegal things. They had sold all sorts of illegal drugs for a man known to them only by the street name of Fat Herman. Fat Herman had allowed the brothers to help him distribute the goods, so long as he got his cut.

They usually cut it pretty close. Once they had money, they would spend it first on their mother, then on their food and rent, and then on Fat Herman's cut. Sometimes they wouldn't have enough to cover it all, and they'd have to think of alternative ways to get the rest of the money. This was one of those months. Business had been slow, and Fat Herman would be after his cut any day now. So, they had to commit little robberies where they found the opportunity. They usually just mugged drunks in the middle of the night, and they usually let them live.

If their victims managed to see their faces or any other easily identifiable feature, however, they didn't have a choice. They had to take care of their mother, and they couldn't afford to get caught.

Davin reached the door of his apartment and hesitated before going in. He knew that he'd have to be honest with his brother, and he didn't look forward to it. When he entered the room, however, he forgot his guilt, because he could not believe what he saw before him. "Jimmy! You did *not* put a sweater on that damned chicken!"

"His name's Ed, Davin. Call 'im Ed, okay?"

Davin glared at the chicken, as it strutted past him, wearing a patchwork sweater and clucking obliviously, and then he looked up and glared at his younger brother.

James smiled proudly. "I made it myself, so he won't be cold."

"Just when I thought it couldn't get scarier." Davin couldn't stand the chicken, but he tolerated it, just barely, for his brother's sake. The chicken had shown up in their yard one morning after a hurricane had blown through, and none of the neighbors had claimed it. James had immediately decided that the chicken had been a sign from God, and that it was his responsibility to feed and shelter it. And it had thus become the fattest chicken in Spring, Texas. Also, quite possibly, the only chicken in Spring, Texas.

"Jimmy, listen to me. You're gonna have to stop bein' so attached to that chicken. Maybe we should let it go live with Mom, huh? The chicken ain't safe with us, James. It just ain't safe."

"He is too safe. I take care of 'im all the time."

"I know, Jimmy, an' that's the problem. We got a lot of work t'do to get that fat fucker his cut this month. I mean, the last deal we made was when Trevor an' Tom came by, and that was two Saturdays ago. We got a lot to make up for."

"Didn't you get some more money when you were out just now?"

Davin looked down at his feet. "Yeah. Yeah, I got some money, but it wasn't enough to cover things. We still need some more, and I think these operations go smoother when you help me out." He looked at his brother expectantly.

"Me an' Ed tried to go with you, Davin. You wouldn't let us, remember?"

"That's just it though, Jimmy! You can't bring the fucking chicken with you everywhere you go! Don't you remember what happened last night? We had to stab that poor ass-hole to death, because your fuckin' chicken started goin' nuts and clucking at the top of its lungs! The chicken's a dead giveaway, James. If it hadn'ta clucked we could have let that guy go last night."

James felt bad. He wanted to make his brother proud, but he had to take care of Ed. It was his responsibility. "Davin?"

"What?"

"Could you let the guy go tonight?"

Davin's face scrunched up, and he looked down. He wanted to cry, but he was a pro when it came to holding back tears. "No. He saw me. He tore off my mask. Belligerent bastard. I wanted to let him go. I tried to, but…" He didn't know what to say. He felt terrible about killing that poor man. All he could think about was that the man he had killed might have had a mother, and how badly this would break her heart. That man might have had a brother who looked up to him. That man might have even had a stupid pet chicken with a stupid name like Blain or something, and who would take care of that fucking chicken now? "It just would have gone more smoothly if I had had some help..." he scowled, "...that didn't cluck!" He glared down at the chicken again. He found himself wondering, not for the first time, if chickens really did run around with their heads cut off.

"I'm sorry, Davin. But God wants me to take care of Ed. That's why he sent him to me."

"God damn it, James! God did not send you that fucking chicken! That fucking chicken somehow managed to get sucked up by a hurricane and live long enough to be blown from wherever the hell it was to begin with and end up in our front fucking yard!"

"Yes. God sent him to me on the winds."

Davin squinted as he looked at his brother. "Are you feeling okay, Jimmy? How old are you now?"

James smiled. "I'll be twenty-seven this Tuesday."

"Twenty-seven, huh? Don't you think that twenty-seven is a little bit old to still be believing in miracles? And even so, what the *fuck* kind of miracle is it for God to look down from on high and put a chicken in somebody's yard?! If God wants to give you a miracle, why doesn't he get you a decent job? Why doesn't he let us win the lottery so that we can get out of this shit-hole life we've been stuck with? Why do you think God, who can do anything he fuckin' wants, would send you a god damned chicken?"

"Maybe 'cause chickens don't yell."

"Oh, don't start that pouty shit with me, Jimmy. You know I only get upset 'cause I love you, and I just want what's best for everybody."

"Well, you shouldn't yell, Davin."

"Oh yeah? And why the fuck not! I need some sort of outlet for all the frustrations in my shitty, crappy life!"

"It scares Ed when you yell all the time, Davin."

"It scares Ed? It scares fucking Ed!? Why did you name that chicken fucking Ed anyway! This is not an Ed! Chickens are not Eds! Ed is a boy's name, and chickens are not boys! Chickens are…" he struggled to pull a female name out of his head. "Chickens are Valeries and Helenas! Why the fuck did you name that chicken Ed!?"

James looked up at his brother indignantly. "Simple name for a simple chicken."

"Of course! Shit! It all makes so much sense to me now."

"'Bout time."

"Jimmy, let me get something through your head! I killed a man tonight! In two nights, I have killed two men! And I lay partial blame on your fucking, God damned, shit-pecking chicken!" Davin reached down and grabbed the chicken, picking it up.

"Davin, stop! Put 'im down!"

"No! Not until I think you understand me!" He carried the chicken over to the window and held it out over the sidewalk below. The chicken clucked and struggled frantically. "I have trouble working with the chicken! You have trouble working without the chicken! I have trouble working without you! If we don't get Fat Fucking Herman his fat, fucking cut, he's gonna cap your chicken's ass to make a point! Do you want your chicken's ass capped!? Do you?"

"No! No! I don't want my chicken's ass capped, Davin! Please, put him down! You're pissing him off? He's gonna kick yer ass!"

Davin put the chicken down inside, and he laughed. "I'm holding the chicken over the pavement, and you're scared he's gonna kick *my* ass? James, he's, I mean, *she's* a chicken! A fucking chicken!"

"I know *he's* a chicken, Davin. But I saw on TV the other day, on this talk show, there was this cop, and this chicken had kicked his ass. 'Cause, ya' see, chickens got claws and beaks, and stuff like that that sometimes cops don't have."

"Sometimes?" Davin started to laugh hard. One thing he never grew tired of about his younger brother was that he usually had a way of wording things that was absolutely priceless.

James didn't know what his brother was laughing at, but it made him happy to see him laughing, so he started to laugh along with him.

Davin went over to his brother, still laughing, and gave him a big bear-hug. "I love you, Jimmy. I'm sorry I yelled. I just hate that I've had to kill people." He let the hug go, but he kept his arm around his brother. "But I swear to God, Jimmy. If Fat Herman even thinks about having your chicken's ass capped, I'll cut him open like a fish. You have my word on that, Brother."

Daniel had been running for hours, thus far successfully ignoring the hunger pains he still felt. It was now 3:00 A.M., not that it mattered to Daniel, and he had finally stopped running in an alleyway somewhere downtown. He caught the scent of blood in the gutter water, and at that instant, he knew that he had lost control. He tried, more out of obligation than hope, to stop the monster from feeding again, but, as he'd come to expect, he was no longer in control, and he found his new limbs moving on their own. He smelled the knife that had been rinsing in the gutter water, and he smelled the living flesh that had been clasped around the knife, and that was the scent the beast chose to follow. Daniel wished that he were dead, as he contemplated the hellish scene that he knew he was about to be a part of.

"Shit! It's late!" Davin Adams looked at his watch. "You'd better get'cher chicken in bed, Jimmy. I'm gonna go outside and get a little air before I turn in."

"Okay, Davin."

Davin walked outside and turned the corner, and just as soon wished that he hadn't. The werewolf howled and lunged forward, tearing flesh and snapping bone, as Davin screamed, involuntarily sending every ounce of his strength and sanity up through his throat in a chilling alarm that was the sound of terror itself. In a matter of seconds, it was over, and there was nothing left of Davin Adams in the wake of the werewolf's hunger.

"Hey! Davin? Oh, God! What've you done to Davin?" James had come outside only to find the monster standing there where his brother should have been. He started hitting the werewolf with both fists, and the werewolf turned and howled again. James stumbled back into the apartment, covering his ears. "Ow. My ears." He took his hands down and noticed that they had blood on them. He continued to stumble back, and he finally fell on his rear on the other side of the room.

Daniel caught the scent of blood in the air. *No! No! Haven't you been fed enough for one night?* Thinking of the man he had just killed, he tried to will his werewolf body to look for Davin's soul, but the werewolf instincts had other ideas about what they should be doing.

Daniel found himself entering the dirty, little apartment, approaching a scared young man who didn't know why his ears were bleeding. *Get up and run, Jimmy! Getup and run!* Daniel knew that even if the young drug dealer could have heard him, taking the advice would have done him no good at all. Daniel was soon within reach of James, and he got in position to make the kill.

It was at that very moment that the werewolf was unexpectedly interrupted.

"Ed! No! Don't do it, Ed!" James cried out as his chicken appeared out of the blue and attacked the werewolf. The chicken jumped on the werewolf's head, and it started clawing and pecking at the monster's shadowy ears and eyes. Though a brave gesture, it was, in the end, a futile one.

The werewolf reached up and effortlessly sliced the chicken in two with its sleek, razor claws. Ed fell to the floor with two sickening splat-thumps.

James looked up angrily at the werewolf. "You capped my chicken's ass! You capped my chicken's ass! Ed!" The werewolf growled as he lunged at the screaming young man. Seconds later, James Adams was gone.

Daniel somehow didn't feel quite as bad about these particular killings, which is not to say much, because the guilt that was left with him was incredibly deep. He found it unsettling that this time it hadn't bothered him as much, but he had known the two people and the chicken. They were the drug dealers whom Trevor sometimes got his marijuana from. Daniel had only met them briefly once before, but he knew they were bad news, and he knew that they had been dealing a lot more than just weed. He assumed that, when he saw their souls sucked into Hell, he would finally be seeing justice. Then he saw them, all three. Davin had his arm around James, and James was holding the chicken. All three glowed inside and out with a soothing, gentle light, and all three were looking right at him, as they walked into the light that shined from above, just as the old man in the fishing hat had done a few hours before.

Then they were gone.

Daniel found himself in control of his body once more, even more confused and enraged than before, and he had no idea where to point his rage, other than at God. *You sent a Sunday school teacher to Hell, you took two drug dealers and a chicken into Heaven, and yet you would not touch Roxanna Stillwaters! You wouldn't touch her! Why? Why!? He* howled with all of his rage and emotion, and the entire building shook.

Again, Daniel ran. He was angry at God, and above all the other horrors of the night, this realization was the what frightened him the most.

***

The rest of the night passed as a blur to Daniel. His last memory, before finding himself back to normal and lying in his bed, was of the moon setting on the glowing, red horizon of dawn, as he continued to run. When he realized that he had returned to his human form and gotten in his bed, he cried. He tried to block out everything he had seen. He tried to tell himself that it had all been a dream. He sobbed endlessly into his pillow. "Please, God, let me wake up in the morning and find that this was all a dream. Please let me see Roxanna alive tomorrow." He cried Roxanna's name, until he fell asleep with her name both on his lips and in his heart.

Next door, Lillian Foster woke up in a cold sweat for the fourth time that night. Her nightmares had been horrible, and they had all been about Daniel. Every time that she had woken up, she had fallen into tears, except for this time. This time, the dream had also been about Jim Jordan. Lillian wiped the sweat from her face and spoke out loud, to let herself know that she was truly awake. "Today, Jim. Today is the day that you call me and fess up. Today is the day that I get some answers."

XII

It was 8:00 A.M. when Robert Mason finally decided to check on his son. "Daniel?" He was startled to find his son lying on top of his sheets, fully clothed in what he had been wearing the previous morning before school. Daniel never overslept. "Son. Are you all right?"

Daniel moaned horribly, as he slowly but surely awoke. "Dad?" he mumbled, with his burning eyes barely opened enough to see. "What time is it?"

Robert looked at his watch. "8:01. You stay up all night, boy?"

"No." Daniel sat up and rubbed his face with both hands. He noticed that he felt woozy, as he struggled to recall the previous night. "But I don't know how much sleep I actually…" Hellish Pictures suddenly filled Daniel's memory. Images of Roxanna's severed head screaming silently in pain, images of a little old Sunday school teacher being dragged into Hell by vile, demonic hands, images of a chicken, sliced in two, hitting the floor with two sickening, wet splat-thumps. *Oh, God!* Daniel's stomach twisted into a nauseated knot, and he jumped off of his bed and bolted for the bathroom, where he vomited violently in the toilet.

Daniel's entire body shook, as he sat on his knees, hovering over the commode, trying to recover from the foul-tasting expulsion. The prospect of opening his eyes again terrified him. He just knew that he would look into the commode only to see Roxanna's once beautiful eyes floating there, staring at him accusingly.

Daniel's father stood in the doorway behind him. "Feel better?"

Oh no! Daniel found himself silently approaching a state of sheer panic. *When he sees what I've puked up, what am I going to say? Oh, God, please make him go away.*

"Here you go, Son." His father's voice was closer now, right next to him.

Daniel opened his eyes slowly. He focused timidly on what had just come out of him and saw nothing that he had expected to see. No blood, no body parts. The only recognizable object was part of what he had eaten in the school cafeteria the previous afternoon.

"Clean yourself off and get back into bed."

Daniel reached up with his left arm and flushed the commode. Without turning his head, for fear of disgusting his father with his vomit-covered face, he then reached out and took the towel that was being offered to him. After Daniel took the towel, his father courteously left the bathroom.

When Daniel finished cleaning his face, he left the bathroom and found his father standing by the bed. "I'm sorry, Dad."

"Sorry?" Robert Mason laughed at his son. "Son, it's all right. Everybody gets sick. You don't have to be sorry." He smiled brightly and shook his head. "You were sick once in kindergarten, remember? You'll be all right. Just get back in bed and sleep it off."

Daniel ran a hand through his hair and spoke absently, "But it's a test day."

"So you'll make it up. That's what make-up tests are for, Son."

Daniel wobbled at the side of his messy bed, trying not to think. "What about my attendance record?" He asked without actually caring at all.

"To Hell with your attendance record. I've never forced you to go to school when you shouldn't have gone. Haven't been many opportunities. You do a good job of staying healthy. You work out, eat right, but sometimes these damned bugs just sneak up and get you, no matter how good a shape you're in." He stepped behind his son and gave him a gentle nudge, causing Daniel to collapse on the bed like a house of cards. Robert chuckled at how badly his son seemed to not want to be weak. "So stay in bed, and get well. I'll see you after work." Robert then grabbed his son's legs and pulled them around, so that Daniel was lying straight. Then he covered his son properly with the sheets and left the room.

He went into the kitchen on his way out of the house to let his wife know what was going on; not that he thought she'd care. He found himself wondering if one of the reasons that Daniel never missed school was because anything was better than staying at home with his mother all day. *I know I never miss a day of work.* "Barbara."

She looked up from the table to face him with a glare that purposely let him know that he was disturbing her.

"Daniel's got a bug, so I told him to stay home. I'd appreciate you seeing to it that he gets plenty to drink."

Barbara looked at her husband furiously. "No. Absolutely not!"

"Damn it, Barbara. The boy's sick as a dog! I just watched him puke out his guts in there!"

"Well then, Robert, why don't you take the day off, and care for him yourself, since you seem so eager for him to give up on his education!"

"He's not giving up on his education! Damn it. The boy is sick. And I would take the day off to care for him myself, but I have an extremely important meeting with my boss today, and to miss it would surely cost me my job."

"Well, if that's your main priority."

"God damn!" Robert knew that he couldn't win. He wanted to strangle her. He wanted to let her know that he thought she was a cold-hearted bitch, and that his father had been right when he had told him to hold out and marry a Texas woman.

Of course, he didn't really regret marrying her—not in the purest sense anyway. If he had taken his father's advice, he would never have had Daniel. It was for Daniel's sake that Robert held his tongue. If he let his wife know exactly what he thought of her, though he suspected she already knew, she would leave him, and he would have no way to shelter his son from the hurt.

Every day that he suffered his continued marriage to Barbara, he held on to the hope that he had thus far protected Daniel from the reality of how much she seemed to hate them both. He knew that Daniel had quietly endured some emotional wounds inflicted upon him by his mother, but so far he still had the illusion that she really loved him. Unfortunately, if she left, she would forever sever contact with Daniel. Robert knew this, and so he continued to endure the pain and misery of his marriage. *God, she makes me want to drink!* "Why don't I call Jeff? I'm sure he could come over for a few hours and look after Daniel."

Barbara almost looked frightened by that possibility, but still she looked more hateful than anything else as she spoke, "Daniel hates his Uncle Jeff!" *He's never said as much,* she thought, *but a mother knows.*

"No! Daniel doesn't hate his Uncle Jeff! *You* do! So, if you won't help your son to get well, I'll call Jeff, because he at least gives a damn!"

Barbara just stared at her husband. *Men think they know everything, but I can see right through all the bluster—right to the core of their arrogant stupidity.* She finally spoke bitterly, "Have a nice day at work, Dear."

Robert rolled his eyes and left the room. As he walked out the front door, he only refrained front slamming it because he didn't want to disturb his sleeping son. He thought to himself, as he walked to his car, *If I'd have been her father, I'd have shot her first!*

It was 1:47 P.M. when Daniel finally woke up again. He was awakened by the sound of a fist pounding on the front door, seemingly intent on knocking it down. He groggily sat up in bed, "Mom?" He hadn't the will to make his voice carry, so he got up and left his room. He scratched his belly, and for the first time noticed his shirt. *It was all a dream. I'm sick, and it was all just a dream.* He clearly remembered taking off his shirt when he was with Roxy in the park. He looked over and saw his jacket hanging on the bathroom door. *I didn't kill her! She's alive! She's alive!* Daniel felt a burst of energy, and he headed from his room to the front door of the house. He saw his mother sitting in the living room. "Mom? Why didn't you get the door?"

The pounding continued, as she answered without looking at him, "I thought you should make yourself useful around the house, since you seem to have given up on your education."

Daniel didn't know how to respond to that remark, so he didn't. He went to the door, eager to stop the noise. He looked through the peep-hole, and his heart sank as he recognized Marc Stillwaters, Roxy's father, banging on the door with uncontained fury. Daniel opened the door.

"You!" Marc Stillwaters' face was bright pink, making what little white hair he had left on his balding head seem to glow. He grabbed Daniel by the shirt and pulled him outside. "What have you done to my daughter! Huh?" He shook Daniel, and Daniel looked him in the face with wide, terrified, brown eyes.

He didn't know what to think anymore. Suddenly, all of the pain and confusion that had just been wiped away was back, and it was more complete now than before, because he had much more to be confused about. He no longer knew what reality was. He felt sure of only one thing—that he had gone perfectly insane.

He found himself questioning, as Marc continued to shake him, whether or not he was even actually on the porch.

"Tell me what you've done to her, you god damned punk! Where is she?!"

"I…" *What is real?* "I don't know. What are you talking about? What happened?"

Marc Stillwaters slammed Daniel up against the wall. "Don't give me that bull shit, boy! Now either you tell me what I want to know, or I'm gonna take you for a little ride in my Cadillac. I'll introduce you to my good friends, Mr. Smith and Mr. Wesson. C'mon boy! Talk!"

Daniel looked over to the doorway and saw his mother walking towards it. "Mom," he uttered pleadingly.

Barbara Mason gave him a cold, disappointed look, as she closed the door and left him to his fate. She then went back to the living room to watch TV, as she thought to herself, *A mother knows. That whore is pregnant, and now Daniel will have to pay the price for his recklessness.*

Daniel heard sirens in the background. *They know! They know I killed her. I did. I did. I deserve to die.* Daniel decided that he was glad Marc Stillwaters had come to kill him. His mind was so unclear, and he was still fighting desperately to separate dream from reality. Two things he knew for a fact though, he remembered killing Roxy, and now Roxy's father was at his house threatening his life. So the memory of killing her must be true. This led him to realize that the memory of *how* he killed her was probably also true, and all the god-forsaken memories of the past night began to flood his tortured mind. Tears started welling up. He wanted to confess. He wanted to be killed by Marc Stillwaters, but he found himself too choked up to speak at all. Daniel heard the siren cut off, as the tires of two separate vehicles squealed to a halt.

"Is she in there?" Marc motioned to the door with a twitch of his head. "My daughter has to abide by certain rules so long as she lives underneath my roof! Maybe you weren't raised as well as she was, and that's why you feel the need to defy my rules! Is that it? Huh?" He pressed Daniel against the wall, with his arm against his throat.

Daniel found himself unable to take a breath, but still he did not fight back. He had wished for death, and now he would have it.

"You'll never be good enough for my daughter! Never! And I'm gonna be the one who ends your relationship! I'm gonna blow your god damned head off!"

Daniel's head was starting to buzz, but suddenly he felt the pressure leave his throat, and he fell forward onto his knees, involuntarily sucking in heavy breaths of air, as he held his burning neck.

Marc Stillwaters was spun around by a fat hand that grabbed him by the shoulder. He recognized the man who had fixed his toilet the month before, in the second before the large man's other hand formed a fist and crashed into his face.

As Marc Stillwaters fell to the ground, unconscious, Jeff Mason picked up a brown, paper bag and offered Daniel a big, gap-toothed smile. "Hey there, Robert Jr.!" He held up the bag and waved it in the air. "I brought soup! Chicken soup, which cures all ills. I hear Jesus used this shit on the lepers! I shit you not. It's in the Bible. 'Truly, truly, I say unto you, eat this shit and rot not more.' Honest to God, I read this once when I was a Christian." He offered Daniel his hand and helped him to his feet. "I would have brought pot, but it seems a wolverine has eaten my supplier. I think it might have been your mother."

Sheriff William Cody approached the men, followed closely by an officer Daniel didn't recognize. He looked at Daniel. "You all right, son?"

Daniel ran his hand through his hair and shrugged pathetically.

"The boy's been sick in bed, Willy," Jeff answered for him. I pulled up at the same time you did, so I'm just as clueless as you are about what this A-hole wanted with him."

"I don't know if that's true, Jeff. We aren't really clueless at all as to why he was here."

Daniel's pulse quickened.

The sheriff looked at the other officer. "Jack, why don't you put Mr. Stillwaters in the back. We'll give him some time to cool off at the station. But we'll keep it off the books. And get on the horn and have his car towed. I'll cover the cost out of my own pocket this time."

The officer nodded his head and started to drag Marc Stillwaters to the car.

The sheriff lowered his voice and spoke in a secretive tone to the two Mason men, "I'm real sorry about this, Daniel. He ran out of the station a few minutes ago, and we could only follow him. There's a lot of weird stuff goin' on this morning, and I just can't help but feel for the man.

"You boys know how his wife died." This was not a question, it was an understanding. Everyone who knew the Stillwaters family knew how Gayle had died. "That bear up in Colorado hardly left enough of her to pick his teeth with.

"So, anyway, to start with, Marc's just pissed off that his daughter isn't in her room this morning. Then he gets wind of some of the crazy things that happened last night, and he calls the school. He finds out that she ain't there, so he comes down to the station and starts tellin' us that we need to find his daughter before that wild animal does. Then he wants us to arrest Daniel. Just goes nuts. But you can't blame him for goin' a little ape-shit, what with all this crazy talk, and the way his wife died an' all.

"'Cause, here's the thing. Last night, Elizabeth Krandall calls in and says that she just heard a *werewolf* bust up Abigail Johnson's house, and she thinks the thing probably got her. So we're all laughin', right? But then, at a little after three in the morning, we get countless calls from all over town. People sayin' they saw a bear, people sayin' they heard a wolf howl. The people from that old apartment building downtown almost all called in and said that there was some sort of monster in the building, and a good number of them said specifically that it was a werewolf with a howl that shook the place all to Hell.

"So, anyway, we send some boys out to see if Mrs. Johnson's all right or not, and these ol' boys about shit their pants. That house had been run completely through. The back wall was busted down, the front wall was busted down, and Mrs. Johnson was nowhere to be found. Her car was still parked outside the house and everything. There were signs of a struggle like nothin' I've ever seen, but there were no fingerprints, no footprints, no blood. Nothin' to go on except for Elizabeth Krandall's werewolf story, and the phone was off the hook, which means that Liz really could have been hearin' all that happened.

"We also sent some boys downtown to check out that apartment building. A homeless woman in the alley told them that she'd watched a demon eat Davin Adams. So, they took a look in his apartment and, y'all know about his brother and their pet chicken. Well, they found that chicken split clean in two. It was the cleanest cut they'd ever seen, like a laser or somethin' had cut through it. And Davin and James were nowhere to be found. But, just like Abigail, their van was still parked outside, like they haven't left at all.

"So now people all over town are makin' like lunatics, talkin' about old werewolf stories their grandparents told 'em. Bunch of 'em are even leavin' town 'til the full moon is gone. Crazy shit.

"So here's where Marc goes nuts on us. There's this wild animal runnin' around, tearin' the town up out there, and his daughter's nowhere to be found. He's scared of findin' another partially eaten corpse."

The sheriff looked directly at Daniel. "Now, I know you kids stick pretty tight. So, if you don't know where she is, 'cause you've been sick in bed, then your friends'll know. If they don't know, then that's when we start to worry."

Daniel was paler now than he had ever been. It was all true, and the police didn't even suspect him. He knew that Roxy was dead now. It hadn't been a dream. He also knew that Marc Stillwaters need not fear finding a partial corpse, because there was nothing left at all.

Daniel started to feel incredibly light-headed. He threw his hand up to his face and spoke through the strain of tears he could no longer hold back, "Roxy." Daniel felt a profound dizziness overtaking him, just before he noticed the ground suddenly flying up towards his face.

Noticing Daniel's distress, Jeff caught his unconscious nephew in his arms before he hit the ground. He set him down gently against the wall in front of the door. He looked to the sheriff, a combination of humor and disdain in his demeanor. "What was that? Some sort of god damned mad-ass science experiment, Willy? See how much fucked up shit you can work into a conversation before a grown man faints like a screaming bitch in a B-movie?"

The sheriff accepted the rebuke with genuine remorse. "Aw, shit! I should'a known better than to say all that in front of the boy. 'Specially since he's been sick. We'll find her, Jeff. I won't rest until we do."

Jeff looked the sheriff in the eyes, his previously jocular countenance suddenly grave. "See to it that you do, Willy. She means a lot to him, and so she means a lot to me as well."

Sheriff Cody nodded earnestly. "I know it, Jeff. We'll do all we can." He shook his head in thought. "You know what's really weird about this situation though? The mayor. He came to see me this afternoon, and he wanted us to enforce a curfew until this situation is under control. I told him that a curfew didn't make any sense in this situation. If there's a wild animal on the loose in Nightfire, it's gonna be out there from dawn to dusk.

"Then he says to me, 'William, that may be true, but werewolves only come out at night.'"

***

Daniel found himself in bed again before he even realized that he'd lost consciousness. He sat up and looked at the clock. It was almost 2:33. Daniel looked around his room, and he found the sack that his Uncle Jeff had brought for him. He looked inside and found a Tupperware bowl full of chicken soup, confirming again that it had all really happened.

Daniel was well rested and knew that he would be unable to escape back into sleep. He realized what had happened to him, what he had become, what he had done. Now it was time to do something about it—either destroy himself, or find a cure. He would have preferred self-destruction, but he knew that, in the eyes of God, it was preferred that he find a cure.

It did occur to Daniel, as he raced outside, that God had not seemed very sympathetic to him as of late.

Daniel intended to walk to Nightfire United Methodist Church, but when he got outside, to his complete disbelief, he found that his car was sitting there. He knew that he had not driven it home, just as he knew that he had never put his shirt back on. Daniel decided that he didn't have the time to wonder at these things. He had too much to do before nightfall. He got into his car, started it, and drove away, intent on getting to the church as quickly as possible.

As Daniel drove, however, he found that he could not keep his thoughts from Roxanna. Her soul stuck, blind in the park. So, with very little conscious thought, that is where he ended up.

He parked *Clunk* and walked to the top of the hill. He found himself still trying to explain it all away. He couldn't help but dream that none of it had happened, and that he had in truth gone completely mad. He looked at the wall where he remembered that they had shared their last truly innocent moments.

He smelled the air. He felt the gentle wind. He remembered how peaceful this place had been only a day before. Yet now he found that this same spot had become a place of personal torture. The once serene sights and smells had become a reminder of the hell he had been born to. They were the smells that had surrounded him as he had shoved her to the ground. It was the scenery that had surrounded him as he had chased her through the night and eventually taken her life.

It had been less than a full day since the happening of those horrific first moments of his new, terrible life, and yet it seemed to Daniel as if weeks, or even months had passed.

He walked away from Hilltop, down into the brush. He thought back with a shiver to how he had almost raped her. Again, he wanted to discover that it had all been a terrible nightmare, but then he caught something from the corner of his eye.

Underneath a small bush, he saw a heart-breakingly familiar pair of panties. He turned his head to get a better look, and he choked up. He realized that if they were found and identified by anyone else, the finger of the law would be pointed at him. He also realized that it was not nearly evidence enough.

Let them suspect me, let them arrest me, he thought. *Perhaps I'll confess. I don't deserve to live, and I don't deserve my freedom.* He looked into the distance, towards the spot where Roxy had died at his demonic hands. *But Roxanna deserves hers. God, please, take her soul.* He closed his eyes and silently wept.

Daniel walked towards that very spot. He wondered if he could find her there as he had the night before. As he approached, he noticed that there was no blood—nothing that would suggest the occurrence of the events he remembered. He saw a puppy walking by, sniffing the ground. It was the same puppy that he had seen the night before, on the old woman's porch.

Oh, dear God, by sparing the puppy, as I murdered his master, have I sentenced it to a life of loneliness and starvation?

The puppy stopped abruptly when he got to a particular spot on the ground. He looked up, staring intently at what seemed to be nothing, and wagged his tail. He then made a small whimpering sound and walked around the spot, as if there were something there that he didn't want to bump into.

Daniel realized that this could only mean that Roxy was still there. He walked to the spot, once the puppy had gone. He put his hands out towards the air there, and he felt a chill. "Roxy." Daniel wanted to see her, but at the same time he never wanted to see her again. He didn't want it to be true. "Please forgive me," he spoke out loud to her. "Please go on. I love you. And I could never love another, I could never deserve another. My life is over without you. I died when I last looked into your eyes. I seem to have stumbled into Hell, and knowing that you are in Heaven is the only way that I can endure it."

He looked down, as tears fell from his eyes. "I never wanted to hurt you. I never wanted to be without you. I would end my life and join you right now, but I have to stay loyal to God.

Maybe that will get you into Heaven. Maybe that will get me out of Hell."

He looked up, still seeing nothing, and he pretended to look into her beautiful eyes. "I have to go now, my love. I've got to try to shed this evil that has claimed me. I plan to do whatever it takes to save both our souls."

Daniel turned then, and walked back to his car.

When Daniel finally arrived at the church, he found Jim in his conference room. The door was already open, so Daniel knocked gently on the wall to let Jim know he was there.

The minister looked up from the pencil he had been contemplating. "Daniel!" He immediately got up from his desk and went to the youth, greeting him with a tight bear hug. "I heard about Roxy. Hang tight, my friend. She'll turn up."

Daniel broke the hug then and stood back, as he looked Jim directly in the eyes. "No, she won't."

The certainty in Daniel's voice alarmed Reverend Jordan. He had been through a very alarming day already, and now this added to his ulcerating suspicions.

He had heard about the previous night's alleged wild animal attacks, he had thought about Lillian's predictions and the secret of 1850, and he had thought about Daniel's alleged possession and Tom's accident in the basement, and he had considered the dark possibilities as to how it all fit together.

He had been visited by the mayor, who had reminded him rather harshly to keep his mouth shut, and had asked to see the beaker of blood. Jim had lied to the mayor and told him that it was sealed in a vault in a secure location, and that he could not risk the security of its location being disturbed. He had told the mayor to come back in two days, and he would have it at the church.

Later, he had been visited by Beth Green, who had insisted on knowing what was going on. She had told him that she wanted to know why the blood had stopped working, because, quite obviously, there was a werewolf in Nightfire, even after nearly a century-and-a-half of security. For Beth, Jim had decided to ignore the mayor's threatening reminder. What would it matter if they all ended up dead anyway? He had told her that the beaker had broken and that she should confirm this quietly to anyone who already knew the story. He had told her that she needed to be as discrete as possible, because the mayor had every intention of keeping the truth buried.

Beth had tried to tell him what she had heard about what Lillian had seen, but Jim had stopped her. He hadn't wanted to know whom Lillian had been talking to, and he hadn't wanted to know who the werewolf was. He had already known that it had to be either Daniel or Tom, and Tom had seemed to be perfectly fine. It was Daniel who had come to him before with the fear of possession—the fear of his own bloodthirsty desires.

A chill ran through the reverend's spine, as he realized that he knew exactly what Daniel was here to tell him. He realized that he was alone in the room with a powerful force of evil—a monstrous killer that he could never hope to defend himself against.

But at the same time, it was Daniel.

"I'm not possessed. I know that now." Daniel felt more tears welling up. His already bloodshot eyes grew redder, and his throat tightened up, as he fought the tears back.

"I know, Daniel." Jim was pleased to find that he had effortlessly overcome his fear. "I'm here for you now, as always. Will you try to tell me about it?"

"Yes." The tears broke free, and the pain in Daniel's throat made it difficult to speak. "I thought I'd run out of tears, but…" He broke down, and Jim took him back into his strong, caring arms.

"Take your time now. There's no hurry. I know it hurts."

Daniel finally broke the hug again, and he blurted out through sobs, "I killed her. I killed her! I killed them all, and I want to join them! Please, Jim. Please help me." He put his hands up to his red face and fell into a chair.

Daniel managed to calm down after saying it all aloud. A weight seemed to have lifted from his shoulders. "I got some of that blood in my veins, and now I'm a monster. I'm a werewolf, and I have no control. I tried to fight it, but it wouldn't let me. The shadow-body. I can control it as long as I plan to kill someone, but if not, it takes over. I refused to kill all those people last night, but still I killed them, it was so…awful." He once again lost his words to his tears.

Jim comforted his young friend. He very patiently waited, until Daniel had shared with him the whole story, with many a painful detail. When Daniel had finished relating the tale, Jim found himself terrified and completely lost to any solutions.

"So, what should I do?" Daniel asked hopelessly. "Should I kill myself?"

"No!" Jim answered sharply. No matter what Daniel had become, Jim couldn't bear the thought of him taking his own life.

"There has to be another way." Jim quickly corrected himself, "There is another way. We just haven't thought of it yet. Keep your faith, Daniel. I know that it feels as if God has abandoned you, but I assure you, he hasn't.

"I don't know what it was that you saw in the park. Perhaps it was just a shadow—some sort of reflection of Roxanna's presence. As you said, she seemed not to notice you at all. I'm positive that Roxanna's true soul is with God right now." Jim had noticed that Roxanna's soul, even amid all the other terrors of the past night, was the part of the experience that was bothering his young friend the most.

"But, you don't understand. I saw everyone I killed. Some went to Heaven, some to Hell. If Roxy had gone to either, I would have witnessed it."

Jim looked into Daniel's pleading eyes. He knew that Daniel hoped his reverend friend would know how to save his lost love's soul. Jim couldn't bring himself to say that he did not. "I will pray for her soul, Daniel. We must trust that God works with a purpose through all things. We cannot believe that God has ignored Roxanna. If she is still there, then God alone knows why. And I'm sure that, whatever the reason, she would only be awaiting her time to enter Heaven.

"And, as with all things, God has a purpose for you—even in your current state. I think that God has a grand plan for you, Daniel. You'll come through this. I refuse to look at it as God having inflicted this upon you, but I do believe that you will come into your greater destiny by staying faithful to him and allowing him to get you through this.

"With enough faith, we can walk on water. Have faith in Jesus Christ, and you will be healed. You have to make yourself *believe* that you will not turn into a werewolf tonight. *Believe* that God will not allow it to happen. Don't just beg. If you truly believe that God will heal you, then he will. Just like when the woman who'd been bleeding for twelve years touched Jesus' cloak. She was healed because she believed she would be.

"I'm sorry that I have no easier solutions for you, but I will see what else I can find out about your situation. Jesus said that, with the smallest amount of true faith, we can command mountains to move, and they will obey. Please, Daniel, put all your faith in God. Don't let your confusion over the spirits you saw weaken you. I personally promise you—God is good, and faith in him will lead you to salvation—always."

Daniel considered Jim's words. *It's true. Jesus did say all of that. I've got to try. If I run away to protect people, it's only because I don't really believe that Jesus can heal me. If I kill myself, I've failed God, because he has presented me with the simple solution of truly believing in his omnipotence.*

"I'm sorry for rambling on like that," Jim said, as he rubbed his temples. "I'm just extremely unprepared for this whole situation. I'll do everything within my power to help you, Daniel. I swear it."

"No, Jim, you've done so much just by rambling. I think you're right. It's all just a matter of faith. I have faith. I will not become a werewolf tonight." *But what if God wants me to be a werewolf? What if God doesn't care at all?*

"That's the spirit, Daniel." *Damn me to Hell. I've become one of those preachers that I detest. They tell AIDS patients and cancer patients the same line of crap, "All it takes is faith." They say it as if it's so easy. It is very easy to say, "I believe," but it is almost impossible to totally eliminate doubt in one's own mind.*

I've never seen anyone move a mountain or walk on water. And when the AIDS and cancer patients fail to recover, the idiots who said that all they needed was faith turn around and speak as if the person has failed, "Your faith just wasn't strong enough." Is that what I'll be stupidly saying to Daniel tomorrow morning, when it turns out that his faith wasn't enough? Damn me to Hell.

"In the meantime, however," Jim said aloud, "I'm going to look into some other possibilities. There's someone I might be able to talk to about this, so, no matter what, come back tomorrow." *If your faith just isn't strong enough—no, I can't encourage doubt.* "Tell me how it goes."

Daniel managed a weak smile. "Don't worry, Jim. I'm a faithful Christian. God will heal me. God *has* healed me. I have faith. This hell is ended." *If God cares. If God is even there.*

He does care, and he is there. I know it. He has healed me already. I have nothing to fear from the coming night. Nothing at all.

Is it a sin to lie to yourself? I suppose that question only matters to people who lie to themselves—not me. I have faith. True faith.

God, I hope you're listening.

XIII

The phone rang at Lillian Foster's house, as she sat reading over some of the old magazine articles she had written. She let the phone ring twice, as she stared at it, mentally preparing herself. "Hello, Jim," she said, when she at last picked up.

"Lillian, how did you… Oh, never mind. How are you?"

"I'm fine, Jim. What brings you to call?"

"I can tell from the sound of your voice that you know this isn't just a social call. There's something I need to discuss with you, and I think I'd be more comfortable discussing it in person."

"All right. I'll be right over."

"Thanks. I think I'll be in the sanctuary praying."

Lillian found herself feeling giddy, as she got off of the phone and raced out the door. Though, for the same reason, she also felt great dread. She was finally going to learn what Jim had been hiding and why. She hoped it wouldn't upset her too much.

When Lillian arrived at Nightfire UMC, she found Jim exactly as he had said he would be. He looked tired and worn, as he knelt before the cross praying. Lillian whispered cautiously, remembering how she had startled him several days earlier, "Jim?"

He turned around and faced her, as if he had known she had been standing there all along. He stood. "Lillian, we need to talk, and there's something that I must show you. Please come with me."

Lillian then followed Jim wordlessly to the basement.

When they got there, Lillian asked, "Jim, what is this about? I'm assuming that it's about the werewolf."

Jim looked at Lillian, worry creasing his forehead, and said, "Yes. I've been counseling him."

Lillian couldn't hide her anger. "Is this what you wouldn't tell me before? Have you known there was a werewolf for all this time!?" If Jim had known over a week ago, when she had talked to him about her visions, something could have been done. The deaths of the previous night could have been prevented.

Then again, Lillian had known in time, and she herself had been unable to prevent those deaths. Her temper cooled, as she realized that there really was nothing that either of them could have done.

"No, Lil, I didn't know that he was a werewolf until just this afternoon." Despair painted the reverend's face as he continued, "That's why I need to talk to you. I need to know what else you know—any information that I can use to help him. He doesn't want to be a werewolf. His soul is dying with the agony of what he's become, and what, against his own will, he has done. I promised I'd help him, but I don't know how." Jim looked away, "He doesn't deserve this!" On the verge of tears, he put a hand up to his face.

Lillian could tell how deeply her friend was suffering for Daniel. She felt his helplessness and wished that there *was* something she knew that could help. Unfortunately, there was not. Lillian's visions had been very specific in letting her know that only disaster was headed their way. The visions offered no solutions—no way to heal a werewolf. The visions, in fact, seemed entirely unsympathetic to Daniel.

She shook her head somberly. "I'm sorry, Jim. I have nothing to offer. I'm afraid you know more than I on the matter. But you know I'm here for you. You're hurting too, because of how much you care. So don't deny yourself the help you need to get through this. You need a friend too, just as much as…" She paused to consider her next words. She decided it was time to lay all the cards on the table. "…Daniel needs you."

Jim looked at her, tears filling his red eyes. It was good to finally have that out. To know for an absolute fact that Lillian knew who the werewolf was. This would make talking about it much easier. "You know," he spoke in a delicate voice, teetering on the edge of tears, "I've never had any children of my own." He paused to collect himself. He closed his eyes, fighting tears. "I've known Daniel since he was three. Tom since he was two. And Roxy…" His voice was gone. He covered his face and began to sob.

This was something that Lillian had never seen. She found herself frightened by it. She didn't know how to deal with this, and yet she wanted desperately to take Jim's pain away. She wanted him not to be suffering so. She went to him and hugged him tightly. "I know, Jim," was all she could think to say. And she did know. She had seen Roxy's death more than a week before. She had seen Marc Stillwaters at the Masons' house earlier that day. She knew exactly why saying Roxy's name had broken Jim's last reserves of emotional strength. It had come to pass, and Daniel had told him.

Jim returned Lillian's hug. He held her so tightly that she found it difficult to breathe. He continued to sob without words, and she continued to hold him until he could again manage words.

When he did finally speak, he broke her hug and turned away. "These youth are the closest thing I've got to children of my own. I've watched them all grow up. They look to me for guidance, just as I look to them as evidence that God is there, and he is good, and all is right with the world, because they're all so healthy, and beautiful, and intelligent, and good. I love them all, and I would die for any one of them if I knew it would help. I swear to God I would!"

"I know you would, Jim. They know it too. That's why they all love you so much. And I'm certain that most of them would just as quickly die for you. You're a good man, Jim, and you're a good friend. But there's only so much you can do. Sometimes you just have to accept that you've done all you can."

"If I've done all I can, then my life has stood only for taking up space in the world. I haven't helped him at all. Not at all! Do you know what I did?" He turned and looked Lillian in the eyes—his own eyes filled with self-hatred. "I told him that all he needed to do was have faith in order to be healed, and then I sent him home with some Bible verses to look up! I would have done better just to have patted him on the head, said, 'there, there,' and sent him home! Instead, whether he knows it or not, I've poured salt in his wounds. I did the two dumbest things I could have possibly done. I was desperate. I couldn't send him away with nothing. He came to me for help. He trusted me, and depended on me for help. Damn me to Hell!"

"You did all you could. I wouldn't have even done *that* well, if it had been me he'd come to. You meant well, Jim. You tried, and trying was all you could do."

"If the road to Hell is paved with good intentions, I believe that most of them have been my own." Jim's voice was no longer weak. His every word was now coated with anger—anger at himself. "Are you sure that your visions haven't given you any hint of a solution? You did only give me the, 'edited version,' after all."

"You were guarding your words too on that day, as I remember it. Is there any light *you'd* care to shed?"

A guilty expression colored Jim's face. "Yes! Yes, of course. That's why I brought you down here. I had hoped that combining our knowledge might present us with the solution."

Jim rushed to a closet and quickly came out with a book in his hands. "Please, forgive me, Lillian. I could have helped you to understand part of your vision when you first told me, but I was afraid of the truth. I was also sworn to secrecy, as I have been for the past fifteen years. I only shared the story with the boys because they found the blood, and I only share it with you now, because I think you're supposed to know."

Lillian looked at Jim with the most puzzled expression he had ever seen her wear.

He put the book down on a small desk and opened it to the antique letter of Reverend David Paul. He pointed. "Here. This is what I want you to read. You told me that you'd seen a horrible conflict in Nightfire's past. You told me that you saw countless werewolves and humans alike killed in a bloody battle. This is what you saw: The Werewolf Plague of 1850. This is the account of a minister who was there. The pastor of this very church.

"I'll leave you to read it. When you're finished, I will tell you more about what has happened to Daniel. I'll tell you everything you need to know."

Lillian just looked at Jim, unsure of what to say, as he left her alone in the basement to read. She read excitedly through what she considered a very badly written story. It was evident to her trained eye that Reverend Paul had not been born to write.

When she finished reading, she found Jim waiting in his conference room. He was staring out the window, deep in thought. Before she could say anything, Jim turned around to face her.

"Thank you," she said. "I always appreciate confirmation of the visions I have. Sometimes even *I* find it difficult to believe in myself."

"Did the letter give you any new insights into the present situation?" Jim asked hopefully.

Lillian considered that. "No. I don't think so," she said with regret. "Unless, of course, it showed me that the only real hope for stopping Daniel lies in you."

"Stopping? I don't think I like the way you said that."

"Jim, you can't help him. I've seen the future, and it's very bleak." She sighed as she tried to think of a way to convince Jim of her beliefs. "I had another vision after we last spoke. I was told that a few may survive, but only if I plant the seed. I saw the town, at least my neighborhood. There wasn't much left. I don't think even my own survival was guaranteed." She thought about her dream. She remembered seeing her own house demolished and looking into her own eyes. "In fact, I don't expect it. I am the werewolf's next-door neighbor after all." She forced a wan smile onto her face.

"Then why don't you leave town? If you've seen such a fate for yourself you should run from it."

"I can't leave, because it doesn't feel right. I've gotten to be as old as I am only because I've learned never to disregard my feelings.

"My point, though, is that I took that message about planting the seed to mean that I should talk to Daniel's mother. I'm afraid that I've failed in whatever God wanted me to do. She didn't believe me. She sent me away furiously—thinking me insane. But that's what my feelings told me to do." She shook her head, lamenting. "I'm afraid that I planted the seed in bad soil. Whatever chance that anyone had of surviving may be lost.

"I have heard the rumors that there's a werewolf, and I don't know how those started, and I don't know if anyone takes them seriously anyway. But you do. You're an ordained minister of God. You can bless some weapons for us like they did in 1850. Maybe that's how some of us will survive."

"Lillian, I could never do that. I'll have no part in hurting Daniel. It was different the last time, because Sebastian Barnes was a truly evil being. Daniel is anything but evil. Reverend Paul's letter suggests that all of the werewolves of the Plague had chosen to become what they were. I know for a fact—Daniel had no choice. If you want someone to bless weapons and dip them in holy water, go talk to Father Scott over at Saint Paul."

"He's a hypocrite, and we both know it!" Lillian protested. "He believes in the Catholic Church, he believes in the Pope, but you know that no matter what he says, he doesn't believe in the supernatural. He would laugh me right out of town if I asked him to bless some silver bullets."

"They don't have to be silver."

"Would you condone it then, if I went to Reverend Scott?"

"No."

"Then what do you suggest we do? How do you expect to help him? Jim, I've seen what's going to happen. I failed to plant the seed!"

"Lillian, what you saw was a possible future. The Bible specifies that God has the right to change his mind. Remember the story of Jonah. He was told that Nineveh was going to be destroyed, and in the end it wasn't."

"But Jonah did as he was told."

"Not at first."

"But, Jim, this is different! This is not Nineveh, where the people can just repent and be spared God's wrath! This is Nightfire, where the people are at the mercy of a monster from Hell!"

"Lillian, I won't hurt Daniel, and I won't refer to him as a monster, or as something from Hell. And I think that you did, in fact, accomplish your mission. I've seen evidence of the seed you planted."

Lillian forgot her anger. "What? How?"

Jim smiled. "Beth Green came to me earlier today. She knew about your talk with Barbara, and she believed in you. It seems that a few people in Nightfire uncovered the secret of 1850 some years ago. That's what started all of the werewolf rumors this morning.

"Because of your psychic warning to Barbara, the people who knew the legend realized what had really happened last night. Several of them are even planning to leave town for the duration of the waning moon.

"You've done your part to help people, Lillian. You've accomplished your mission. Get out of town. If you truly believe that there is no averting the future you've seen, then you have no reason to believe that Daniel can be stopped anyway. Your convictions contradict themselves. Either we have the option of helping him *and* the option of stopping him, or we have neither option. Because the simple fact is, either your vision can be eluded, or it cannot."

Lillian spoke absently, as she considered Jim's words, "You're right." She looked him in the eyes again. "So now I believe that he can't be stopped."

"And I believe that he can be helped."

"Jim, the future I saw was written in stone. I can feel it."

"God warns us about dark futures so that we can avoid them," Jim said.

"Or prepare for them, as with the droughts and floods of the Bible. These things were not to be prevented."

"So why don't you get out of town, if you fear your own life is now in danger? You've played your part!" There was nothing but honest concern in Jim's voice as he spoke.

"I told you already. I can't leave, because it doesn't feel right when I consider the possibility. I'm supposed to be here for the disaster. Maybe I'm meant to be a witness, or maybe it's just my time to die. I don't know, but I'm not going to leave."

Jim smiled once again, nervously. "It's obvious that we're not going to sway each other. I think that if we continue to argue, it would serve only to make us angry at each other. I think at this point, that we should just agree to disagree. We each have to do what we feel is right, and we should each respect the other for doing so."

Lillian smiled. "Agreed." A thought then occurred to her. "Now, maybe you can tell me how all of this came to be in the first place. You said earlier that Daniel had no choice. So how did it happen?"

Jim then told her how it happened. He told her about how Trevor had found the blood, he told her how Tom had accidentally broken the beaker and passed out, and he told her how Daniel had rushed to help Tom and, in the process of cleaning up the glass, had cut himself and gotten the smallest amount of the werewolf blood in his veins.

"That's awful," Lillian said. "He couldn't be more innocent. How do you intend to help him though?" *Futile effort though it is.*

"Just as I can bless the weapons to hurt Daniel, I can bless the tools to help him. I intend to steal some actual holy water from Saint Paul, just to be sure. Then I intend to mix it into the bread and wine for the Holy Communion I will serve to Daniel in private."

"I thought Methodists used grape juice instead of wine."

"Yes, but you know me. Besides, Jesus didn't use grape juice. I just want to be sure."

"And what do you hope to accomplish by this?"

"I hope to expel the werewolf entity from Daniel's body."

Lillian was concerned. "Even if that works, Jim, you don't know what the final result will be. What happens to the werewolf entity? Where does it go?"

"I'll pray for its destruction."

"So will I. I hope that this plan doesn't backfire on you, Jim."

"Yeah, me too." Jim chuckled through his deep worry.

When Lillian had gone, he returned to the sanctuary, where he resumed his vigilant prayer.

Daniel sat down on his bed and unfolded the piece of paper that Jim had handed to him as he'd left the church. On the paper, Jim had written, "Matthew 5:3-10—You are all of these things!" Daniel reached over and got the Holy Bible off of his nightstand. He looked up the verses that Jim had written down, and he read them silently.

"How blessed are the poor in spirit: the kingdom of Heaven is theirs. Blessed are the gentle: they shall have the earth as inheritance. *Blessed are those who mourn: they shall be comforted. Blessed are those who hunger and thirst for uprightness: they shall have their fill. Blessed are the merciful: they shall have mercy shown them. Blessed are the pure in heart: they shall see God. Blessed are the peacemakers: they shall be recognized as children of God. Blessed are those who are persecuted in the cause of uprightness: the kingdom of Heaven is theirs."*

Daniel considered the verses. *Am I all of these things? I am poor in spirit, but I can no longer claim to be gentle.*

Yes I can! God has healed me. I am gentle.

Daniel looked at the next part of the passage. *I mourn.* He put the Bible back on his nightstand, leaving it open to that page for further contemplation later. He put his head in his hands and thought about Roxy.

He was immediately interrupted by a rapping on his window. He pulled up the blinds and saw Trevor Stevens and Tom Don. They waved and motioned for him to open the window. He smiled and did as they asked. Trevor and Tom then crawled in through the window and onto Daniel's bed. "Hey guys," He greeted them somberly. "What's up?"

Trevor put his finger right in Daniel's face and answered, "*You* were absent today. *You* were absent!" Trevor then proceeded to chuckle wickedly.

Tom closed the window and pulled down the blinds. "We came by to make sure the monster hadn't eaten you."

Daniel went pale at Tom's intended joke and looked away, once again on the verge tears.

Tom noticed this with deep concern and more than a little fear. "Are you all right, Daniel?"

Somehow, Trevor managed to pinpoint Daniel's thoughts. "You don't know where Roxy is, do you?"

Daniel looked at Trevor with sad, helpless eyes.

"Shit! We thought you'd skipped together. I take it you've heard all the weird shit that happened last night. Jim was being totally straight with us that night. It's like, a lot of other people know that old story too. And they take it totally seriously! You know, Brenda and her family are leaving town even as we speak, because of an old family diary her grandmother has. It had the whole story written down just like Jim told it to us. This is really freakin' me out."

Both Daniel and Tom had fallen to guilty contemplation, and they were both having the same thought: *This is all my fault.*

Trevor noticed the two long faces on either side of him. "Hey, it's all right. This whole thing'll blow over soon. Roxy'll turn up. She's probably just pissed at her dad or somethin'. I'm sure she'll call over here any minute."

Tom found himself sinking into potent guilt. He hadn't really considered it before now, but if there was really a werewolf in Nightfire, it was his fault. He had broken the beaker. He had practically invited the werewolf. And if anything had happened to Roxy… "Oh, God."

"What's wrong, Tom?" Trevor asked. He studied Tom's expression. *Why does he look so guilty?*

"Nothin'," Tom replied, without meeting Trevor's gaze. "I'm just not feeling so good all of the sudden."

Trevor looked over at Daniel, who wore an expression on his face similar to the one on Tom's, and a thought occurred to him. "Why did you stay home from school today anyway?"

There was another rapping on the window, and everyone turned towards it. Tom pulled the blinds up and opened the window to let Nic and Bert crawl in.

Daniel forced a smile. "Haven't you guys ever noticed the front door?"

"Yes," Nic said, "but we've also noticed your mother."

Trevor and Bert both laughed at this, but Daniel and Tom sat silently.

"What the hell's wrong with them?" Bert asked.

"Shut up, Bert," Nic said. "You know what's wrong." He looked at Daniel. "I hear Roxy's dad was over here earlier today. What a jerk."

"Oh." Trevor decided that this was the reason Daniel had missed school. He had probably heard the werewolf/wild animal rumor and learned that Roxy was missing long before the rest of them. "Your cop dad sure does talk a lot. Lucky you."

"I got no reason to complain. I get lots of useful information that way." Nic looked back to Daniel. "I hear Sheriff Cody is making it his top priority to find Roxy. There's no evidence that she's been hurt by that wild animal, or whatever it is. She's probably just off somewhere. Maybe she's just pissed off at her asshole dad."

Tom found himself being smothered by grief. He needed to be alone, so that he could consider all that he had learned this day. "Trevor, I've gotta get home."

Trevor looked at Tom inquisitively. "Oh, all right. I need a cigarette anyway, and it's not worth the wrath of Daniel's mom to smoke one in here." Trevor and Tom promptly crawled back out the window. As Tom walked to Trevor's car, Trevor leaned back in and said, "See y'all later." Then he closed the window, lit a cigarette, and walked after Tom.

"So, what brings you guys by?" Daniel asked, once again forcing a smile.

"That's a forced smile if I ever saw one." Nic laughed. "We're just here to see how you're doin', bud. My dad told us what was goin' on when we went by my house after school. We're just worried about'cha.

"Roxy's fine, Daniel."

Daniel looked away, not wanting to hear it.

"I know there's a bunch of weird stories goin' 'round right now, but if y'ask me, none of'm're true.

"My dad was tellin' me about this dead chicken they found at one of the crime scenes. They can't figure out what cut it up like that. It wasn't any identifiable wild animal. They haven't found any animal hair at either scene, 'cept for some golden retriever hair on Mrs. Johnson's back porch. But no golden retriever tore through her house like that. I think what we're dealin' with is someone with a lot of expensive equipment and a very sick sense of humor. And the reason I just can't believe that the same sicko got Roxy is that this guy only seems to attack people in their homes, and no one's torn up Roxy's house. She's just run off somewhere. You've got nothin' t'worry about."

He put his hand on Daniel's shoulder. "Why don't you come with us? We're just gonna go look for some trouble. You need to get all this off your mind for a while."

"I don't know, Nic. That might not be such a good idea." *I can't risk their lives. I can't risk hurting anyone else that I love.*

Wait, I don't have anything to worry about, I'm no longer a werewolf. If I don't go with them, it's only because I have no faith, and I do have faith. This is exactly what I need. I must prove my faith to God.

"What're you talkin' about? It's a great idea!"

Daniel shook his head, as if to clear it, and he looked at Nic and Bert. "You're right. I need to get out and do something." *I need to go on as if there's nothing to fear.*

"That's right, Daniel! We can't all fit in my truck, so why don't you follow me to my house in *Clunk*, so that I can park, and we can all ride with you."

"All right." Daniel stood up and let the blinds down over his window. "Follow me, boys. I'll introduce you to my front door."

The rest of the afternoon passed slowly. Nic led Daniel to a completely rural area just outside of Nightfire, known to most people as The Middle of Nowhere. Once there, Daniel pulled off of the dirt road they had been driving on and parked. Nic then led him and Bert to a small pond, surrounded by incredibly tall, dead grass. He showed them the fishing pole he had made out of a branch and left at the pond. This was where Nic often came to think and be alone.

Nic proceeded to fish, while Daniel and Bert skipped rocks across the pond. They ended up talking mainly about college and what they planned to do with their lives. They also talked about girls.

Daniel found himself unable to deal with either conversation. They both made him think of Roxy, and how she was no longer there, and would never be there again. Any future he had envisioned was gone. All he could think about was how he wished to be dead, but he could hardly talk about that, so he sat in almost complete silence.

Daniel was relieved when Nic finally decided that he had to get home. Daniel looked forward to getting home as well and letting himself fall apart. They all got into the car, and Daniel drove most of the way down the secluded dirt road in The Middle of Nowhere. Then, suddenly, the car broke down, and Daniel felt the tight squeeze of panic gripping his heart, as he looked to the horizon and noticed the swiftly setting sun.

Nic found himself puzzled by the look of absolute terror that had captured Daniel's face. "It's all right, Daniel. Prob'ly nothin' we ain't had t'fix before." He got out of the car and went around to the front of it. "Pop the hood, and let's take a look."

Daniel popped the hood absently, the death-white look of shock never leaving his face.

"Shit!" Bert said from the back. "Weren't you supposed to have a new car by now? I don't need this! I'm sick of this piece of shit always breakin' down! Damn it!"

Daniel again spoke absently, as he stared off towards the horizon without blinking, "I'm sorry." He closed his eyes and barely whispered, "My God, I'm so sorry."

He was jerked back to full consciousness by Bert's hand on his shoulder, shaking him. "Hey! You all right, man? It's not like *Clunk's* never broken down before. You know? Come on, I think you need some air." Bert got out of the back and opened Daniel's door.

Daniel looked up at Bert and said nothing.

"Shit, you're pail, Daniel." Bert then remembered why they had all gone out in the first place. "I know. You were eager to get back home and see if there's been any news about Roxy. Don't worry. Any news that's come in will still be there when you get home. We'll have *Clunk* up and running in no time, just like always."

Nic called out from under the hood, "I can't figure it out. Nothin' seems to be wrong." He walked around to the driver's side, where he got his first real glance at Daniel's sickly pale face. "What's wrong, Daniel?"

Daniel answered in a strained voice, "*Clunk*'s not going anywhere."

"Why not?"

Daniel pointed to the gas gauge. "Out of gas."

In less than a second, the expression on Nic's face went from shock, to disgust, to worry, to amusement. "Well, I guess we've got a lot of pushing to do. That has to be healthy." He patted Daniel on the shoulder. "I know you've been preoccupied today. It's all right, brother. You aren't going to suffer alone. We know what you'd do for us." Nic looked down at Daniel more closely. "Are you strong enough to help us push, or do you need to rest for a little while?"

"No!" Daniel's panicked voice shot out. "Don't wait on me!" *There isn't any time before the moon comes out, and I kill you both! What am I going to do?* "I'm strong enough! In fact, go on without me, and I'll push it myself."

Nic and Bert both chuckled at this.

"Don't be retarded, Daniel," Nic said. "Why would we leave you to push *Clunk* alone?" He laughed some more. "Well, if you think you're up to it, why don't you push from the front, and Bert and I'll push from the back? That way you can steer."

Daniel had no patience. He stood abruptly and shouted, "I said, I'll push it myself, Nic!" Daniel was so desperate for them to leave before it was too late, that it didn't concern him at all whether or not he offended them.

"Shit! I guess he told you."

"Shut up, Bert." Nic was filled with concern. He knew now that there was something far more than anyone had guessed bothering Daniel. "Daniel, are you all right?"

Daniel looked at the ground in raging frustration—fighting to stay calm.

"Now, you *know* that me an' Bert are not the type to leave you alone out here pushing a station wagon—no matter how strong you are. So you'd do yourself a favor to just give up on that particular fight right now. 'Cause you're not getting' anywhere with it. And I'd like you to at least consider telling us what's up your ass tonight. What's got you so freaked out, brother?"

Nic, you're such a good friend. Daniel thought. *Why can't you be a jerk and abandon me just this once? Why can't I just tell you?*

Wait!

Where's my faith? Why am I upset like this? I've got nothing to worry about. Nothing! Jesus has healed me. I have faith in that fact. When the moon comes out, it will only be proven that I am healed. The more I freak, the less I believe. I must believe completely.

I do.

I am not a werewolf.

Daniel shook his head and looked back to Nic. "Nothing. I'm fine. I'm just stressed out. Sorry I snapped at you, Nic."

"Don't give it another thought, Daniel. It happens."

Oh, Nic, you're so true blue. "I owe you guys for this."

"You got that right," Bert said from the back of the car, where he had already taken his pushing position.

Daniel only forced a chuckle at Bert's reply. "Hey, Nic, why don't you take the front. I'd like to push from the back."

Nic grinned. "You're not gonna kill Bert, are ya'?"

"No." *Oh, God I… No I'm not.* "Of course not." He forced another smile onto his tense, young face.

"Okay, whatever."

"Thanks."

The three young men pushed the old station wagon down the road, singing old camp songs to keep their minds off of their burden, until the dying light of the sun was gone—deposed by the soft, shining light and deceptive beauty of the rising moon.

Daniel's body started to tingle. *I'm not going to change. Not going to change. God's hand has saved me. He will not allow me to cause any more harm to the innocents.*

The tingle began to grow into a stinging pain. *Oh, Jesus, please! Don't let me hurt them! I've given myself to you! What more would you ask of me?*

No. I have nothing to fear. Nothing at all. I'm just tired, and my limbs are falling asleep from pushing this big, old car for so long. I have nothing to worry about. Nothing at all.

As I walk now through the valley of the shadow of death, God is with me, and he will not forsake me.

Oh, God, please don't leave me.

The pain grew too intense, and Daniel collapsed where he stood, hugging himself to fight off the pain.

Bert saw this and let go of the car, rushing to his fallen friend. "Hey, Nic! Com'ere!"

Nic looked behind him and saw Daniel on the ground, gripping himself in pain. He left his position and went to his friends. "What happened? Daniel, what's wrong?"

Bert put his hand on Daniel's arm. "Hey, Daniel! You all right, man?"

The shadow-body began to emit itself from Daniel's human body.

"Woah! Shit!" Bert stood up with lightning speed and backed away, physically numbed with fear.

Daniel was cold with the horror of the moment. He was unable to move, unable to speak, unable to warn them away, though it was now too late for any of those things to matter. *Oh, God,* Daniel thought, *if you let this happen to them, I fear I may hate you.*

The werewolf body enveloped Daniel, just as it had the night before. He felt its hunger, and his eyes found Bert, standing before him, wide-eyed in terror. Daniel went numb. He knew what it meant to fight against his werewolf instincts.

Nothing.

Bert was too frightened to run, too frightened to scream, and his final living thought was a testament to his very hollow understanding of life: *My God. I'm going to die a virgin.*

The werewolf lunged forward with a hellish growl, and Bert was no more. In all truth, Bert had been an innocent, and now he would never live to outgrow his youthful naïveté.

Nic felt himself going mad. He was unable to cope with what he saw before him. The werewolf, having finished Bert, turned its glowing, red gaze on Nic, who stumbled backwards, towards the open driver's side door of the car, unable to complete the only word that his petrified mind could form, "F-f-fu-fu-f-f." As he crawled into the false security of the car, barely managing to close and lock the door, Nic felt a loss of bladder control soaking his pants. He huddled down on the floorboard and shivered, as tears began to fall from his eyes in the horrible silence of what he knew to be his final moments.

Even after the consumption of one youth, the werewolf's body still felt the burning flames of its preternatural hunger. It approached the old car, having followed Nic with its eyes.

God, Daniel thought, as his soul despaired in the agony of his defeat, *you have left me. I do hate You.*

Daniel resigned himself to Hell.

The werewolf tore through the car as if it had been made of paper. It found Nic, who was too frightened even to blink, and it devoured him in less time than Nic would have even been able to shut his tortured, green eyes, had he thought to.

No! Run! Daniel threw back his monstrous head in a soul-piercing howl of agony. He closed his werewolf eyes, for the first time, and ran. He felt himself crashing through countless trees, though he felt no pain from it. He felt no pain at all, except for the ever-haunting hunger of the werewolf.

He knew that, had he chosen to stay, he could have seen the ultimate fate of his friends, and that is why he ran. The spirits he had seen the night before had left him too confused, and with too much pain. If either Nic or Bert had failed to make it into Heaven, Daniel refused to know.

Daniel soon found himself in a lonely alleyway, where he caught the scent of human meat, and the hungry instincts of the werewolf called his running to a halt. His eyes opened, by his own will, for he wanted to see where he had stopped.

He heard the squeak and rattling of little wheels, and the raspy voice of an old woman singing, "Amazing grace! How sweet the sound, that saved a wretch like me…!" The woman continued to sing, as she turned the corner, pushing her battered, old grocery cart full of the garbage she lived on.

Though the werewolf was now in her sights, she did not even slow her approach. Her singing only stopped during the moment that she looked up at the werewolf, as she passed by, and said, "Hello there, big fella." She then resumed her singing and continued to push forward.

The werewolf pounced upon her. Her body was gone, and her grocery cart was destroyed.

In the next instant, Daniel looked up and saw the woman continuing on, as if nothing had happened. "…Through many dangers, toils, and snares, I have already come; 'tis grace hath brought me safe thus far, and grace will lead me home." She turned the corner, and passed out of sight.

Run! Run! Run! Daniel did not want to think. He had no desire to unravel, or even contemplate, the mysteries of the afterlife. He ran, his eyes open this time, and he noticed that his hunger seemed satisfied. He ran faster and faster, the world passing by him as a blur. As long as he kept running, he did not have to think. As long as he did not have to think, he did not have to feel. He ran on; dawn his only destination.

Robert Mason was mildly annoyed to be caught in traffic at such a late hour, but this fact failed to dim his glowing joy. He had stayed at work late in a meeting with his superiors; a meeting that had resulted in both a hefty raise and a hefty promotion. Life was finally starting to look up. Now he would be able to help Daniel buy that new car, which his boss' son still hadn't sold.

Even in the normally infuriating instance of a massive traffic jam, Robert's thoughts were only on how happy he was. As soon as he got home, he had decided, he would kiss his evil wife, wake his sickly son, and buy them all a fantastic dinner.

The stink of the giant eighteen-wheeler beside him filled Robert's nostrils. Wondering if it had sprung a leak of some sort, he switched on the car radio to take his mind from the potency of the stench, and he was instantly delighted with a song that he felt perfectly matched his mood. *Ah, the Beatles! Neither before nor since has there ever been a greater band!* He started drumming the steering wheel and singing along to the upbeat tune of "Ob-La-Di, Ob-La-Da," as it filled his ears.

Daniel closed his eyes again, as he continued to run faster. *My God, where are you? Are you anywhere at all? Is there no mercy for me at all? I need to know that you have mercy, if only for Roxy.*

No! I won't think! I refuse to exist!

When Daniel opened his eyes, intent on replacing his thoughts with his sight, he found himself approaching the freeway—about to slam into a huge diesel truck. There was no time to turn, and he hit the truck with the full force of his speeding body.

As the truck tipped over, Daniel leapt to the top of it and, without looking at them, ran across the cars below. Before the truck had finished its fall, Daniel was gone from sight.

***

Terror gripped Robert Mason's heart, as the cursing of the truck driver called his attention to what was happening around him. Robert realized that the traffic was too thick, and he wasn't quick enough to abandon the car before the inevitable. *Why! It's not fair! Why, God? Why?* Though he had the time to think these words, he did not have the time to vocalize them before the truck's trailer hit, mangling both his car and body, crushing them both completely—as were crushed the dreams of a noble father and husband, who had never been granted by life a moment of selfishness.

In the instant before the leaking trailer exploded, a few people managed to abandon their cars. Some of them could even hear the muffled sounds of a once happy song, now filling the cold night air with the eerie music of bitter irony, for Robert Mason's car radio had somehow managed to keep going. The explosion ended the song, as well as the dreams of many others.

Daniel ran on, more intent now than ever on not thinking. He soon found that he no longer had the strength to fight. *Oh, God. Please don't let anyone be hurt by that truck. I didn't mean to hit it.*

He stopped running.

None of this is my intention! None of it! Why is this happening to me!? Where is my salvation? Daniel howled his raging questions up into Heaven, the one place he was now certain would turn a deaf ear to him.

***

Daniel woke countless times to find himself in bed, drenched with sweat, though he could not recall ever returning home. Every time that he awoke, he turned over immediately, intent on sleeping forever.

During his last moments of restless sleep, Daniel suffered a disturbing nightmare.

In this nightmare, he sat up in bed to find an angel with jet-black wings, sitting at the foot of his bed. "Hello, Daniel. Don't be afraid. Isn't that what angels are expected to say?"

"Angel? What do you want? What angel are you?"

"What I want, is to help you; to save you and claim you among my flock. My name, is Lucifer."

"No! Go away!"

"But you invited me yourself. You said that you hated God. I heard you. That is why I am able to appear in a more attractive form to you, unlike the last time you dreamt of me.

"It seems to me that you are right. God has abandoned you. I, on the other hand, am here. You are now a creature of my domain. I can offer you guidance, and love. I love the things that I saw you do tonight. I loved laughing at them. Yet, I pity you, Daniel. I pity your agony. I can help you end your agony.

"You probably noticed that the pain of your transformation was less tonight than it was before, and last night you barely noticed it at all, after your first transformation. That physical pain will pass by the next full moon,

I promise you. The hunger, too, will not be so bad. This is your birthmoon. After this, you need take only one life each night of the full moon to sustain yourself, and you know that you don't really have a choice in the matter.

"You will find that, if you will only give in to what you are, you have a great deal more control than you've been displaying. You can do anything you want. Anything at all. This Hell, as you call it, can become an absolute paradise. Please, Daniel, just give me your hand."

"No! Go away! Go!"

"Daniel, has God not left you? Am I not here, offering help? Be rational. Who is your master?

"Take my hand."

As Daniel watched Lucifer offer out his hand, he shouted, "No!"

He sat up in bed, awakened from the dream, and noticed that it was raining outside. He looked to the nightstand and saw his Bible still open to the pages he had turned it to earlier. "Who is my master? Who is my salvation?"

An unnatural wind suddenly passed by Daniel, and he watched as the pages of his Holy Bible turned over. When they stopped, a drop of water fell from the ceiling and landed on one of the open pages. Daniel looked closely and realized that the water had marked a particular verse: Revelation 12:18. He read out loud, "And I took my stand on the seashore."

The phone rang. Daniel picked it up, half expecting God or Satan to be at the other end. "Hello."

"Daniel," it was Trevor, "I think we need to talk."

"Trevor? What's wrong?" *Oh, no. He knows.*

"I'd rather talk to you in person. Can you meet me at Hilltop right away?"

Daniel looked at his clock. It was 6:17 A.M. The moon was gone, and the sky was filled with clouds. "All right," Daniel spoke with little thought, as he was still struggling to get his bearings. "I'm on my way."

After getting off the phone and walking outside, Daniel remembered that he had eaten his car. He would have to walk to Hilltop, and Daniel knew that this would be a thoughtful walk. He hoped that Trevor would have it all figured out, and be waiting to kill him.

He hoped, but he dared not pray.

XIV

When Daniel finally arrived, wet and on foot, at Hilltop, the rain had stopped, and the clouds were blowing quickly towards the east. Trevor was waiting under the cover of the roof, and smoking a cigarette as usual. As Daniel somberly approached him, Trevor slowly stood up from the little wall he had been seated on. His expression was haunted, as though he had just taken Death by the hand. "What took you so long?"

Daniel shrugged, as he stepped under the cover of Hilltop. "No car."

Trevor was visibly disturbed by this. "No car? What happened?"

"I'll tell you later. Right now I'm more concerned with why you wanted to talk to me." Daniel found himself blind to taboo. After last night, he no longer cared who knew the truth, and thus had every intention of telling Trevor exactly what had happened to *Clunk*. Daniel had no fight left in him. He wanted only for the nightmare to end. He waited, in the warmest depths of hope, for Trevor to tell him that he knew who the werewolf was, and that he had every intention of killing him. "So, what's up?"

Trevor looked away from Daniel's eyes, smoking as though his cigarette were a prayer. "I think I know who the werewolf is." He looked up, gauging Daniel's reaction.

Daniel's expression remained dark. He showed no reaction whatsoever to the news. "What do you intend to do about it?"

Trevor was puzzled by Daniel's mood. "Well, I was hoping you could help me figure that part out. We need to help him."

Help him? Daniel was confused by Trevor continuing to refer to the werewolf as if he were not standing right before him. "How? Wouldn't it be better to—" *…just kill him?* Daniel's mouth refused to open. He had been stricken silent by the self-preserving instincts of the werewolf. It mattered not that the moon had long since passed out of the sky.

"Better to what?"

Kill him! Kill me! You have to kill me, before I kill you and everyone else in Nightfire! Why can't I speak? Kill me, Trevor! You know it's me, and I can't be helped, so I must be destroyed. Daniel looked down helplessly, away from Trevor's gaze.

"Don't you even want to know who it is?"

Daniel now realized how lost he had been in this conversation. He looked back at Trevor skeptically. "Who?" He was relieved to note that he could speak again, but he was not yet ready to push his luck.

Trevor seemed quite upset suddenly. His voice was weak and quivered with remorse at having to speak his next words. "Tom. I think it's Tom."

Daniel was completely baffled. "Tom? What makes you think that Tom is a werewolf?"

"Well," Trevor forced his emotions steady, "he has been acting pretty weird lately. He looked so guilty yesterday afternoon. We were supposed to go out and get wasted or something last night. You know, since Brenda's out of town and all. But, I was on the phone with him just as the moon was coming out, and he suddenly got sick or something. He sounded all panicky and told me he had to go. Then he never called back. I mean, it all makes sense." He inhaled deeply on his cigarette and looked Daniel dead in the eyes. "He is the one who fell with that glass beaker. Maybe he got cut by some of the glass and got infected by the blood. You know, like sharing needles with an AIDS victim."

Trevor found Daniel's stare unnerving. He quickly changed the subject, making it obvious that he was no longer sure that he should have spoken his concern out loud, "So, did you ever hear from Roxy?"

Daniel continued to stare darkly into Trevor's eyes, as he slowly shook his head. "No. And I'm not going to hear from Roxy. Roxy's been dead since Thursday. And Tom is not the werewolf."

A chill coursed through Trevor's body, as confusion gave way to comprehension. "Wha… I mean… Why…? What…?"

"I am."

Daniel's stone-face crumbled then, revealing the depth of his sorrow.

Trevor felt his own grief wash over his soul as he went to his silently weeping friend and hugged him.

Daniel pushed him away. "No. Don't hug me. Don't pity me. I don't deserve it."

"Daniel, I'm going to do whatever it takes to help you through this."

Daniel was enraged. "Why? Why help me? Why sacrifice anything for me? Why will no one desert me?" His tears continued to stream.

"Why should anyone desert you?" Trevor answered sharply. "*You* would never desert anyone in need. You're a good person, Daniel. A righteous person. That's why there has to be a way out for you."

"So that's it," Daniel spoke bitterly. "I'm chained to damnation by my own righteousness, and my life is nothing more than a divine joke. You ask why anyone should desert me? I would suggest that you ask Nic, or Bert, or Roxy! But you can't, because they're all dead!" Daniel could no longer fight back his true, desperate emotions. He broke down into sobs, and fell to the ground, holding his red face. "They're all dead because of me."

Trevor was jolted by the news of Nic and Bert, and he had suspected since the day before that Roxy was not just missing, but he knew he had to block his emotions for them. He had to put them away for a later time. Right now, he had to be there for Daniel. He had to be a rock, as Daniel had always been for him. He sat down on the ground beside Daniel and hugged him tenderly.

Daniel returned the embrace, and wept on yet another friend's shoulder. He could not bring himself to push Trevor away again. He was desperate for friendship.

Trevor spoke to Daniel, as he held him, "I'm your friend, Daniel, and I love you. I'm not going to let you go through this alone. I'm not going to leave you, no matter what. So, if you don't want to kill me, you're going to have to let me help you."

After a while, Daniel found himself able to talk to Trevor about what had happened to him. He told him everything that he could. The two friends talked for many hours. Daniel wanted to die. He had no problem confessing this to Trevor, but he still was rendered unable to utter the phrase: *Kill me.*

Barbara Mason is going to die.

"No!" Lillian Foster awoke with a start at noon. She had suffered a near sleepless night—plagued by visions of death. She had seen a number of terrors, all of which promised to happen that very night. In her many nightmarish visions, she had continued to see the ruins of her neighborhood, and she had continued to find herself staring into her own eyes—her bodiless head lying within the wreckage of her house.

The last occurrence of this vision had been different from the others. Instead of the vision ending with her finding her severed head, it had ended with her turning away from it. When she had turned away, she had found herself in the arms of a tall, blonde stranger who looked like an angel.

As much as the visions of her own mortality disturbed her, she found herself more urgently driven to save her neighbor from the coming night's disasters. Lillian shook her head and had a perplexing realization "Barbara isn't going to be eaten by the werewolf. She's going to die another way." It didn't matter. Lillian knew that the death could be prevented, and she alone could prevent it. She just had to convince Barbara to get out of town.

She jumped out of bed, threw on some clothes, and ran next door to the Masons' house.

Lillian felt like a deviate for opening the door and letting herself inside, but she had been knocking for ten minutes, and she *had* to get inside to talk to Barbara. She walked softly, feeling more guilty with every step she took. She had no right to just walk into someone else's house like this, but she knew better than to ignore her feelings.

She found Barbara sitting in the kitchen, staring into space. "Barbara?" she spoke cautiously, not knowing what to say next, having barged in as it was.

"Hello, Lillian," Barbara answered her absently. "Won't you sit down?"

Lillian sat across from her neighbor at the small kitchen table, and she became more uncomfortable with every passing second, for though she now sat directly in front of Barbara, Barbara continued to stare wide-eyed at nothing. "Barbara, I hope this isn't a bad time. I need to talk to you about something."

"Yes. You need to say, 'I told you so.' Well, that you did, Lillian. You did indeed. But I told you as well, didn't I?"

She released a long sigh, and then turned her blank eyes on Lillian. "I've decided to rid myself of the men in my life. You know, Robert really was a terrible husband. He was a lousy provider, a monstrous father, and he wasn't much of a lover. You know, he only fathered one son. What does that say about his manhood? I'll tell you the truth. It was an accident in every sense of the word.

"He's dead you know."

"What? How?" Lillian had certainly not seen this.

Barbara answered her without emotion, "He was working late last night. On the way home, a diesel tipped over during a traffic jam and crushed every bone in his flabby body. If he had ever gotten a better job, this wouldn't have happened. He was such a fool. I should never have married him."

"Oh, Barbara, I'm so sorry." Lillian knew that her words wouldn't help, but she didn't know what else to say, and she felt like she had to say at least something.

"You know," Barbara said, "my grandmother hasn't spoken to me since before she died."

"Excuse me?"

"But I saw her. This morning, after I got the call about Robert. Daniel wasn't in his room when I went to deal with him, and when I turned to leave his room, I saw her standing in the hallway. She said nothing, and she faded so quickly.

"People saw the monster again last night. They saw it at the scene of Robert's demise. They saw it tip over that diesel. You were right about Daniel, but you weren't the first to warn me.

"Was there anything else?"

Lillian was lost. This was not what she had expected to find. It seemed that the death of her husband had driven Barbara mad. Was there any point in even talking to her? "Barbara, I'm afraid for your life, and I'm afraid for your soul."

"Why, Lillian? I've taken care of myself thus far."

"Yes, but I had a vision. I saw your death. You need to get out of town before sunset, or someone is going to kill you."

Barbara's reply didn't dare to argue, "How will I die?"

Lillian paused and took a breath. She hated seeing death visions. She hated remembering dark visions of any kind. "You're going to be shot."

"By Daniel?"

"I don't know."

"Why would a werewolf shoot me?"

"Barbara, I didn't see who pulled the trigger. I just know that it can be avoided, if you get out of town! Please, Barbara. I'm afraid that you're going to Hell!"

Lillian covered her mouth with both hands. She couldn't believe she'd just spoken those last words. She was horrified at herself. But it was done nonetheless.

"No, Lillian. I'm not going anywhere."

Lillian felt defeated. There was little else she could say. Everyone must make their own choices in life. Barbara now had the choice to accept or disregard Lillian's vision.

"Barbara, do you pray?"

"Are you asking me to pray for my salvation? I don't pray, Lillian. I talk to my grandmother, but never to God. God is a sexist."

Lillian stood up and put her hand on Barbara's shoulder, preparing to leave. "Then I'll pray for you."

After Lillian had left, Barbara Mason stood up and walked over to the kitchen counter. She opened the smallest drawer and removed from it her sharpest knife. Alone, in the darkness, she admired its shiny blade.

***

The afternoon grew later. Reverend Jim Jordan had been waiting nervously in his conference room all day long. He had been suffering with concern. Concern both for Daniel and the people who may have crossed his hungry path. It worried Jim to no end that Daniel had not come back yet.

Jim jumped in his seat when he heard the door creak open. He looked over and saw Daniel standing in the doorway. Trevor was with him. "Daniel! Trevor! I'm so glad to see you both!" He got up and hugged them both at once.

"I told Trevor everything," Daniel said. "Now he refuses to leave my side."

Trevor spoke up, saying what Daniel had omitted, "I'm afraid that he'll try to kill himself the moment he's left alone."

Jim nodded. "Daniel, how did things go last night?" He knew that the answer was evident in the fact that Daniel had talked to Trevor and was still having suicidal thoughts, but he felt the need to feign ignorance. He needed to at least pretend that he thought his advice to Daniel had been beneficial, as he awaited the answer with silent dread.

"I killed three more people last night. I can't go on, Jim. I just can't do it. There's no point."

Jim hugged Daniel again. "You have friends and family who love you to live for. And God."

Daniel made no comment, and his face remained somber.

"I want to try something, Daniel. I'm going to try to expel the werewolf entity from your body."

Daniel looked up—a wave of hope lifting his dying soul. "How?"

Jim smiled. "Good ol' fashioned Christian ritual. Come with me into the sanctuary."

He turned to Trevor. "Trevor, do you mind waiting outside? I don't know exactly what will happen if this works. I don't want anyone in there who doesn't have to be."

Trevor agreed reluctantly, "Okay." He lit a cigarette.

Jim led Daniel into the sanctuary and instructed him to kneel at the altar. Just after sunrise, Jim had broken into the Catholic church next door and stolen a Thermos full of holy water. He had mixed it with wine and now intended to use that very wine to expel the werewolf entity.

"What are we going to do?" Daniel asked.

"Holy Communion, with some very special wine. You know that Communion cleanses you of your sins. In this case, you are not the sinner. The demon attached to you is. My hope is that the act of this ritual will cleans you of the sinful entity completely, and then I pray that it will be destroyed."

"Sounds like a plan." As Jim picked up the loaf of bread, Daniel made a confession. "Jim, I'm afraid that I've lost my love for God."

Jim looked sad. "I understand." He paused. "You do *want* to love God."

"Yes!" Daniel spoke as though pleading. "I do, but where is he? Why is he deaf to my prayers? Why has he abandoned me in my time of greatest need?"

"He hasn't abandoned you, Daniel."

"Yes, he has!"

"What evidence do you have that he has?"

"What evidence do you have that he *hasn't*?"

Jim thought about that. "Though you are going through a very difficult time, you are still surrounded by very expressive love. This is how God, who did not inflict you with this trouble himself, is showing you that he is with you even now, and that he will guide you through to the end.

"You have me.

"You have Trevor beside you.

"You have Tom, sick with grief for dropping the beaker. I spoke with him on the phone earlier. He's literally worried sick about you and Roxy. I didn't tell him anything about you though.

"As long as you have us, you know that you have God. It takes a powerful love to stand by a friend at the risk of one's own life. You have two people doing just that in this very building: the house of God."

Daniel let Jim's words sink in. He could have given a thousand arguments, but he didn't want to. He wanted to believe. He wanted to love God.

Daniel thought about how he had expressed his hatred to God the night before. *It's true. God is with me, and I have a sin of my own to be washed away by this Communion.* "Thank you, Jim. You make a valid point."

Jim broke the bread. "Take and eat this in remembrance that Christ died for you, and feed on him in your heart by faith and with thanksgiving."

Daniel took and ate.

Jim put a glass of wine before his young friend. "Drink this in remembrance that Christ's blood was shed for you, and be thankful."

Daniel lifted the glass to his lips, and his stomach turned. He put the glass back down. "I can't. The thought of it makes me sick."

"That's because I put holy water in the wine. This is the most important element. You must drink."

Daniel again lifted the glass. His stomach again turned, but this time he took a swig of it into his mouth—only to find that he could not swallow. He spit it out. "I can't swallow it. The shadow has self-preservation instincts. It won't let me drink this."

"Don't worry. Try again, and don't spit it out."

Daniel didn't know what difference it would make, but he did as the preacher said. He held the wine in his mouth, fighting the violent urge to spit it out.

Jim walked around behind Daniel. "Hold still," he said, just before he grabbed Daniel by the chin and held his mouth closed with one hand, while using the other to hold his nose closed.

Daniel's eyes started to bug out.

"If these self-preservation instincts are any good at all, you'll surely be allowed to swallow before you're allowed to suffocate." Jim soon heard the pleasing sound of Daniel swallowing and was satisfied that the deed was done. "How do you feel?"

Daniel grabbed his stomach. "It hurts! It hurts! Oh, God, Jim, it hurts!" He hunched down onto the floor. With great suddenness, he bolted back up, wide-eyed and wanting to run to the bathroom, but there was no time. Daniel's stomach churned loudly in the instant before he vomited. He vomited with a force so great that it knocked a hole in the pulpit, and the howling, and growling sounds that accompanied the expulsion were loud enough to shatter every stained-glass window in the sanctuary at once.

When Daniel recovered enough to open his eyes, he noticed Jim lying on the floor. Daniel walked over to him, holding his stomach. Jim's ears were bleeding, but he was breathing. *Good.* "I'm sorry, Jim. I guess it didn't work. There's only one way out of this now, and I haven't got very much time to get it done. Please forgive me."

Daniel ran out through the front doors of the sanctuary, where Trevor wouldn't be able to see his departure.

Moments later, Trevor came into the sanctuary to see what had happened. "Jim! Jim!" He went to the pastor, just as he was starting to sit up.

"Ouch! My ears are ringing like crazy." He looked at Trevor. "Did it work?"

Trevor looked at the windows and the splintered, vomit-dripping pulpit. "I think not, Jim."

"Huh?"

Trevor shook his head exaggeratedly.

"Where's Daniel?"

Trevor looked around, suddenly near panic, until he saw the open sanctuary doors. "Oh, shit! He took off. I've got to go stop him!"

Trevor was out of the building and in his car before Jim could protest, and Jim was left to wonder whether or not he actually would have protested. On the one hand, preventing Daniel from committing suicide would save Daniel's life. On the other, at this point, as Jim was out of ideas, saving Daniel would be effectively murdering countless others.

Jim wept alone in silence, not even bothering to stand up off of the floor.

Trevor circled Daniel's house for hours, with the knowledge that Daniel would eventually end up there.

Lillian watched both Trevor and the sun, as the hours passed by. She waited for the inevitable.

Daniel went to the spot where Roxanna had died. He talked to her for a while with the assumption that she was still there, and he told her that he'd soon be back with a gun.

Daniel entered his house, conscious not to risk the added sounds of closing the door behind him, as he didn't want his parents to notice his coming and going. He crept into their bedroom, which he found empty, and he opened the drawer in their nightstand. There he found the gun his father kept for prowlers—fully loaded at all times. He held it in his hand, as he glanced out the window. *Too late, I'll never make it back to the park before the shadow takes over. I need to act now. God, please forgive me.* He cocked the hammer. *I'm going to Roxy.*

Daniel lifted the antique pistol to his right temple.

At that same moment, unknown to Daniel, Trevor was driving by and noticed the open door, and Daniel's mother was walking towards the room.

Daniel closed his eyes, resigned himself, and readied to pull the trigger—only to find that he could not. He opened his eyes and saw a translucent shadow covering his hand and wrist. The shadow entity would not allow him to kill himself. He put the gun down at his side, looked out the window, and noticed the darkening evening sky. "No. Why can't I die?"

"I always knew you would end up like this."

Barbara Mason had entered the room, and Daniel turned to face her—ashamed for how she had found him.

"You're weak and cowardly. You're a monster—an abomination! You killed your own father when you knocked over that truck last night! You set out to kill your own father! You're the Devil's bastard! I've known it since the day you were born!"

Daniel went cold. His voice was barely more than a whisper, as he remembered hitting the truck, "Dad?" His skin was whiter now than ever before.

"You don't have the guts to pull that trigger! You're pathetic! One more thing I have to do for you." Her voice was filled with undisguised hatred and coated with motherly disgust. She revealed her kitchen knife.

Daniel's heart broke into a thousand wounded pieces. His mother hated him. She wasn't ashamed that he was attempting suicide, she was only ashamed that he hadn't succeeded, and she now intended to kill him herself.

Painful tears fell from Daniel's reddened eyes and streamed down his ghost-white face. *Let her kill me. Let this all end. Let me go to Roxy.*

"If you want to go out a crybaby, that's just one more reason to get this done." She stepped forward. "I swear I'll send you back to Hell!"

Daniel's arm flew up, covered now in the translucent shadow of the werewolf. "No! Mom!"

His finger squeezed the trigger.

Trevor had just entered the house when he heard a loud gunshot. "No! Daniel!" He ran into the master bedroom, where he found Daniel holding a gun, and Daniel's mother with a bullet hole right between her eyes. The wall she was lying against was covered in blood, brain matter, and shards of skull. "Oh, God. Daniel."

Daniel fell to his knees, holding the gun with both hands, crying like a little boy. He couldn't recall any of her flaws through the dark shockwave of grief that now carried him. "Mommy!" He dropped the gun to the floor, and he started to feel the tingling all over his body.

Trevor knelt down and lifted Daniel off of the floor. "Come on, buddy. We've gotta get you out of here."

"Trevor. Run," Daniel spoke plainly and with authority, though his voice barely surpassed a whisper.

"What… Oh, fuck!" Fear threatened to stop Trevor's heart altogether.

"*Run*!" Daniel was frantic.

Trevor let Daniel go, and he ran.

The shadow consumed Daniel once again, hiding his terrified human form within its solid black mass, looking at the world through hungry red eyes. Daniel denied it his will, as a matter of course, and the werewolf took over, as it had both nights before.

Trevor opened his car door and, at the same instant, heard the ear-splitting howl of the werewolf. His body began to shake involuntarily, at the same time going numb with fear. "Oh, fuck. Oh, shit." He turned his head, and the werewolf was standing right behind him. It lunged down and took him in only an instant.

Daniel had shut down. His mind was gone. Though he saw Trevor's spirit standing before him, watched the spirit say, "Damn it. This sucks," and saw the spirit light a cigarette and vanish into thin air with no hint of a colored light, he did not comprehend it.

Mommy.

His mind was gone.

XV

The werewolf was hungry. It smelled the air and again caught the scent of human meat on the wind. It followed this scent to the house next door.

Lillian Foster knelt praying in her living room. She was scared, having heard the monstrous howl just outside of her home, and she was beginning to wish she had never listened to her feelings at all.

Oh, Lord, please get me through this night. Please have mercy on all of the souls that will receive judgment this night. Please be with Daniel. Please, even if I am meant to die this night, let me know how you have worked through me. Let me know why I was moved by the Spirit to stay. Please let no death linger this night.

Lillian spun around with a scream, as the wall behind her came crashing down, followed by the howl that she realized may signal the coming of her own judgment. "Oh, God! Please no!"

Viewing the scene through the werewolf's eyes, Daniel knew that he was about to kill Lillian Foster, but he refused to let himself think about it. He was finished thinking. He was finished fighting. There was no point in it. The werewolf would have its way regardless, and when it was done, Daniel would simply slip into catatonia. The werewolf could just have his body, for he had no desire to occupy it any longer.

Lillian knew that it was futile to run. She closed her eyes and prepared her soul for what lay ahead. *Lord, forgive me for all my sins. I beg you.*

The werewolf leapt towards her. Lillian squinted her eyes tightly shut, hoping that it would be quick and painless.

She never felt the werewolf's jaws close on her. Instead, even though her eyes were closed, she saw a bright, white light. She opened her eyes and was astonished.

The werewolf was stopped in midair and thrown backward by an invisible force. A bright light filled its devilish eyes, and Daniel was alive again—alive with hope.

An angel was suspended in the air between Daniel and Lillian—an angel of God. Daniel could tell this by the white light surrounding and emanating from it, and from the whiteness of its beautiful wings. It spoke to them both, soundlessly, as if it were simply placing the words into their heads.

"Do not fear me." It fixed its gaze on Daniel. *"Lest you should try to harm this Woman. She is under the protection of God."*

The angel then looked to Lillian and smiled. *"I am here blatantly, only because your death was otherwise unavoidable. Take heart that I am with you always in the name of God, but do not be arrogant. It is not for you to know if God may be finished with you ten minutes from now. It is only for you to know that God is not finished with you yet."*

Lillian wept in the presence of God's messenger. *Oh, God. How will I ever deserve the beauty of this vision?*

Daniel was desperate with hope. He hoped that the angel could hear him from within his demonic shell. He knew that the angel could save him. *I don't want to hurt her.*

The angel turned its attention to Daniel once again.

Encouraged that it had heard his thoughts, Daniel pleaded his case. *I don't want to hurt anyone! Please, help me! Save me! I've spent my life in loyalty to God! I can't believe that he would leave me because of something that wasn't even my fault. This happened to me when I was helping someone! Please have mercy, and free me from this evil! I want everything the way it was!*

"God has not overlooked your righteousness, Daniel."

Hope reached a peak in Daniel's soul. *Then please release me from this horror! Please end my suffering!*

The angel looked sadly into the depths of Daniel's troubled soul, answering as gently as it could, *"No. It was not meant to be."*

As quickly as hope drained from Daniel's heart, outrage leaked in to replace it. *What.? How can you say that? Is this my evidence then? My evidence that God has forsaken me! Where is the Shepherd who would risk all for any of his flock!?*

The angel's look of sorrow deepened. It looked as if it had so much that it wanted to say, but could not. *"God is a shepherd, yes, and like all good shepherds, God occasionally loses one of his flock to the wolves."*

But I'm not lost! I'm here before you! I'm begging to be taken back! Take me away from this horror. Please!

Oh, God! Why won't you save me?

"God will not heal you, for God has no further use for you as you were before. In God's eyes, the life of the lamb you once were is over." The angel offered a sad smile. *"It is now time for you to take your place as…"*

Damn you! Daniel's rage would not allow him to hear any more. He had gotten the message. God had given up on him. He'd been abandoned for nothing of his own fault. *Damn God! Damn Heaven, Earth, and everything in between! Damn you all!*

As Daniel's soul raged, the werewolf howled accordingly.

The angel vanished sadly from Daniel's sight, and the walls began to crumble.

Lillian looked at the crumbling walls, and she smiled, as tears fell down from her joyful eyes. She was no longer afraid to die.

Daniel howled once more, with all the might of his bitter resentment, and the house came crashing down on them both.

Moments later, Daniel, the werewolf, crawled out of the rubble. He had accepted that his love of God was lost for all time. And the night was still so young.

XVI

After destroying Lillian's house, Daniel went on to destroy every house on his block in exactly the same way, sparing only his own. Though he was hungry still, he did not take the time to consume any of their inhabitants. He knew that he would eat later and found himself in control of that decision.

When Daniel at last approached his own house, he surveyed the rubble of the former homes that now surrounded it. He noticed all of the spirits that had been disturbed by his rampage—all of the various ways that they appeared, disappeared, and expressed themselves. He refused to be affected by it. If they had a problem with him, he thought that they should take it up with their loveless God.

Daniel wanted to enter his house one more time as a human, and he found that at the instant he thought it, the shadow body was gone.

Now I am in control.

Daniel entered into his empty house. He looked around the kitchen and the living room. No ghosts. At least, no literal ghosts, although nostalgia threatened to break his callous air. *I've lost it all. I have no one, not even God.*

He went to his bedroom and took one last, good look at what he had been. He noticed all of the academic awards and little league trophies that decorated his walls; the Holy Bible sitting open on his nightstand. He looked at his drafty, old bathroom and thought about how much his father had loved him, and how much he had loved his father. He even thought of how much he had loved his mother, though he now knew that he had loved her in vain.

He thought to himself, *This is what I was. This is what I shall never again be. That lamb is dead now—torn apart by the wolves. The Good Shepherd only shrugs.*

Daniel looked at the bookshelf in the hallway. His eye was caught by a particular volume. It was a children's book that his mother used to read from when he was a child. He picked it up and flipped through it, hearing his mother's voice.

Why didn't she love me? What did I ever do wrong? I lived my whole life not knowing what I had done wrong, but she would never explain. I thought she loved me, but that was a lie. A lie that I told myself, because she never perpetuated the myth.

His throat became sore, as he felt the welling up of tears.

No. No more tears.

Daniel was again covered in the shadow body of the werewolf. The werewolf that he now was, without doubt, and without hope. He replaced the weakness that was his sorrow with the strength that was his hatred, and he poured that passion into the destruction of his home and the erasure of his past.

***

Over the next few hours, Daniel attempted to understand his new body. He learned to stop seeing it as an invader and to start seeing it as an addition. It wasn't *like* an extension of himself, it *was* an extension of himself. He knew that he had to accept this. He had always excelled at everything he had tried. Why should being a werewolf be any different? Daniel was confident that he could be the fiercest of all werewolves, if he put his mind to it. He would cause God to regret ever leaving him. He would become everything that God hated. He would become everything that the world feared.

Daniel learned that he could cause the werewolf body to extend from and retract to his human body at will. He found that he could extend and retract specific limbs without the others if he chose. He could even walk as a human, while viewing the world around him with the eyes of a werewolf.

Daniel knew that there were many more things that he could learn, but he also knew that he could never hope to learn it all in a single night. He had to prioritize.

He was still hungry. What better time would there be for him to learn to kill without self-hatred? Daniel went forth into the night, in search of sustenance—sustenance he knew by name.

He ran aimlessly, unsure of where he wanted to go, soon finding himself on Oak Street; the part of Nightfire inhabited almost entirely by people over the age of seventy. The mailbox of the Tylers caught the attention of his werewolf eyes. The house that it marked was the home of Ned Tyler and his much younger wife Amy.

Ned had been a constant personality in Daniel's life. When Daniel was a very small boy, attending vacation bible school with Trevor, Ned had frequently gone into their classroom and given them candy when the teacher wasn't looking. Over the years, Ned had been a great supporter of the church's small youth group. He had led several bible studies, and he had always been handy to brighten up any gloomy faces he found in the church. Ned was a good old man.

He would be a perfect candidate for Daniel's next kill.

Daniel shed his werewolf skin and knocked on the Tylers' front door.

"Who is it," came Amy's friendly voice.

"Daniel Mason." Immediately after he spoke, Daniel realized that he couldn't bear for them to see him. He couldn't bear for them to fear *him* in their final moments. He returned to the shadow skin.

Amy Tyler spoke as she opened the door, "Daniel Mason. Well this is such a nice surprise! I—" She saw the werewolf, and she screamed.

Then she stopped screaming and closed the door.

Daniel knew that this had to be done. He had to kill them, and he had to resist the guilt of it. He broke through the door.

Amy went into the bedroom to wake her ninety-eight year old husband. "Ned! Ned, wake up! It's that damned werewolf you're always tellin' the grandkids about! He just knocked on the door!"

"What the hell? Are you sure, Amy?"

"If you don't believe me, just go look in the living room, and see for yourself."

"You let him in?"

"No, he let himself in. And we just had that door replaced after you ran it over with the motorcycle."

"Well, did ya offer 'im anything to drink? It'd be a damned shame ta' piss a guy like that off by refusin' hospitality." Ned cackled at his own warped amusement.

"Ned! How can you be laughing!"

"Better'n cryin'. Welp, I guess we'll have to start runnin'. Where're my slippers?"

As Amy handed Ned his slippers, the werewolf walked into the room. He sliced Amy in two from top to bottom, and she slowly pealed apart.

"Well, shit. Guess I outlived another one," Ned said, as he put on his slippers.

As Daniel devoured Mrs. Tyler, Mr. Tyler opened the window and crawled out. Daniel's hunger was satisfied. The pain was gone, but he had not accomplished his task. He hadn't really known the latest Mrs. Tyler all that well, so he still had to kill Ned, and he had to kill Ned without regret.

He looked over at the window, and Ned stuck his head inside.

"You know, wolfie, you're gonna have to move pretty fast to catch me. I was the fastest man of the class of 1917. 'Course, now I'm the *only* man of the class of 1917." Ned laughed out loud, stuck out his tongue, and rasberried the werewolf. He then turned and ran as fast as he could.

Daniel mentally prepared himself. *Ned must die, because I hate God. I will not feel guilt for killing him, I will feel satisfaction for spiting God. This will not hurt me—this will hurt God.*

Daniel smashed through the wall of the house and chased after Ned, who was cackling insanely as he ran down the street in nothing but his long johns and house slippers. Daniel also noted that Ned ran surprisingly fast for a man nearly a century old.

When Daniel had finally set his mind to it, he caught up with Ned. *I hate You, God, and this is how I hurt You!* He bit Ned in half. *I feed on your sheep.*

Not only did the bottom half of Ned continue to run, but Daniel swore that he could still hear Ned's mad laughter as it did so. Daniel was far too disturbed to chase after the running legs, so he simply sat and watched, as they turned the corner and vanished from his sight. Daniel had given up on understanding the diversities of the afterlife. He had killed Ned, and that was all that mattered. He had killed Ned, and thus he had wounded God. Daniel ran from the scene.

As for the rest of Ned, though many people witnessed this scene from their windows, his legs were never found.

Daniel was no longer hungry, but the night still called to him. He wanted to do more. He wanted to offend God in every way. He wanted God to know how it felt to be forgotten.

He found himself at Carey Jonson's house. She had been his girlfriend before Roxanna Stillwaters had replaced her. Daniel had never loved Carey in the way that he had loved Roxy. He had never even come close. Carey had only wanted Daniel for sex, which he never gave her; though he had wanted to, for the pure, physical pleasure of it, but he was loyal first to God, and would not have premarital sex with anyone.

He had wanted to become one body with Roxanna, because he loved her more than any other person. He had wanted to make love *for* her, and she had wanted him just as passionately. It was the one thing that she had asked of him that he had ever denied her. All because of his loyalty to God. If not for that, he could have given Roxanna everything. If not for his loyalty to God, he and Carey might never have broken up, and it would have been she whom he had killed on that first night, and Roxanna might still be alive.

Now God had left him.

All the lights in the house were out. Daniel hoped the Jonsons hadn't left town. He retracted his werewolf skin and tapped on the window.

Carey opened it, wearing nothing but a skimpy, blue bra and panties. "Hey, Daniel. What's up? Aren't you afraid of the wild animal?"

Daniel actually laughed. "No."

She put her elbows on the windowsill and cradled her chin on her fists. "Ooh, so brave and strong. So did you and Roxy have a fight or somethin'? It's pretty late to just wander on over to your ex-girlfriend's house you know."

Daniel looked at the ground. "No. We never had a fight." He spoke, remembering the fact that they honestly never had.

Carey ventured jokingly, still clueless as to what Daniel could possibly want from her, "Then you must be here because you're having regrets about never letting me give you the time of your life." She giggled playfully.

Daniel looked up at her and spoke solemnly, "Yes."

"What?" Carey would have never expected that reply from Daniel Mason. Not even if the world had been coming to an end. *Of course,* she thought sarcastically, *he probably would have already been taken up by the Rapture anyway.*

He smiled up at her, a haunted gleam in his brown eyes. "So, what're your plans for the rest of the night?"

She replied seductively, "Why don't you come in and show me?"

Daniel held out his hand, she took it, and he climbed in through the window. He kissed her deeply, as they stood next to her bed, all the while in hatred of God.

Moments later, Daniel surrendered to her the last of his innocence.

Afterwards, she fell asleep with her arms around him. Daniel lay in silent contemplation, thinking about how meaningless it had been. How much better it would have been with Roxy. He also thought about how powerful he now felt. He had chosen to kill Ned and Amy, he had chosen to give his virginity to Carey, and God had done nothing to stop him. It was as if God were powerless to enforce his own rules. Daniel realized now that he could do anything he wanted. God was a barking dog who had no teeth. Daniel could not respect him. God had ruled Daniel's life with empty threats and empty promises. For the first time, Daniel felt that his life was truly his own.

He sat up, waking Carey.

"What is it, Daniel? Hungry for more?"

Daniel looked down at her, filled with disgust. "You know what, Carey?"

"Hm."

"It should have been you that died first."

She didn't even have time to scream, as he returned to the body of the werewolf and consumed her.

Daniel returned to his human form, put on his clothes, and left, never looking back even once.

Thomas Raymond Don sat up in his bed. He looked at the clock and saw that it was 5:03 A.M. He had been awakened by what sounded like his mother screaming. He sat, listening to the silence. He felt a potent sense of terror squeeze on his heart, as he listened for the sound to repeat itself.

It never did.

He gasped at the sound of footsteps in the hallway—footsteps he knew were not his mother's.

"Tom? Are you up? It's me. Daniel."

Daniel? Something was clearly not right. Tom felt as if someone had just stepped on his grave, when his bedroom door slowly creaked open. "Daniel? Is that you? What are you doing here…" he glanced at the clock, "…so early?"

Daniel stepped into the room. "I have some bad news, Tom."

Tom was terrified, though he could not figure out why. That fact alone intensified his fear, but it seemed perversely wrong that he should be afraid of Daniel. Tom looked closely at his friend, trying to pinpoint what was different—what was scary. When he realized what it was, he began to shiver and did not stop. Daniel didn't *feel* like Daniel. His presence had lost its warmth. Daniel now stood before him, unsmiling—his presence colder than death. It was as if he were in the room with someone else; someone who looked a lot like Daniel, but had a completely different manner. "Daniel, what's wrong? A- Are you okay?"

"I've never been better, and I have you to thank for it. You took God away from me."

"Wh- What are you talking about?"

"I'm a werewolf, and it's your fault. I cut myself on the beaker that you broke. The blood from inside of it infected me, and now God has left me, and I'm going to kill you for it, even though I feel freer now than ever before.

"If you don't believe me, ask your mother when you get to the other side. I just killed her a few seconds ago, and I did it just to piss God off." Though Daniel had changed drastically, there were some things that still remained the same. "And I enjoyed it." He was still lying to himself.

Tom felt tears filling his eyes. Why was Daniel scaring him like this? It was such a cruel thing to do. "Why are you talking like that? You're lying, and you're scaring me. Please stop. Would you turn on the light at least?"

"Tom," Daniel's willed his eyes to be covered by the red, glowing eyes of the werewolf, "I'm not lying."

Daniel saw Tom's mother standing beside her son protectively, so he reverted to his normal eyes as he walked right up to Tom.

"Daniel, I'm sorry. I didn't mean it... I... I never wanted..." Tom started to whimper, as tears streamed down from his glistening, young eyes.

Daniel got right in Tom's face. "Tom, tell it to God."

"Daniel, please don't kill me." Tom met Daniel's hateful gaze with his own teary, blue eyes. "I never meant to hurt you. I hate myself for all of this. I hate myself."

Daniel felt his heart ache. He knew what it was to feel self-hatred, and as much as he wanted to hate Tom, he couldn't. He, in fact, felt a deep sympathy for him. He wished he could make Tom stop hurting. He wanted to hug Tom and tell him that it would be all right. Try as he may to fight it, Daniel was still human.

He backed away slightly. "Oh, Tom, I'm so sorry. I *have* to kill you." Daniel thought he would feel better if he made Tom understand. "I have to! I need to erase my past! I can't be what I intend to be if my past is still with me. You're the last embodiment of my dying humanity! I have to kill you before I can go on."

"No you don't, Daniel. You can stay, and we can work it all out together. Daniel, you're the best friend I've ever had."

Daniel turned his back to Tom, fighting back tears.

"I love you, Daniel."

Daniel closed his eyes and felt the tears begin to fall. "I love you too, Tom."

With his eyes still closed, Daniel willed his left arm alone to be covered by the shadow skin. *I have to kill him, but I don't have to watch.* He back-handed Tom with all of his werewolf strength.

Tom watched in horror, as the giant, black, clawed hand came racing towards him. When it hit him, Tom felt himself go numb. It didn't slice through him as he had expected. It just pushed him, really, with all of its might. Tom watched everything grow farther away as he flew backwards into the air. Before he knew it, he was looking at the house from outside, having flown through the wall. He slammed into a tree.

After that, Tom knew only darkness. His broken body slumped to the ground, blood pooling beneath his fractured skull.

Daniel, satisfied by the sound of the breaking wall that Tom was dead, walked out of the house, weeping, and never looked back.

He now knew that he still had humanity, but it was far too late for him to turn ever back.

The night was no longer young. In fact, it was nearing its end when Daniel arrived on Deerbrook Road. He had decided to revoke his great sacrifice. He had given up a car for his father, and now God had taken his father away. The sacrifice was rendered pointless.

Daniel broke through the front of the large, white house at 7748. He found his way to Steven Kile's room, killing and eating Steven's parents along the way. When he walked through Steven's bedroom door, his only supernatural features were his glowing, red eyes, as he looked at Steven and said, "Keys."

Steven got out of his bed, shaking, and reached for the keys on his dresser.

Daniel never let him get that far. He saw where the keys were, and he minced Steven where he stood, letting the pieces fall to the floor. He then took the keys, and he drove off in the '93 Mustang convertible of his dreams.

Daniel knew that he had to leave Nightfire, Texas. He knew that he would eventually crack if he stayed. His new life would be lived elsewhere; a place where everyone was a stranger.

He had only one bit of business left to take care of before he left, and it had to be done quickly, because the sun was about to rise, and he had no idea what effect the absence of the moon would have on his newfound power.

As the sun peeked over the horizon, the survivors of the night were gathering their emotions. Those who had believed in the werewolf rumors, but chosen to stay, breathed a sigh of relief that the monster had not found them. Those who had seen the werewolf, and avoided its wrath, slowly began to come out of hiding. Still others went about life as if nothing had changed, and for some, nothing had.

The little puppy still wandered. He had grown so weak and thin, so hungry and cold. Being a puppy, he was sensitive to certain truths, and he knew that he would soon be dead if no one would have mercy on him.

He had wandered out of the park and into the suburbs. Still, no one would feed him, no one would love him. It seemed there was no one who would not shoo him away.

The puppy was tired, and he needed to rest. He knew that he couldn't keep walking forever. He wanted to sleep, but it was so cold.

The puppy made it to the top of a small hill, which to him was a mountain. He looked down and saw a boy sleeping next to a tree. *Maybe no one will love him either. I can love him. Maybe he can love me. Maybe he'll pet me, call me Heresamson and Goodboy. He has no fur. It's cold.*

The puppy scampered weakly down the small hill and approached the boy. The puppy felt that the boy was in pain. He noticed that there was blood on the tree and beneath the boy's head. He noticed the rhythm of the boy's chest rising and falling as he breathed.

Heresamson yawned. He was tired. He snuggled next to the boy, whose body felt warm. *When he wakes up,* Heresamson thought, *I will help him to feel better.*

The puppy drifted off to sleep, and he dreamt of the boy and the games they would play.

Lillian Foster climbed out of the rubble of what had once been her house. She noticed her torn clothes, her bruised and cut body, and the deep, red horizon of dawn.

It was over.

She looked all around her and saw nothing but ruin. She wondered if she had died, but then she thought that death couldn't possibly hurt like this.

She took in the eerie, dead surroundings and wanted to cry. She turned back to look at her house, and she saw what she had dreaded. She was staring into her own eyes. She screamed and turned quickly around.

She was startled to find a man standing there. He was a very tall and muscular man, and he was wearing a suit and tan trench coat. His clean-cut, blonde hair rustled in the wind, as he took her urgently in his arms.

"There there, my lady. It's going to be all right."

Lillian pulled back. "Who are you? I know you're not an angel. I've seen an angel before."

"Why would I be an angel? You survived." He spoke with an accent that she could not place.

She looked at him skeptically. "But I… I saw my own head in the rubble." She pointed, too afraid to look back.

The man laughed. He walked over to the spot she was pointing at, and he picked something up. "It's all right. You can turn around."

She did, and she covered her face with astonishment at her own foolishness and breathed a massive sigh of relief. She then broke out in uncontrolled laughter, and the tall man joined her.

"See?" He threw the broken shard of mirror to the wind. "You were all worked up over a piece of glass." He stood and went to her. "I'm Julius."

She smiled back at him. "Lillian."

"Well, Lillian," he smiled. "Everything is going to be all right."

She looked at the ruin around her. "Yes." She laughed at her own anxiety. "I think you're right."

XVII

The moon was now just barely visible in the lighting sky. Daniel stepped out of his car and entered the church sanctuary. He found Reverend Jim Jordan kneeling at the altar in perpetual prayer. "Hello, Jim."

Jim spun around. "Daniel!" He rose instantly, a broad smile lighting his face, and he went to the youth to hug him, but stopped just short of it. "Daniel, did it work? Did the Communion heal you?"

"No." Daniel's face remained expressionless. "It didn't."

Jim found himself unnerved. Daniel seemed to be carrying himself differently. Jim backed away slightly. "Daniel, what's wrong?"

Daniel snarled, "You are, my *friend.* You, who told me for so many years that God was good, that God was salvation and love. You told me to have faith, and everything would be fine! Because I took that advice, Nic and Bert and some poor, old bag lady are dead! You know what though, Jim? You were right about one thing. I did want to love him. The only problem is, he had already given up on me."

"Daniel, don't say that."

"No, Jim. I found the evidence you were talking about. I spoke to an actual angel of God, and it told me that God, being a shepherd, occasionally lost a sheep to the wolves. No big deal! He's got lots more! I wasted my youth praying to a God who couldn't possibly care less! I wasted my time letting you tell me that he was my hope and would always be there for me, no matter what. Now here I am, Godless, and I never even wanted to hurt anybody. I've lost everything and everybody that I ever cared about, Jim. Everything!"

"Daniel, you still have me."

Daniel turned away in disgust. "Jim, you are blind. You have no idea what I've been through." He turned back to face him. "I'm leaving Nightfire, and I'm leaving my past. The lamb that I once was is dead. The Daniel you knew is no more. When I'm gone, I want you to give God a message from me, his once faithful follower."

Jim was very pale now. He was lost to words of comfort. "Daniel, I… We can give him this message right now. Will you pray with me?"

"Jim! Will you give him my message, or not?"

Jim accepted defeat. He had lost Daniel. "Yes. Of course. What is the message?"

"The message," Daniel's werewolf arms extended, "is goodbye!" He slashed with both arms, slicing his one-time mentor into twelve, bloody pieces.

Before Daniel left the church, he took a candle from the altar and lit the splintered pulpit on fire.

He went back to his car, and he drove away. He drove towards the future, for whatever it was worth. His ties with God had been broken, his human life was over, and his vengeance had just begun.

Daniel drove away from Nightfire.

He drove into the sunrise.

www.ingramcontent.com/pod-product-compliance
Lightning Source LLC
LaVergne TN
LVHW020537100826
845148LV00010B/1509

* 9 7 8 1 6 1 8 1 5 0 9 5 0 *